SINEMA 2:

SYMPATHY FOR THE DEVIL
Rod Glenn

www.rodglenn.com

A Wild Wolf Publication

Published by Wild Wolf Publishing in 2011

Copyright © 2011 Rod Glenn

ISBN: 978-1-907954-06-1

www.wildwolfpublishing.com

FURTHER WORKS BY ROD GLENN

The King of America (2006)
Sinema: The Northumberland Massacre (2007)
The King of America: Epic Edition (2008)
Radgepacket: Tales from the Inner City (2008, contributor)
The Killing Moon (2009)
Holiday of the Dead (2011, contributor)

PRAISE FOR SINEMA

Thank you to Suzanne Davies for her invaluable input on policing and forensics and Roger Parkinson for his expert knowledge of Thornes Park. Thanks also to Tony Wright as my ever-reliable sounding board and to Laura Harvey and Debbie Heffernan for their polishing skills.

Exorcise your demons …

FOREWORD

Sinema: The Northumberland Massacre was and continues to be a major part of me. Writing it took something out of me, but, in doing so, also replaced it with something else. Whether that is a good thing or bad is not for me to say, but it affected me deeply. It was published in 2007 and now, four years later, and a great deal wiser (and some would say darker!), the sequel that I originally said I would never write has finally torn itself free through my calloused fingertips.

Han Whitman is ... well, me. I'm not saying that I'm a serial killer, but a great deal of his persona is mine and visa versa. Han Whitman is the dark side of me; of that, I have no doubt. He is the monster that I keep shackled deep within and, I suspect, the monster that lurks deep inside every one of us. So, this man – or monster – call him what you will, is an integral part of me and writing this sequel became more difficult than I could possibly have imagined. This sequel delves into the psyche and background of the man we know as Han, and so, in a way, also delves into mine.

Every question you may have asked at the end of the first novel *will* be answered. Grab yourself a stiff drink and enjoy the ride.

Footnote on HMP *The Weare*: the UK's only prison ship did in fact leave service in 2005 and is no longer in operation.

Pleased to meet you
Hope you guessed my name, oh yeah
But what's confusing you
Is just the nature of my game

Just as every cop is a criminal
And all the sinners saints
As heads is tails
Just call me Lucifer
'Cause I'm in need of some restraint

So if you meet me
Have some courtesy
Have some sympathy, have some taste

Use all your well-learned politesse
Or I'll lay your soul to waste.

'Sympathy for the Devil' by The Rolling Stones
(Mick and the lads are legends and a source of tremendous inspiration)

CONTENTS

Leave your lights on, you better leave your lights on,
Cause there's a monster living under my bed,
Whispering in my ear.
'Put Your Lights On' by Santanna

PROLOGUE

Not your time, son. The words were whispered, fragile, like they could disperse with the slightest breeze. There was something strangely familiar about them, but at the same time, terrifying. The four words seemed to hang there for a moment and then melted away.

Lisa stood before him, her hands clasped together against her bosom, trembling, frail. "My ... Angel ..." Her contorted lips ejected the words like bullets. The nauseating combination of fear and anguish that had contorted her normally pretty features was abruptly consumed in a wave of undulating rage.

The petite barmaid swelled and distorted in front of his eyes, transforming into a hunched and snarling beast, her broad back a pulsating mass of vicious black barbs and gnarled outstretched arms like an eagle's talons.

Han staggered backwards, his eyes wide with horror. He threw his arms up in desperate submission, his lips moving soundlessly.

A guttural snarl emanated from the back of the beast's throat, like an approaching freight train. Its haunches quivered then

15

it leapt forward, slamming into Han. He fell backwards, his back hitting cold concrete. The creature pinned him down and razor sharp claws raked at his chest, drawing trails of blood through his torn shirt. He screamed, but nothing escaped his taught lips. The only sounds came from the monster's snapping jaws. Its hairy dog-like muzzle drew close to Han's face and, although it had lost any resemblance to Lisa, the eyes still revealed its true identity.

"Lisa, please!" His mouth had finally found a voice.

The creature's black snarling lips hovered close to Han's, stinking saliva dripping from extended canines. Then it spoke and the words did not synchronize with the beast's lips. "You murdered my angel." It was Lisa's sweet, melodic voice and the hatred was gone, only a deep sadness remaining. Its eyes welled up with tears.

"I'm—"

"A monster," the creature said in Lisa's voice.

"Pot calling kettle, hon," Han managed with a fearful snort.

"I *trusted* you." A tear splashed onto Han's cheek and it burned like acid, a wisp of smoke rising up to be drawn into the beast's nostrils with its grunting breaths.

"It wasn't personal," Han said weakly, desperately trying to pull his face away from the abomination.

Its eyes narrowed into yellow slits and its jaws snapped open with a thunderous roar. Glistening teeth engulfed him.

... a shell of a man, a burnt out, desolate man, a man haunted by the demons of his past, a man who wandered out into the wasteland.
Mad Max 2: The Road Warrior

(HAPTER 1

The man known to the residents of Haydon, Northumberland as Hannibal Whitman awoke with a cry strangling his throat. He was bathed in sweat and the duvet and bed sheet were knotted around his feet.

Outside, the dawn was beginning to take hold, seeping in through a narrow gap in the curtains.

Panting, Han craned his neck to glance around the room. Everything was as it should be. There was no John Landis creation lurking in the shadows, ready to give the now rather clichéd second unexpected scare. He was alone in the gloom of his bedroom.

He sat up and wiped the sweat from his brow with the palm of a trembling hand. "Fuck me, Freddy," he said to no one in particular.

The sound of his master's voice caused a stirring under the bunched up duvet at the bottom of the bed. Gradually, the sandy-coloured snout of Jumanji, Han's faithful companion, nuzzled its way out of its cosy bed.

y, Ju," Han said as he felt the dog's wet nose nudge his
stroked Jumanji's head and his lingering fears gradually
"Good boy," he said after drawing several shaky
breaths.

His eyes were set into bruised sunken hollows and he
appeared gaunt and malnourished. Several days' growth dusted his
sallow face.

Over a year had passed since his narrow escape from
Haydon. The public and media furore had scarcely diminished
since. What the papers had nicknamed the 'Northumberland
Massacre' had become the stuff of legend. Nearly four hundred
men, women and children had been butchered days before
Christmas, and the authorities had yet to catch up with the prime
suspect, the ghost-man known as Hannibal Whitman. The media
had afforded him almost supernatural powers, despite the
authorities remaining unconvinced that one man could have been
responsible for all three hundred and ninety six murders.

Of course, what no one else knew was that Hannibal
Whitman was only responsible for three hundred and ninety five. A
certain Doctor Larry was responsible for one, the old dog! But, no
matter, that still made him the single most prolific serial killer ever
(not including mass murders orchestrated for religious or political
purposes, unsubstantiated legends or a certain granny killing GP).

Three hundred and ninety six dead and one survivor ...
Carol Belmont. Arguably the most damaged and pathetic individual
in Haydon and she ended up being the one to survive. Ironic? Or
just irritating? Luckily, she had been so badly traumatised by the
events that she had only managed to give a sketchy description and
had been of very little help to the investigation. After recovering
from her wounds, she had been given a new identity and was
currently in hiding with round the clock police protection. Yeah, a
little irritating.

Han swung his legs out of the bed. The movie posters and
memorabilia filling walls and shelves had lost some of their lustre of
late. Even his prized signed poster of Anthony Hopkins in his
Hannibal Lecter role appeared flat and lifeless. He looked into
Lecter's cold intelligent eyes and could almost feel the two

dimensional character mocking him. *Oh dear, it's just a movie or didn't you know?*

"My therapy is going nowhere," he muttered with a humourless grunt.

After showering, Han poured some tea into a *Planet Terror* mug (his favourite *Lord of the Rings* one had committed suicide in the dishwasher a few months ago). He prepared toast with honey for breakfast and stood at the kitchen worktop in thoughtful silence. The tea tasted bland and the honey-coated toast stuck in his throat. He gave up, scarcely halfway through and poured the tea down the sink and dumped the rest of the toast into Jumanji's bowl.

This time, it was more than the nightmare that had left him with an uneasy feeling. *Not your time, son.* Those words were something new ... so disembodied and yet so familiar. They had struck a chord deep in the pit of his stomach and yet he couldn't recall anyone ever saying them to him. *Not your time, son ...*

The more he thought about it, the more ridiculous they seemed.

"Snap out of it, you ponse!" he berated himself loudly to Ju's tail-wagging approval.

***

Han's DVD and game store, *Movie Maniac,* harboured a solitary spotty teenage boy browsing/scoping when he walked through the door just after 10am.

Sidekick and Tarantino wannabe, Perry, was stooped behind the counter, staring intently at a double page spread of a pouting and scantily clad Megan Fox.

Looking up, Perry said, "Hey, boss." His eyes lingered on Han's unkempt appearance, but instead of commenting, he nodded at the magazine in front of him. "Megan Fox is in the new *Empire* edition. Christ on a bike she just gets hotter and hotter." He lifted the magazine to show Han, who scarcely noticed. "Bloody criminal that she got dropped from T3."

"Yeah," Han muttered, distracted.

"You okay, boss?" Perry asked, frowning.

19

Han offered a thin smile. "Rough night."

"She must've been a real animal," Perry leered, his concerns forgotten.

Han managed a laugh and headed through to the back office-come-kitchen. "You have no idea. Cuppa?"

"Does Megan take it up the arse?"

"In your dreams, aye."

"You have to be a jobby-jabber not to spank it to the Foxster!" Perry shouted after him. Turning back to the photos, he placed a hand on them and added, "We have something special, you and me."

***

Soundless footfalls. Han glanced down at his feet. He was walking over gravel, but there was only silence. Looking up again, he saw the Bryce family farmhouse up ahead. The lights were on and the faint aromas of a Sunday roast filled his nostrils.

Han smiled. He liked John and his wife, Sally. Where was Lisa? He could have sworn that she was supposed to be coming with him. Maybe she was already there.

He walked up to the front door and placed his hand on the handle. It felt warm to the touch. He began turning it, but then paused, suddenly and oddly troubled. Something didn't seem quite right.

Scoffing at his ill ease, he pushed the door open and entered the hallway. He could hear voices coming from the lounge, so headed in that direction. The cooking smells had been replaced by something else. He didn't notice at first, but ... what *was* that? It smelled sickly sweet, but earthy and caught in his throat, almost causing him to gag.

Frowning, he called out, "Hello? Sorry I'm late."

The door to the lounge was open ajar. Light and laughter beyond. The crackle of a fire, the clinking of glasses.

Sighing with relief, Han stepped inside. "Hell–"

The conversation abruptly ceased. John and Sally, their son, Anthony, one of their Border Collies and Lisa all turned to stare at him. That was not what caused Han's sharp intake of breath.

John had a gaping hole in his chest and blood and intestines were spilling out down his legs and pooling around his boots. Sally's throat was sliced wide open and the front of her shirt was stained crimson. Her head kept lolling backwards in an almost comical fashion. Anthony had no head at all ... or arms, just dribbling ragged stumps. Cody was sat by the fire and, when the dog turned to look at the newcomer, its head fell off and rolled across the floor, leaving a dark smear on the wood.

Han's gaze then fell upon Lisa. She was naked, but between her pert breasts, there was a festering open wound. As he watched, steaming puss began oozing out of it and splashing onto the floor.

They stared at him through lidless opaque eyes, with crooked smiles frozen on their blue-tinged lips.

Lisa raised her arms and beckoned him. "My ... *angel* ..."

As Han remained rooted to the spot, gaping at the Lovecraftian apparitions in front of him, someone whispered into his ear, "*Not your time, son.*" Startled, Han spun around ...

... and sat bolt upright in bed.

"Jesus and fucking Mary Chain!" he cried out, blinking and wiping his hot and sweaty brow. "This is ridiculous!"

Jumanji whined softly and nudged his hand. He recoiled away at first, but then, realising that it was Ju and not some Romero creation, he gently ruffled his collar. "Sorry, Ju. All this shit is affecting your beauty sleep too, eh?"

***

The nightmares continued and, more often than not, he would hear those disembodied words ... *Not your time, son.* He could not tell whether the voice was male or female, but there was a familiarity to it that was unmistakeable.

It's fair to say that Han was not in the best of fettles, so being hounded into a catch up coffee at a local Costa with his brother was not exactly perfect timing.

Karl was the slimmer and taller of the two. He was a few years Han's senior, but many thought Han was the older brother. Tough paper round, Han would always retort, adding with a mischievous glint that it was mixed with a near-lethal concoction of alcohol and hard drugs. There was no denying that he was a bit of a drinker – if it was a sport he'd be performing at a County level. But he had never been into drugs – he still had the occasional joint with Perry every now and then, and had tried Speed and Coke, but they didn't really do anything for him.

With Karl dressed in a tailored suit and Han sporting faded jeans, *Get Carter* t-shirt and Converse, they made an odd couple. Karl placed two Massimo lattes onto the table and sat down opposite Han.

"How are ya, bro?" he asked. His tone was good-humoured enough, but Han knew him better than that. He was concerned. He had probably been speaking to Mum.

Still, always more fun to play the game first before seeing the results. "I'm canny, thanks. Good to see you – it's been a good couple of months or so since that poker night."

"Four, I think," Karl corrected and took a sip of coffee.

Han feigned surprise. "Has it really been that long? Jesus." Changing the subject, he added, "So you on your way to head office?"

"Aye. Quarterly board meeting. Should be a barrel of laughs." He laughed, but it lacked any sincerity.

"Well, it was nice of you to stop by as you were passing."

Karl studied Han over the rim of his mug. He had always been fitter than his younger brother – Han had been stronger and thicker set, but Karl had always beaten him in the stamina stakes. Karl had always participated in a variety of sports, including football, tennis and squash, whereas his brother's main fitness regime was solo gym work. They had both been fiercely competitive when training together, which they used to do at least a couple of times a week before Han had moved away. He missed those times.

Looking at Han now, he seemed a ghost of his former self. He was scrawny, pale and jittery. Like a second-rate transparent replica. He scarcely seemed like his brother at all anymore. Finally, he said, "You don't look too well, bro. Is everything okay? I mean, *really*?"

Han smiled and sat back, nursing his mug in his hands. "You've been talking to Mum, eh?" Han laughed, but, like his brother's earlier, it sounded insincere and hollow.

"Yeah, she's worried about you. So am I. You were so distant and quiet at the poker night. You didn't look well then, but you look worse now."

Han gulped down some coffee then said, "Look, I've just had a lot on my plate the last few months. It's been a bit of a crap twelve months really, but I'm okay."

Karl stared at him, his features pinched, apprehensive.

"Honestly," Han added. "I've been under the weather too – bit of a lingering cold that just doesn't seem to want to shift."

Karl sighed. "You know, we're here for you, bro. You know that, don't you?"

For the briefest second, Han felt an overwhelming compulsion to blurt out everything that had happened in Haydon. Here and now, in front of a bustling late morning coffee shop full of punters. It was the strongest urge to just get it all off his chest once and for all. But the moment passed in a heartbeat and he came to his senses once more.

"I know, bro," Han said eventually. "It's been a bit of a struggle of late, but things will get better. I'm sure of it."

After finishing their coffees, the two brothers hugged outside.

"I'm gonna have to keep an eye on you," Karl said with a wink. "I promised Mum."

Han laughed and it felt more genuine this time. "Have fun at the *bored* meeting."

***

23

Another quiet day at the shop passed like a film montage. As evening set in, and the imminent prospect of bed, Han's mood grew darker.

In an attempt to lift his spirits (and postpone sleep), he picked up a copy of Michael Caine's *Harry Brown* and two bottles of *Campo Viejo Reserva* then ordered a Chinese from his local takeaway.

He finished off one bottle of red within an hour whilst listening to the *Dark Side of the Moon* album on his iPod. Gradually, the tension in his neck and temples began to mellow.

Feeling a little more chilled, he decided to pop in the DVD.

He had heard from Perry and from a number of reviews that *Harry Brown* was Michael Caine's best work since *Get Carter*, but had not got round to seeing it himself. As a Caine fan, it was inexcusable.

He knew he'd like it. What's not to like about Michael Caine killing off chavs? What he didn't realise was how deeply it would affect him.

Half of his Singapore chow mein was left uneaten as he quickly became captivated. It took the rest of the film to polish off the second bottle of rioja.

As the credits rolled, Han poured himself a Jack Daniels and stood in the doorway of the living room, watching the television. He sipped the whiskey, savouring the taste and lost in thought.

Performances, production and story aside, the film's premise crashed over Han like a tidal wave. As the film returned to the menu screen, Han suddenly stumbled against the doorframe, sloshing some of the whiskey onto the floorboards. He stood with mouth agape and eyes wide with anticipation.

It was all suddenly so glaringly clear. He had to laugh at himself at not having thought of it months ago. The sudden revelation smacked of the original dream that had been the catalyst for the Haydon experiment. Like then, a plan began to formulate immediately with utter clarity. Details rushed into him with each panting breath. *Yes! Of course!*

That night, he slept like the dead and awoke from the most restful sleep he had experienced since Haydon.

As he prepared tea and toast, he decided that there was no time to waste and he would begin preparations immediately. After a quick telephone call to Perry to get one of the other lads to cover his shift, he settled down in front of his computer.

The screensaver was showing various stills from *Inglourious Basterds*. As Han watched, an image of Brad Pitt holding a sub-machinegun atop a pile of slaughtered Nazis appeared with the slogan, *A Basterd's work is never done.*

"So true," Han said as he moved the mouse to banish the screensaver. Several minutes of Googling quickly rewarded him with several different information sites and forums. A few chat rooms popped up as well, but he wasn't that desperate, not yet anyway. After another hour of browsing dozens of forums without posting, a link posted anonymously on one site took him to a web page entitled, *Paedophiles Living Near YOU – You have a right to know!*

"Nonces, eh? A good place to start," Han said and sipped his second cup of tea. He typed in a Wakefield postcode (close enough for an easy hop down the M1, but not too close) in a box below a map of the United Kingdom. After a brief egg timer moment, a list of names with distances from that area popped up.

He clicked on the first name that happened to be within one mile. Albert Livingstone. A black and white photograph appeared with statistical and address information below. Height, weight, hair, eyes, date of birth, marital status and a brief history, which included convicted offences. Whoever had set up the site had clearly done their research.

"Albert, you have been a naughty boy." Han scrutinised the list of offences. There were a few, but the more serious ones were indecent conduct towards a young child and possession of indecent photographs of children.

Sitting back, Han stared at the photograph. Albert Livingstone appeared to be Mr Average Joe. In his late forties, a little over weight, clean-shaven, glasses. There was no indication of a profession, but he could easily be an accountant or a judge, for all Han knew. He didn't look like the life and soul of a party, but basically inoffensive. A little like a white version of Cleveland Brown …

"So, part two of the experiment will start with you, you lucky dog, you."

***

Lunchtime traffic was light. The January weather had been mild so far – it was cold, but clear as Han headed south on the M1. Big Al lived in the suburb of Alverthorpe, so Han found a quiet spot near the golf course and parked up.

Wearing a heavy bomber jacket and beanie hat against the cold, Han set off at a brisk walk the half a mile or so to a quiet row of red brick semi-detached houses. Clipped hedges and green lawns painted a quiet and uninteresting picture of suburbia. The place had probably never made the news for anything ever.

No CCTV, no traffic, only a couple of parked cars. Perfect.

Han spotted the right house and headed straight for it with unhurried, purposeful steps. The wrought iron gate squeaked its displeasure, startlingly loud in the hushed street.

Han set his rucksack down to one side then rapped on the green door. Where lawn was still in shadow, he could see a light ground frost had endured the morning sun. It was an ordinary house on an ordinary street, with an ordinary paedophile living in it. It didn't look dissimilar to his mum's house.

He heard muffled footsteps then a bolt slid back and the door opened ajar. A security chain prevented it from opening further. Albert Livingstone had aged a few years since the photograph on the website and had actually lost a few pounds, but it was unmistakeably him.

"Albert Livingstone?" Han asked, his tone genial enough.

"Yes? Can I help you?" No fear, just open curiosity.

"DC Wright: West Yorkshire Police. Can I come in?"

Livingstone's eyes widened a fraction and his cheeks flushed. "Err … why? What's the problem?"

"No problem, Mister Livingstone. In fact, it's actually more something you can help us with."

26

Uncertainty. His cheeks were now crimson at the centre and white around the edges and his jaw clenched and unclenched. In a strained, but polite tone, he asked, "Can I see some identification?"

"Of course." Han pulled out the doctored ID that he had taken from Wright's still warm corpse back in Haydon. He flashed it, showing his picture with Wright's credentials. A keener eye might have noticed that it was actually a Northumbria Police ID. He had prepared an answer for that all the same: on secondment, but it wasn't needed.

Livingstone reluctantly unhooked the chain and withdrew into the hall, pulling the door fully open.

Han snatched up his rucksack and walked past him into the living room. The room was in semi-darkness with heavy burgundy curtains still drawn. There was a faint musty aroma; like that of a house that had stood empty for some time, perhaps with some mothballs thrown in for good measure. But it was clean and tidy – maybe obsessively so.

As Livingstone came in behind him, Han flicked the light switch to illuminate the room, not wanting him to open the curtains. He dumped the bag at his feet.

Livingstone walked over to a small cheap circular dining table set at the far end of the room, near a door that most likely led to the kitchen. A clothing catalogue was sat open on it. He closed it and set it aside on a bookshelf that was filled with mainly well-thumbed paperbacks.

Han observed him in silence, guessing what section the catalogue must have been opened at.

Livingstone then stood in the centre of the room and wrung his hands together, glancing from rucksack to intruder. Other than the bookcase, there were very few signs of personal inhabitation. There were no photographs or memorabilia of any kind on mantelpiece or walls. As Han took in the room, Livingstone, unable to bear the silence, said, "So … how can I help, officer?"

Han stared at him and, his tone even, said, "Sit down, Mister Livingstone."

Livingstone complied immediately. Sitting on the edge of the sofa, he asked, "Would … err … you like a cup of tea?"

Han ignored the question. As he slowly walked over to the seated man, he drew a pair of rubber gloves from his pocket and proceeded to pull them on. It was casual, unhurried, but such a bizarre act should have rung alarm bells, but Livingstone simply gawped at him, with a mask of utter confusion.

With gloves on, Han drew a simple kitchen knife from another pocket. His smile was almost apologetic, like a nurse reassuring a patient. *Don't worry, we'll have this over with in a jiffy.*

With the glint of sharp steel, confusion finally morphed into fear. Livingstone immediately started to rise, mouth opening to speak.

The movement a blur, Han thrust the blade into Livingstone's fleshy stomach and shoved the man back onto the sofa.

Livingstone slumped back in the chair, clutching the wound. The crimson spot around the neat tear in his shirt was growing rapidly. "What? What are you doing?" Livingstone gasped, his face contorting with both pain and shock.

"I thought that was pretty obvious, Al. I'm killing you."

Rising panic stretching his vocal cords to breaking point, Livingstone managed to shriek, "Why? Please, no!"

"Keep your voice down, Al, otherwise I will make this very painful indeed."

Livingstone's mouth fell open, but only managed a low whine. Thick oozing blood was seeping through his fingers. He looked from it back to Han, fully dilated pupils pleading.

"Thank you, Al," Han said. As if chastising a naughty child, he added, "Now, you're a paedophile – a kiddie-fiddler, if you will. So that should be reason enough."

Realisation dawned on Livingstone's face. His worst fears had finally caught up with him. His mouth started working before his brain could kick in. Stammering, he managed, "Please … please, that was so long ago! I … was sick. I'm all better now! Please!"

Han put the bloodied knife close to his lips and said, "Shhh."

Livingstone bit his lip and began visibly trembling. *"Please,"* he managed in an overwrought whisper. Moaning and rocking in the chair, he gripped his stomach, as if his intestines might spill out.

"As I was saying, that is reason enough for me to gut you like a fish, but as it happens you're going to be part of something much bigger. As you're the first, I shall tell you. I'll try to keep it brief because I don't want to monologue like a Bond villain. It's so clichéd." He laughed at that and suddenly a fleeting image of Steve Belmont's angry and terrified face sprung to mind.

"I ... I don't understand." Tears were streaming down Livingstone's cheeks and the blood was now soaking into the fabric sofa.

"No, but you will. Do you recall the Haydon massacre in Northumberland just over a year ago?"

"Y–yes."

"That was the first part of my masterpiece – although I didn't know it at the time, but I digress. I murdered three hundred and ninety six essentially innocent people, not-so-good doctors' aside."

"Oh ... *God* ..." Livingstone was ghostly pale. He had stopped rocking and sat as still as a corpse, only his bottom lip quivering to betray him.

"He had nowt to do with it, as Reverend Dunhealy would attest to; if he could. Now, to redress the balance I must murder the same number of the guilty. As you can imagine, I've got my work cut out, but you should feel honoured to be the first."

Livingstone appeared to regain some of his composure. Cringing as he eased forward, he said, "I ... I paid for my crime!"

Han snorted. "That line ain't gonna work with me, Al. You're a guilty man and you must die. If it makes you feel any better, there will be three hundred and ninety five more who will follow you."

Livingstone's shirt, and the sofa around him, were drenched and blood was now dribbling onto the carpet. Despite the blood-loss, Livingstone still managed to push himself into an unsteady standing crouch. "I refuse to be ... party to your absurd game!"

Han let him rise and laughed at the angry rebuke. "This isn't a game show, mate. You don't get an opportunity to open a box to win your life. You were a dead man the second you fiddled with that little girl."

Livingstone threw out his arms, groping for Han's neck. Han easily swatted them away and then planted a punch in the middle of the pervert's face. The man's nose crunched under his gloved knuckles and specks of blood and spittle sprayed in all directions.

Livingstone sagged back to the sofa, weeping. A hand half-heartedly rose to his bleeding nose, but then flopped back down to his side.

Han crouched down to Livingstone's level and gently lifted his chin to look into the man's bloodshot eyes.

"*Please* ..."

"Release me, let me go ..." Han sung, using the knife as a microphone. Han chuckled, but seeing the hopelessness in the man's teary eyes, he cut it short. He wasn't the sort to get a kick out of humiliation.

"Albert Livingstone," he said in a formal tone. "This is your death." Han offered him a consolatory smile then thrust the knife into his eye.

Livingstone managed soft mewing sounds as his body twitched with the impact of each thrust of the knife. The first blow split Livingstone's eye in half, spurting blood and fluid out onto his chest. The subsequent thrusts tore open cheeks and nose. Han repeatedly stabbed the man in the face until it was nothing more than a gory void. Albert Livingstone was dead long before Han finished, but he liked to be thorough.

Han stepped back from his handy work, wiping the dripping blade on a cloth. He nodded, like a craftsman finally satisfied with a long and arduous commission.

He spent more than an hour cleaning up. He wiped the light switch and splashed bleach everywhere that he had walked for good measure. Once satisfied, he undressed on plastic sheeting beside the front door and placed all his bloodstained clothes into a plastic bag. After dressing in clean clothes, he stepped outside and retrieved the sheet.

As he stuffed the sheet back into his rucksack with the stained clothes, he unhurriedly retraced his steps back to his Peugeot then drove back to Leeds. On the way, he would find a secluded area and burn the soiled clothes.

At first, he felt a sort of righteous elation – as if he had performed a genuine service to society. That passed quickly. This was a chore – part of Phase Two of the experiment, nothing more. But, for a few minutes, he actually felt like one of the good guys. That absurd concept made him roar with laughter. So much so, that he had to pull over into a lay-by to hold his aching stomach. Tears rolled down his face for several minutes.

He sat there with the engine idling as icy sleet began to spatter the windscreen. Wiping tears from his eyes, he switched the wipers on to a low setting then put the engine back into gear.

Not your time, son ...

The words crowbarred their way into his head. Those same four fucking words. Where the hell had he heard that?

His mood ruined, he set off once again in brooding silence.

Yeah, you're gonna bring yourself down,
I got soul, but I'm not a soldier ...
'All These Things That I've Done' by The Killers

CHAPTER 2

The rear ramp of the RAF C-130 Hercules military transport aircraft lowered to reveal several soldiers in desert fatigues. A tall well-built man at the front of the group slung his kitbag over one broad shoulder and strode down the ramp onto the tarmac of RAF Lyneham. The others followed. The men looked haggard and their fatigues, although clean, were faded and tatty. Despite exhaustion from the journey and a gruelling tour, they still chatted animatedly amongst themselves, all except the leading man.

A six tonne truck was waiting to ferry them back to 40 Commando Royal Marines barracked at Taunton.

The others spoke to him here and there on the journey to the barracks. His responses were always only a nod or a single word, but it did not seem to irritate his comrades. They understood.

Once there, the big man was ushered into his commander's office. A couple of his comrades watched him go with sombre expressions.

"Ah, Sergeant Wright. Sit down, son." The major was a wiry man, almost as tall as Wright when standing, and with the patient face of a school teacher.

"Thank you, sir." Wright sat down in front of the officer's desk.

"We're all going to be sorry to see you go, son. You're a bloody good marine and a fine leader."

"Thank you, sir. That means a lot." Wright shifted in his seat, but his expression remained dispassionate.

"However," the major continued, "I would be bereft of my duty if I neglected to mention the glaringly obvious."

"Sir—"

"Let me finish, son." There was no sternness, only a fatherly concern. "What happened to your father in Haydon was appalling and for you to continue with your duties afterwards, including a tour of Afghanistan, is highly commendable. However, we'd be kidding ourselves if we pretended not to know why you're leaving us. All the lads know that you're going to try to find out who was responsible for your father's murder and for the rest of those poor buggers killed up in Northumberland."

Wright was silent for a moment, then, choosing his words carefully, he said, "Sir, after everything that's happened – and everything I've been through – me heart just isn't in it anymore. I did want to find the bastard at first, but now … I'm tired, I just want to go home and spend time with me sister and her family."

"Some of the brass may buy that line, but I know you, Wright. You're a fucking warrior and a damn good one." Leaning forward, he sighed and added, "Look, the entire resources of the police, along with a host of intelligence agencies, combed through every centimetre of Haydon and every piece of evidence and information remotely relating to the case. They came up with precisely zero. Nothing. Just what the hell do you expect to achieve?"

"Me dad's dead, sir. There is nothing to achieve." A flicker of pain marred his unyielding features for a brief moment.

"Take my advice, Will; go home and start building a new life for yourself. Don't waste your life chasing a ghost."

After demobbing, Will Wright, son of Detective Constable Tony Wright, boarded a train bound for Durham. He was indeed planning to spend some time with his sister in the cathedral town. He needed to see her and to be around her family for a time, and not just because of Dad. Helmand had taken its toll as well. He needed to clear his head and recharge the batteries. But after that, the hunt was on.

The last known survivor of Haydon – Carol Belmont – was first on the list. Then, the mass murderer known as Hannibal Whitman.

As rolling Devonshire countryside hurtled by, Wright's only thoughts were of Whitman. *I will find you, Whitman. And I will kill you with my bare fucking hands.*

***

The internet café was bustling with lunchtime browsers of all persuasions: kids, students, office workers and silver surfers. Han Whitman had chosen a public access point after his first target, so as not to draw unnecessary suspicion if the authorities were monitoring access to the 'hit list' site. He would have to make more permanent arrangements in the future. An exposed public place like this made him a little twitchy.

He had already checked that this particular café did not have any CCTV. He had also strategically positioned himself at a terminal that was not easily visible from fellow surfers.

He called up the same site, but this time typed in a York postcode. Again, he clicked on the first name, which amazingly was once again less than a mile from his chosen postcode. *Dirty fuckers are on every doorstep. I should be getting paid for this shit!*

A photograph of a particularly pug-ugly chav by the name of Darren Horner appeared, along with statistics and offences. This delightful fellow had previous for burglary and assault, in addition to his numerous child offences.

34

After jotting down the pertinent details and burning the face of the piece of shit into his brain, Han deleted the web browser history, wiped down the keyboard and mouse, and then left.

This one was no accountant; Darren had the face of a boxer and the shoulders of a brickie, so Han decided that a little more preparation would be in order for number two.

As well as his usual gear, Han procured a pistol – a rather 'well-used' former gangland classic 1976 Beretta 92. It wasn't a patch on the Walther P99 he had used up in Haydon, but it would serve its purpose. It also came with an attachable suppressor for more clandestine work. Silencers were notoriously unreliable and certainly nowhere near as quiet as they were depicted in films, but it was better than nothing.

Darren's street was a tad down-market in comparison to old man Livingstone's. It was a rough-arse meandering council-hovel estate, perhaps in Scud missile range of York Minster. Han had visited York on a number of occasions over the years and had no idea such a picturesque town could harbour such puke-stains, but that's just ASBO Britain for you. Where there's a Maccy Ds there's a chav nest, regardless of the local per capita income.

There was no one home the first try, which was bloody inconsiderate. So, Han partook in a spot of spontaneous sight-seeing, taking in the Castle Museum, the York Art Gallery and the Railway Museum.

On returning after 4pm, the dirt-smeared door, that looked as though it had been jimmied more than once, opened to reveal a young teenage girl. She was dressed in a grubby school uniform, with a skirt that was too short and a blouse that showed her pierced belly button. Her dirty blonde hair was loosely tied back with a scrunchie and she was chewing incessantly.

"Wot?"

Yes, it has to be said, the girl was a real charmer.

"Hi." Han offered a friendly smile. "Is Darren Horner home?"

"Na." She folded her arms across her chest – the push up bra wasn't helping her boyish frame. "What's he done now, like?"

35

"Actually, it's something he might be able to help us with." Scrunchie Lolita had assumed one thing and he wasn't about to correct her. "Do you know how long he'll be?"

"Dunno. Not long – he doesn't get his giro till tomorrow."

"Can I come in and wait?"

"S'pose so." A baby started crying from within. "I'll have to see to Nikita-Jade." She started walking through to the kitchen.

Han hesitated, picking up his rucksack that, as with Livingstone, he had left out of sight to one side of the door, then followed, closing the door behind him. He dropped the bag just inside the living room as he walked past to the kitchen.

Scrunchie was picking up a chocolate-smeared toddler off the sticky linoleum. Han stood in the doorway and said, "Cute baby. Your sister?"

Scrunchie shot him a glaring sideways glance. "Fuck off. She's me little angel."

Lisa's face flashed before his eyes. *My angel* ... He had to blink a couple of times and gulp in some baby-puke air to heave himself back into the present. *Focus, you ponse! There is no Lisa. Lisa is gone.*

Well, at least that explained the name then. "Nikita-Jade, eh? Pretty name." *Jesus, that actually sounded sincere. Those Oscars are beckoning. The award for best performing serial killer goes to ...*

Han noticed bruising and scratches on the back of Scrunchie's legs as she cradled the child. She was wiping away some of the chocolate and grime from her face with some balled up toilet paper. "Must be hard juggling a baby with school," he said finally, leaning against the doorframe.

"It's not the little un that takes the looking after it's the big prick who helped make her." She seemed to catch herself and quickly added, "Me sister helps out – she's been fucking great. She's been helping us with me SATS Stage 3 too – dunno what I'd do without her." Under her breath, she muttered, "Probably be stuck in this shit hole for the rest of me natch."

"What about your mum and dad?" Han asked, initial prejudices giving way to a form of begrudging pity.

She stared at him again, but saw only sincerity in his kindly features. She suddenly had to choke back a sob and turned away quickly to conceal it. "Kicked us out, like," she managed after a moment. "When Darren got us knocked up. Said I brought shame to the family getting pregnant so young."

Han stepped forward and put a hand on her shoulder as she buried her face into her daughter. He felt her shiver under his touch. "What are you doing with this loser?"

Without looking up, she said, "He looks after me and Nikita-Jade. Without him I'd be on the street and the social'd take my angel away from us." She glanced at him briefly, adding passionately, "I *won't* let that happen."

"I know he hurts you – don't even try to deny it."

She concealed her face against her daughter again. She did not respond, but he heard a soft snivel and her shoulders trembled.

"There's help out there for young mothers, you know. People who care." *What the fuck am I saying? Shut up, you tosser!*

She stared at him through bloodshot eyes that appeared twenty years older than the young teenager they belonged to. "No one will help me. Darren only keeps us to be his easy fuck."

"Darren is a convicted paedophile, a thief, a bully and a general all round piece of shit." No point in beating round the bush. With a nod to the grimy bundle in her arms, he added, "Think of your daughter!"

"What?" Genuine shock bit into her despair. "He's a fucking paedo?"

Han shook his head in disbelief. "Does that really surprise you? Come on! He's been having sex with you since you were what? Fourteen? Maybe even earlier?" Why was he saying all this bollocks?

The shame in her eyes said more than words could. "I – I didn't … he was nice to us … at first."

Han grabbed her shoulders firmly. The toddler gurgled then smiled at him. "Look, get some things together right now and go to your sister's. She can help you speak to the right people who'll help you."

"I can't! What about Darren?" she implored.

"You let me deal with Darren. You just promise me one thing; whatever happens and whatever you hear; you saw nothing today. You came home from school, gathered your things and went straight to your sister's house. You know *nothing*." He didn't like where he was taking this.

Her trembling subsided and her eyes widened. "What … what are you going to do?"

"When you're settled I'll send you some money to help get you started." He caught the change in her expression and added, "You will never see me again after today. I'll send you a little money to help start you off, because I think you deserve a break – that's all. No deals, no favours – just a one off bit of no questions asked help. For you and your daughter. But you have to leave now before he gets home and you can't mention anything about me to anyone. Ever."

As Scrunchie Lolita threw clothes and baby paraphernalia into a bin bag, Han pondered on what had just happened. Happened, rather than what he had actually consciously decided to do seemed more appropriate. He was now, for want of a better word, gob-smacked.

He was effectively allowing two witnesses to walk out the door, knowing fine well that he was about to murder the boyfriend/father/paedo/scrunchie-beater. What the fuck was he thinking? Could this be another aspect of the experiment that he hadn't considered? Not just the erasing of bad elements, but also coming to the aid of the victims? It all seemed a bit *Little House on the Prairie*, but he hadn't made a conscious decision and also the elimination of innocents was strictly forbidden in Phase Two of course. Thinking about it, what else could he have done other than abort altogether? So, he supposed that it could stand … this time. He had no intention of making a habit of it though!

Scrunchie hesitated in the hallway with baby-stupid-name and a bin bag full of crap. She seemed to shuffle from foot to foot, with uncertainty etched into her features. "I … I don't even know your name."

"It's best if you don't. When you walk out of that door, you forget everything about me. And forget about Darren too. Your new life starts right now." Your *new life*? Christ, what was the matter with him? He sounded like a right twat. He used to piss himself laughing at shit like that in films. *You've just been erased,* Han mused in a mock Arnie voice from the confines of his own head.

She opened her mouth to speak, but instead she suddenly threw her free arm around him and hugged him, fresh tears streaming down her cheeks. He felt her delicate frame trembling against him, the gurgling toddler dribbling against his neck. His first reaction was to recoil, but instead he rather awkwardly returned the embrace and then watched them leave.

He stared at the closed door for a time in silence. Then he shook his head and sniffed his jacket. "Great, now I smell like a fucking happy meal mixed with kiddie-vom."

Rolling his eyes, he clapped his hands together and said, "Right, let's get this party started."

After closing the curtains in the living room, he then laid out plastic sheeting over most of the carpet. "Plastic sheeting … check! Can't have a party without plastic sheeting," he said, back to his old self once more.

As he finished his preparations, he heard keys jangling at the front door, along with inaudible mutterings.

Han stepped behind the living room door and plucked a claw hammer out of his inner jacket pocket. Barely containing a snigger, he whispered, "Claw hammer … check!"

"Kelly?" a voice shouted from the hallway. "Kelly, where the fuck are ya?"

Ah, so that was her name. Scrunchie Lolita had more of a ring to it.

Heavy footsteps through to the kitchen and then, "Kelly? No fucking tea on! You better not be in bed, you lazy bitch!"

Damn, Darren, you are a real catch! How do they resist you? Ah, yes, with extreme force, I should imagine.

After a great deal of cursing and grumbling, the door to the living room pushed open and a stocky man in his early thirties swaggered in. He could've been the poster boy for a national chav recruitment campaign. Kappa baseball cap pushed right back on his skinned head, tracksuit and lairy over-sized trainers. Complete the

39

picture with chunky Argos gold sovs and chain and a latticework of homemade tattoos.

Here, ladies and gentlemen, is a specimen that epitomises the very substructure of modern western society's gene pool. How proud you all must feel.

Darren Horner stepped into the room and failed to notice the plastic sheeting until he was several steps in. He looked down at his feet and frowned. "What the fuck? Has that fucking brat pissed all over the front room?"

"No." Han appeared behind him and, as Darren began to spin round, he cracked the hammer across the top of his head. The baseball cap flew across the room and bounced against the safety guard on the gas fire. Darren dropped to the ground without a word, unconscious and bleeding from a deep gash in his scalp.

"Okie-dokey, then," Han said, his tone cheery now that he was doing what he did best. First, he stripped Darren down to his Y-fronts (he had no desire to stare at another man's penis – call him old fashioned!) He then bound his wrists and ankles with cable ties and wrapped the body in the sheeting. He then dragged him up the stairs, pausing only to catch his breath at the top of the staircase. Holding his side, he said, "Note to self: If I'm to continue with Phase Two I must get back to the gym."

After some more wheezing and straining, Han managed to place the body face up in the bath and started running both taps. As Han recovered, the bath quickly filled so that only Darren's face and knees remained poking out of the water.

As Darren gradually regained consciousness, Han proceeded to empty a packet of sodium hydroxide granules into the tepid bathwater.

"What?" Darren muttered. As his blinking eyes began taking in his surroundings, he added, "What the fuck? Who the fuck?"

"Wakey, wakey, sleepy head," Han said as he stirred the water with a wooden spoon borrowed from the kitchen.

Darren's foggy brain finally began to process his predicament. "What the fuck yer doing?"

Han smiled. "Glad you asked. This is much more fun with audience participation. I have submerged you in a bath that I have just filled with pure sodium hydroxide – caustic soda to you and me. In its pure form it is extremely corrosive."

"What?" He was still too confused to feel fear or anger yet, but it would come.

"They speak English in 'What'?" Han asked with a chuckle. "Your skin will quickly start to burn and will, over time, dissolve, whereupon the soda will then go to work on the meat." *Here it comes ...*

"Cunt!" Darren cried. "No! Get me the fuck out of here!" A mixture of terror and rage coursed through Darren as he twisted and contorted against his bonds, splashing water over the garish violet carpet.

Without a word, Han produced the hammer and smashed Darren in the teeth with it. Several teeth shattered, leaving his mouth a bloody mess. Before Darren could scream in agony, Han pulled out a roll of masking tape and wrapped a long strip several times around Darren's head, covering his bloody mouth. Once secured, Han washed his gloved hands thoroughly before turning back to Darren, who was whimpering and trembling.

With marked delight, Han noticed that Darren's body was already starting to turn an angry red. "That should be starting to smart some now, kiddo."

Fraught mumblings were all Darren could manage as he continued to squirm.

"This is no good, Darren, old buddy. Can't have you splashing around like this and causing a ruckus." Han took his jacket off, hung it on the back of the door and then rolled up his sleeves. "Where's my head at?" he said to Darren, shaking his head in mock disbelief. "Should've thought of this earlier." Darren's struggling was feeble and disorientated, given his concussion, smashed mouth and bonds, so Han was easily able to manipulate his legs into a manageable position.

Gripping each knee in turn, whilst whistling *Whistle While You Work*, Han then proceeded to repeatedly smash the hammer down onto both of Darren's exposed knees until they were crushed beyond recognition. Blood oozing from his wounds quickly turned the bathwater a deep scarlet. Sometime during the onslaught, Darren passed out.

Han man-handled him into a sitting position and then took the claw to the inside of Darren's elbows, gouging at the flesh and tendons. Darren woke up briefly, but quickly passed out again.

Satisfied, Han set Darren back into his original prone position and then thoroughly cleaned the room and then himself.

As Han pulled his coat on, he took one final look at Darren. "No goodbyes?" It would've been a nice final touch for the dirty little prick to wake up before he left, but he obviously wasn't feeling in an obliging mood.

On the plus side, his skin was starting to blister badly already. Hopefully, he would wake up a few times to feel the scolding agony over his entire body before dying, probably of blood loss. As long as the body remained undisturbed for a few days there'd be very little left after that.

***

Detective Chief Inspector Karen Carter stepped past the ashen-faced uniform standing on the landing and into the bathroom. The room was small at the best of times, but with a pathologist and a SOCO already at work inside, it was standing room only.

Carter had fifteen years on the Force and had worked several departments, including Scotland Yard's renowned CO19 unit, before settling on CID. She had seen a lot of dead bodies in her time, but none like Darren Horner.

As she took in the grim scene, she picked at an annoying dinner fugitive lodged in her teeth.

"Hi, Karen," the pathologist said, glancing up. He was kneeling in front of the bath, gloved hands fishing amongst the brown soupy goo that was a blend of skin, flesh, blood and water. The remains of the body had slipped beneath the surface, but two smashed knees were still visible, skin gone and flesh jellified and oozing. Despite the horrific sight – and smell – the man had a cheerful tone. "How are you doing?"

"Better than Mister Horner, I'd guess," she said humourlessly. She ran a hand through her tightly cropped raven hair and said, "So what's the score, Andy?"

"Well, he's definitely dead, I'm afraid."

"I hope you at least attempted mouth to mouth."

"I would've, but he didn't have a mouth left to try," Andy said and chuckled to himself. Switching to a more businesslike tone, he said, "We have a Caucasian male, positively ID'd as a one Darren Horner." He nodded at the SOCO as the white protective suit-clad man stepped outside to speak to the uniformed officer. "According to Phil, the victim was attacked in the living room, knocked unconscious and dragged up here. He was bound and gagged and then placed in the bath, which was filled with water mixed with sodium hydroxide. Something like a claw hammer was used to further immobilize the victim. He was then left – still alive at this point – to gradually erode. Victim died of blood loss, which I'm guessing came as a huge relief to him. Time of death estimated at around sixty hours ago."

"Sodium hydroxide?"

"Caustic soda – highly corrosive. If the bath hadn't been enamelled steel it probably would've corroded right through it too. Our perp or perps also cleaned up after themselves. No tools, no mess, not even a stray flake of soda."

Carter clicked her tongue. "What's the availability of–"

Anticipating the question, Andy said, "Sodium hydroxide – even in pure flake form – is easily obtainable from any number of stores or online."

A younger detective popped his head around the door. "Ma'am."

Carter rolled her eyes. She hated Richard calling her that. It sounded so bloody decrepit and out-dated. Boss, detective, DCI, Carter, anything rather than ma'am. "What, *Howie?*" she asked tetchily. She always resorted to his nickname when he irritated her.

Richard frowned, but then said, "Horner was on the sex offenders register."

Carter snapped her head around to stare at him. "Like the other two?"

43

***

Over the following two weeks, Han eliminated two more perverts from the hit list website before police and media attention began cottoning on to the paedophile angle. Although Darren was second to be eliminated, he ended up being third to be discovered. The newspapers had used evocative headlines like *Gruesome Find* and *Shocking Discovery*, so he must have been a pretty sight.

His instinct to let Kelly go had been sound. She had been interviewed several times, but had stuck vehemently to the story that Han had suggested. And, true to his word, Han had sent £500 in an unmarked envelope to help her with her new life. It wasn't much, but it was a gesture. Any more might have risked the authorities taking notice.

Han sat in the same coffee shop that he had met his brother in several weeks ago. Thinking about that last visit, he realised how much had changed since then. He felt like a completely different person to that jaded husk. *Han reborn ... Han Rising, maybe? Nah, that was the worst film of the franchise.*

Someone had left a crumpled copy of the Yorkshire Evening Post on the table, so Han absently thumbed through it. He rarely read newspapers these days – he picked up all the news he needed from the internet usually.

A headline caught his attention – WORST FAMILY IN BRITAIN. And underneath, *One family crime wave hold entire community hostage.*

With growing interest, Han read the story. A family of rogues were responsible for terrorising a Leeds housing estate. Collectively, they were responsible for everything from burglary, car theft, mugging, vandalism and drug dealing to public disorder, assault and even animal cruelty. Move over Ed O'Neill, this is Britain's modern family. The Dixon family made the Maguires look like the Waltons.

This was a turn up for the books. Ma, Pa and three sons. Five for the price of one. Bargain! They had all done time in one way or another, even the youngest, who, according to the

44

newspaper, at fifteen had already enjoyed three spells in a juvenile prison. That made every man jack of them fair game.

Goodnight, John-Boy ...

CHAPTER 3

It's fair to say that the Dixons' stomping ground had probably seen better days. The local shop was boarded up, with delightful slogans adorning it, including *Al-Qaeda Cunts!* and *Pakis Fuk Off.* It comes to something when graffiti artists can't even spell swearwords. Is the education system at fault or the individual? Or, is it just pure text-speak laziness? Hey, at least they spelled Al-Qaeda right. They could manage to spell the name of an Islamic militant group correctly, but not rudimentary English words. What does that tell us, kids?

There was a local boozer and a betting shop, of course, but they resembled fortified bunkers, with barred windows, reinforced doors and barbed wire topping walls and flat roofs.

A burned out car of some description, a scattering of derelict council houses and a shopping trolley completed the picture.

A police car cruised slowly by. Han kept his head turned slightly to the side to avoid any chance of identification. He was dressed in a combat jacket, Nike baseball cap and trainers, so he didn't exactly stick out.

Dusk was throwing long shadows over the broken bottles and lager cans.

The Dixon residence wasn't hard to miss. There were three cars in various stages of decomposition and a Subaru Impreza that had been modified almost beyond recognition. Vin Diesel would've been impressed. There were a couple of motorbikes, dog kennels and an assortment of engine parts and rubbish littering what had once been a lawn behind a chain-link fence. The iron gate had a hand-painted sign that read, FUCK THE DOG, BEWARE THE OWNER.

As Han reached the gate, a grubby Staffordshire Bull Terrier raced out of its kennel and charged the barrier. Han knelt down and stared into its eyes as its drooling jaws snapped in between the iron bars.

It continued to bark as he stared at it. "That shit usually works in the movies," he said, deciding that he wasn't going to unnerve this little ball of rage.

"Who the fuck are you?" a voice snapped, not dissimilar to the dog's.

Han rose to see a monster of a man emerging from the front door. Bald, barrel-chested, tattooed and wearing a grubby vest and tracksuit bottoms, he was exactly what Han expected from Pa Dixon. He was around forty and looked like a bouncer who had been put out to pasture.

"Raymond Dixon Senior?" Han asked.

"What do you want, pig?" the man asked, folding massive arms across his chest in defiance.

Why did everyone think he was a copper? He wasn't sure whether he should take that as a compliment or not. But, it did serve a purpose. "I'd like to come in for a quiet word, if you don't mind." Han kept his tone friendly as the Staffie continued to bark incessantly on the other side of the gate.

"We make some fucking headlines in some fucking rag I wouldn't wipe my arse on and you come sniffing round like a bitch on heat." It's safe to say, the man didn't have a whole lot of gushing respect for the boys in blue.

"I've just got a couple of questions to ask and then I'll be out of your hair," Han said. "Or we can do it down the station. It's up to you."

"Sabre," Ray snarled at the dog, "shut the fuck up and go to your bed."

47

The Staffie snapped one final time and then trotted back to its kennel.

"Let's get it fucking over with then," he muttered and walked back into the house.

As Han walked in, a man in his late teens – the middle son – shouted from the top of the stairs, "Who's this cunt?"

"Mind your own fucking business, Tyler," Ray replied, walking into the living room. "And take that fucking mutt for a walk!"

Han followed him, allowing the baton to slip down his sleeve and into his hand.

Ray started to turn around, saying, "So what's this about?"

Han leapt at him, bringing the baton down hard onto the top of his head. The blow dazed the bigger man and he stumbled backwards, knocking over a coffee table that was overflowing with empty lager cans and a butt-filled ashtray. Cans scattered everywhere.

"Cunt!" the man screamed as Han waded in with a second and third blow onto his head.

Han could hear a commotion upstairs, so he knew he didn't have long. He battered Ray several more times until the man fell back onto the leather sofa with a grunt, blood trickling from one ear.

"Da!" Tyler was shouting as he rushed down the stairs.

A female voice was also shouting from the kitchen. "Ray? What the fuck's going on?"

Han stepped to one side of the living room door and raised the baton. Tyler was first through. He was bald and tattooed, like his father, but wiry. His neck was covered in love bites. Han brought the baton down onto the back of his neck.

Tyler went down like a sack of spuds.

A fat lolloping woman, wheezing and cursing followed. She had a moustache that would put Tom Selleck's to shame and a six-inch kitchen knife.

Han could have stunned her like Tyler, but the stinky creature was so offensive to his senses that he batted the knife out of her hand first. The crack signified a definite fracture in either the

48

Radius or the Ulna or both. She would have to shovel pie and chips in with the other claw for a while.

Her scream reminded Han of Medusa and it almost made him wince. With thoughts of polished shields from the gods, he proceeded to batter her several times in the face for good measure. As her screams turned into gurgles, he stepped back and rubbed his temple. "Jesus, woman. You're giving me a headache."

Ray was stirring on the sofa, so Han wasted no time in binding his arms and legs with cable ties. He then dragged Tyler over to the sofa and deposited him next to his father after binding him as well.

He then looked down at the mother. Blood from her broken face was staining the dirty grey carpet. She was dressed in stained black leggings and a t-shirt that could've doubled for a tent.

"Who the fuck are you?" Ray muttered, grimacing.

"That doesn't matter right now," Han said as he continued to stare at the piece of filth that was bleeding on the carpet. "I'm just debating whether to kill your munter of a wife where she fell or truss her up like you two first." Han glanced over at Ray who had now fixed his livid stare on him. "What do you think? To be honest, I don't think I'm strong enough to move it."

Ray started struggling against his bonds, but even his considerable strength was no match for the ties. "I'm going to fucking kill you! Is it the Malloy brothers? Did those cunts send you?"

Han laughed as Tyler began stirring. "Glad you could join us, Tyler." Turning back to Ray, he said, "No, this isn't some drug-related hit, matey. This is a … let's call it a retribution-related hit."

"Who? Who fucking sent you? I'll kill him, his family, his friends, everyone who ever laid eyes on him! I'll even kill his fucking pet cat, you cunt."

"Well, that's not very nice. What's Mister Flibble ever done to you, eh?" Jolly Moe's chubby and heavily tanned face sprung to mind.

"What?" Ray spat. "Who the fuck is Mister Flibble?"

Han shrugged. "Never mind. Let's get things moving before your other two walking abortions return home, eh?"

After pulling on a pair of gloves, while both father and son spat and cursed at him, he then picked up the knife that Mrs Blobby had dropped.

With a nod towards the unconscious whale on the floor, Han said, "Do you still shag *that*? Do you have any pride? It stinks of shit, for Christ's sake."

Ray continued to struggle, screaming, "I'll fucking rip your tongue out!"

Han rolled his eyes. Kneeling down beside Ma Dixon, he grabbed a handful of her matted hair and lifted her head off the ground. "Jesus, her head's like a bowling ball!" he said and laughed. Without any further fuss, he tore her throat open. A torrent of blood gushed onto the carpet.

"No!" Tyler screamed in utter disbelief.

"Motherfucker!" Ray spat, his body bucking and thrashing on the sofa.

"One down, four to go," Han said and walked over to Tyler.

As Tyler wet himself, his father stopped thrashing and asked, "Why? What is this about, you piece of shit?"

Han stared at him, incredulous. "You really need to ask? You and your family are a stain on this country. Every last one of you is scum – evil down to the core." Shaking his head, he added, "Well, it's time to pay the piper, mate."

"Please …" Tyler whimpered as Han stood over him.

"Don't even fucking try it," Han said. "I've read all about your exploits, you little shit stain."

As Tyler tried to shuffle towards his struggling father, Han knelt on the sofa and grabbed the young man's head. With one swift movement, he drove the blade up through his chin and into his brain. He was still twitching as Han wrenched the knife free and turned to Pa.

Ray had turned beetroot and his sweating, trembling face glared at Han as he walked over to him.

"Just fucking kill me then, you cunt!" Ray shouted. "Just get it over with."

"I will," Han replied evenly. "I haven't really got time to mess about. Just so you know though, I will sort your other two out when they get back."

"No …" the big man managed weakly.

"Now, hold still …"

***

Han sat in the armchair opposite the sofa, silently staring at the gaping sockets where Ray's eyes used to be. He made the prick suffer a little longer than the other two. He was the head of the household after all, so deserved some special treatment.

He was surprised that Pa's screams hadn't roused any interest from the neighbours. He had kept one eye on the street outside the whole time, half expecting the police car from earlier to turn up. But it didn't. No one came. The neighbours had probably heard worse. Nobody gave a shit. He was ridding the world of a few more scumbags, that's all.

As he considered that, he heard the squeaky gate open. Peaking through a crack in the curtains, he saw the other two boys. The Staffie had been unusually quiet throughout the whole episode, but now it chose its moment to bolt for freedom. It pelted straight past the two brothers and disappeared down the street.

They shouted after it but then looked at each other, confused. "Fuck it," the elder brother said. "Fucker'll come back when he's hungry."

Han stood up and waited behind the living room door.

The two brothers entered the hall, the elder saying, "Bit quiet, like. Are we being good now that we're celebrities?" The younger brother laughed.

They stopped at the open door to the lounge and Han heard them gasp. "What the fuck?" the elder blurted out.

"Ma!" the younger one cried and rushed into the room, falling to his knees by his dead monster-mother.

Elder stepped in behind him, mouth agape. Han stepped out, gripped him hard around the neck and sunk the blade into his side. As he cried out, Han stabbed him twice more in the stomach

51

and let him keel over. He stumbled over his mother's legs and struck a cabinet with his head.

"Billy!" the younger one cried, tears streaming down his face. He jumped up and rushed at Han. "Bastard!"

Han let him come and, at the last minute, punched him in the face then followed up with a swift kick to the family jewels. The boy crumpled.

As the younger one gasped for air, Han finished off Billy by stabbing him a couple of times in the heart.

He then grabbed the youngest one and shoved him into the armchair. "Time to join the rest of your scum family."

Gasping, the boy cried, "Please! Me Pa battered us! Me brother used to fiddle with us!" Between gasps, he began sobbing, his head in his hands. "I hated em all!"

"Sorry, matey, but that ain't good enough," Han said, shaking his head apologetically.

"Am only thirteen, man! I don't deserve this!"

Han was leaning in to finish him off. He stopped, inches from the boy. "Thirteen? The paper said you were fifteen."

"Cunts can't even get me age right! Said I went to Juvie three times. I went to an STC once for nicking. Me da made us do it!"

Han stepped back and frowned. A secure training centre wasn't exactly Strangeways. Thirteen years old and one conviction for theft? Could the newspaper have gotten some of the details wrong? It certainly wasn't beyond the realms of possibility. The question was, did one minor conviction and a poor upbringing still make him fair game?

"Bit of a dilemma," he said aloud.

The boy looked up through his hands, sudden hope in his eyes. "They were horrible people – they deserved everything they got. Please let me go. I can be a good person if I can get out of this shithole. Please, mister!"

Han sighed. Another bloody victim. It was all rather inconvenient. But he had let Scrunchie Lolita go. That had worked out alright, so maybe this boy was another example. It was one less for the tally, but if he was going to complete Phase Two correctly, he had no choice.

"Alright, kid," he said finally with a disgruntled sigh. "I'll let you, but I've got a couple of conditions."

The boy wiped snot away from his top lip. "Anything!"

"You say you chased after the dog when it escaped, so your brother entered the house alone. When you returned you found everyone dead and no sign of anyone. You never saw me or anything else."

"Aye, no problem! I didn't see shit!" The kid was actually starting to smile.

"And," Han continued. "You get your ass back into school and make a life for yourself. If you stray from the path, I will hunt you down and I will show you pain you wouldn't believe before I kill you. You got that?" Han glared at the boy, knife hovering close to his streaked face.

The boy nodded vigorously. "Got it, yes, I got it. Back to school – no more nicking or owt."

"Okay," Han said, dropping the knife down to his side. "Walk out the door and go looking for your dog. Don't come back for at least thirty minutes. Then wait another five or so for the shock factor and then ring the police."

The boy sprung to his feet and headed for the door.

"Be good," Han said after him. *Be good? What the fuck? You're starting to sound like a fucking god-squader.* Shaking his head, he watched the boy open the front door.

The boy glanced outside then turned back to Han. The look of fearful relief evaporated. He suddenly burst out laughing and said, "Fucking wanker! You're a dead man!"

As Han blinked in surprise, the boy darted out the door and ran up the street.

"Bollocks!" It took a second too long to recover and then he was sprinting after him.

The boy was laughing as he ran down the street. Lights were on in houses, but luckily there was still no one about on the streets. Han's legs were screaming as he pushed them to beyond normal limits.

Panting, the boy glanced over his shoulder and his smile vanished. Han was gaining ground. Panic etched into his red face and he let out a tirade of curses and darted up the path of the nearest house with lights on.

Banging on the door, he screamed, "Help! There's a fucking killer after me! Help us, for fuck's sake!"

The living room curtains twitched, but then quickly closed again.

Han reached the gate and stood, gulping in deep breaths, knife behind his back. "You try to give someone a break and this is how they repay you?" There was genuine sadness in his tone. "Society really has reached new lows."

"Fuck you, you fucking bender!"

"What is it with kids these days? The only insults you can come up with are race or sex related. How about some originality, for Christ's sake? Or, failing that, how about just the truth – call me a psycho killer or something."

The boy gaped at him. With raw terror in his eyes, he resembled the proverbial rabbit in the headlights. "Please ..."

Han shook his head. "You had your chance, kid. I was going to let you go – give you a second chance. You blew it." As he stepped forward, the boy darted left across the patchy lawn.

Rolling his eyes, Han gave chase.

The boy cleared a low wall into the adjoining garden, but stumbled and fell to his knees. Han landed right next to him and stamped on one outstretched ankle, snapping it like a twig.

As he cried out in agony, Han knelt down and clamped a hand over his mouth. Pressing the tip of the knife against the soft flesh of the boy's cheek, he said, "You fucking people are beyond salvation. If I was Pontius Pilate, I'd be washing my hands right now ... in your *fucking* blood." With that, he pushed the knife into the boy's flesh and he felt the boy's lips contort under his palm.

***

DCI Karen Carter swallowed the last bite of her bacon buttie then stepped inside the Dixon residence, ignoring the shouts and jeers from the crowds gathered beyond the police cordon.

"Hey, Andy," she said, seeing the pathologist kneeling beside the bodies of the mother and eldest son. "Quite a few happy people outside, eh? It's starting to look like a street party out there."

Andy glanced up. "Hi, Karen. Fancy meeting you here. Yeah, quite a few suspects!"

"I'd say the whole estate, plus a good size chunk of Leeds," Carter replied as she took in the carnage. "All five of them?"

"Yep. Daddy and middle son capped on the sofa. Mummy gets it as she comes through the door. Eldest and youngest arrived around thirty minutes later and the eldest buys it here, but the youngest manages to escape and makes it about five hundred yards up the street, where he's executed in a neighbour's garden."

"And nobody heard or saw anything?" Carter asked, shaking her head.

Andy's snorted. "Nobody hears or sees anything around here. Ever. That's the rules."

Carter sighed and walked over to the window. She needed a cigarette and a drink. Five more murders. This wasn't South Central, for Christ's sake. Could this be linked to the other recent murders or was this completely separate? They had just been in the papers. It could be just coincidental – there were quite literally dozens of potential suspects for this lot. Even the thirteen year old had a string of convictions. But still, thirteen? Executed. Christ, what was going on? What the hell was she up against here?

***

Ten down. Three hundred and eighty six to go. Hmm, this was going to take a while! The Dixons had certainly helped a little, but he still had a mammoth task ahead of him.

Han sat at the computer, feeling his initial jubilation ebb away. Despite the recent successes, he could not help but feel despondent at the sheer scale of the task ahead.

Physically, regular exercise and healthy eating had added half a stone of muscle and his skin had taken on an altogether healthier tone. The sunken pallor was a thing of the past. Perry had been the first to notice and, as was his way, he put it down to a woman. Han just laughed it off and told him that it was just a late New Year's resolution.

The second phase was very different to the first phase of the experiment. He couldn't just eliminate the whole lot in one go. He had to weed out the bad from the good. That took research and planning. The Pervert Yellow Pages had helped, but he couldn't continue to rely on that. The Dixons had been a lucky bonus, but what now? He had to find alternative ways to locate his targets. If he averaged one scumbag per week, it would take … over eight bastard years! *Bollocks to that!*

"There must be an easier way," he said finally.

The screensaver was showing the gleefully twisted face of the Jew Hunter, Colonel Hans Landa. He stared at the SS officer's face for some time. Just as it began to change to the next image from *Inglourious Basterds*, Han had an idea. *That's a bingo!*

He wiggled the mouse to expel the image of Mélanie Laurent in a red evening gown who had just replaced Christoph Waltz. He called up Google and began sifting through dozens of chat rooms. He spent the next three hours surfing through pages of inane drivel from mainly bored or horny teenagers, only pausing to grab a sandwich for lunch.

Rooms with such charming titles as *Pakis Out, I Fucked MY Sister, Naked and Wearing My Wife's Underwear* and *Camming Naked for $1* were skipped through with a growing sense of despondency. Even rooms with quite innocent sounding descriptions were mainly filled with who wanted to fuck who, how and when. Eventually, when he was close to changing Phase Two to hunting down and slaughtering all the complete fucknuts who inhabit chat rooms, he finally fell upon a relatively quiet room entitled *Britain Going to Sh!t*. Not overly subtle. Promising.

There was a lot of talk of chavs, gang violence, drugs, knife crime, disassociated youth, binge-drinking, teenage pregnancies and a whole host of related topics. There were a dozen or so angry posters. Some were hard-liners wanting to bring back hanging, some were liberals suggesting ways to 'help' these poor souls. Some were being purposely argumentative, but many were genuinely concerned.

Han played it cool, talking about how concerned he was at the slow demise of civilisation and wondering what could be done about it. He pretended to be angry about a neighbour who had been attacked and stabbed in the street for his mobile phone. After chatting for another two hours, someone with the username of CB1 privately messaged him.

The user had been lurking for some time without posting. But now the person said, I'VE BEEN READING YOUR COMMENTS – YOU SEEM TO BE PRETTY SWITCHED ON AND ON A SIMILAR WAVELENGTH TO ME.

Staying in character, Han typed a reply, AYE BUT WHAT THE HELL CAN ANY OF US DO ABOUT IT? I FEEL SO HELPLESS.

CB1's response bounced back. POLITICIANS AND THE POLICE ARE SO WRAPPED UP IN LIBERAL RED TAPE AND EU LAWS THAT THEY ARE THE REAL HELPLESS ONES.

A smile played across Han's lips. A definite possibility. Keeping the hook dangling in the water, they chatted privately for several hours, testing each other, each holding their cards close to their chests and gradually revealing a little here and there.

It was nearly three in the morning when Han signed off after exchanging email addresses and agreeing to chat more another day. The email address he gave was harry.brown2010@hotmail.co.uk – not particularly understated, but could still be construed as just a film fan. The account information was false and untraceable and his IP address, thanks to a great deal of research and tinkering, was now routed through more than a dozen countries, including Kazakhstan and Bangalore, so cyber crime eyes would find it impossible to trace. It never ceased to amaze him what you could learn off the internet.

Something that both tickled and further excited Han was the fact that CB had turned out to be the initials for none other than the late *Death Wish* star, Charles Bronson. A film fan with a keen sense of irony. Well, what could he say? They hit it off right away. Some things just happen, but then occasionally some things happen for a definite reason.

***

After spending a couple of weeks with his sister and her family, Will Wright began his investigations in earnest.

He began by camping out in the local library, reading up on every scrap of information and evidence and every rumour circulating on the internet. There was a lot to wade through and hard evidence was drowning amidst a sea of rumour, speculation and conspiracy theories. He shook his head in disgust as one forum discussed a possible government cover-up to conceal a failed alien invasion attempt. Another suggested the government testing a new biological weapon.

He also called a couple of his father's old mates who were still active in Northumbria Police. One politely refused to offer any assistance, but the second, a community beat sergeant named Leigh Simpson, who used to work CID with his father, came up trumps.

They met in a bustling coffee shop, overlooking Grey's Monument in Newcastle city centre. After rather awkward introductions, Leigh handed over a slip of hand-written paper that held the alias and last known address of Carol Belmont. She didn't say a word, but her grim expression revealed just how at odds she was with handing over such highly delicate information.

"You don't know how much I appreciate this, Leigh," Will said, with barely suppressed exultation.

"Your father was a good friend of mine. He was there for me when I went through a really messy divorce. He kept me sane and helped me get back on my feet." The petite sergeant's eyes welled up as she spoke. She looked away and took a sip of her coffee.

"Were you two …" Will started, but couldn't find the words to complete the sentence. He looked down, embarrassed for even asking.

58

Leigh looked back at him. "No. I think there was a mutual attraction there, but neither of us wanted to jeopardise our friendship."

They both sipped their coffee in silence for a while, both seemingly lost in their own thoughts. Will looked up from his nearly empty cup and stole a moment to study her. She was at least ten years younger than his father had been and pretty, in a tough, no nonsense way. She was really quite short, so they must've looked quite the mismatched pair. But he could certainly understand his father's attraction to her. It also sounded like they both had messy divorces in common too, but he thought best to keep that to himself.

Leigh finally said, "I'm sure I don't have to tell you what will happen if it gets out that I gave you that information."

"No. I understand. If anything happens the buck stops with me."

Leigh offered a thin smile. Then, almost wistfully, she added, "You're your father's son."

At twenty-six, Will was maybe eight years Leigh's junior, but he suddenly felt compelled to hold her hand in a purely fatherly gesture. "I will find me dad's killer." There was no bravado in the words, just grim determination.

"I believe you," Leigh said. "That monster didn't only kill your father and all those people in Haydon. He ruined hundreds more lives. Your father's partner, Mitchell had a young family. Parents, partners, children – victims stretched out across the whole country. Even the head of the investigation didn't escape Whitman's legacy. Chief Superintendent Hewitt died of cancer six months into the investigation. The strain of it – having all that pressure from the Force, the media, the public – that did him in in the end. His body had nothing left to fight the cancer with."

Leigh fell silent one more time then, before Will could speak, she added, "When you do find him, *don't* call us. Kill the bastard."

Will was taken aback by the venom in her words, but he accepted them and, more importantly, agreed with them.

59

I can't seem to face up to the facts,
I'm tense and nervous and I ... can't relax,
I can't sleep, cause my bed's on fire,
Don't touch me I'm a real live wire.
'Psycho Killer' by Talking Heads

CHAPTER 4

Charles Bronson was a Godsend. It was downright bizarre. Surely, if there was a god, after Haydon he'd be giving old Hanny-boy a bloody wide birth, but here he was throwing the old serial killer a bone. Here was the kicker – Charles Bronson was a prison officer. A particularly disillusioned and bitter one at that.

It took a couple of weeks of regularly conversing via email and Live Messenger before Charlie really opened up and began trusting his newfound friend. Even once they really began getting to know each other, they made a pact to use their pseudonyms only and not to ask or give real names. Even in those early conversations, they both knew the direction they were heading. The destination may have still been obscured, but they both knew what roads they were planning on taking.

On the Friday of the third week after their virtual meeting, impatience got the better of Han. He found himself cruising the city centre of Leeds at 2.30am. He knew it was reckless, but a few JDs had sealed the deal.

He wore a thick coat with the collar turned up, *Outpost #31* baseball cap and scarf to mask his features from the CCTV cameras that operated in and around the many bars and clubs.

The streets were filled with drunken revellers and police officers, with the occasional paramedic thrown in for good measure, treating broken noses and alcohol-fuelled catatonia at the curb side.

There was far too much activity on the main drag, so Han walked off the beaten track to find one of Leeds' more dingy nightspots. If you were looking for trouble, *Malaga's* would surely have some on tap. Snakebite? Wifebeater? One double trouble coming right up, squire.

The nightclub lurked down a poorly lit back lane. Several patrons were milling around the open door, where two brick shithouse bouncers were standing with arms folded across ample chests.

Han walked past the cluster of swearing and cackling youths. They were all too pissed to notice, but one of the bouncers did. The man's eyes traced Han's passage across his field of vision. They both had the obligatory black overcoats, secret agent earpieces and skinheads, but this one seemed pretty switched on and, despite all the furore, noticed one person that for some reason just seemed a little out of place.

As Han rounded the corner, his demeanour changed instantly to that of a swaggering pisshead. He pulled out a wad of twenty-pound notes and held them in plain view in his right hand. He knew from experience that this area of interlocking lanes was a hotbed of crime, so all he had to do was pretend to be carrion and wait for the vultures to start circling. He didn't have to wait long.

Two youths spotted him from further down the lane. They were smoking and chatting animatedly. Steam was rising from their wet hair and short-sleeved shirted torsos, having recently vacated the club from larging it on the dance floor. The shorter of the two, with a skinhead and arms and neck plastered in tattoos, nodded towards the new arrival. It would've been barely noticeable to the casual observer, but not to Han. He caught the signal and the subsequent subtle changes to their body language.

Han was lurching almost parallel to them when the short one said, "Here, mate. You got a tab?"

As Han turned to them, he dropped one of the notes onto the wet cobbles. Slurring a curse, he bent down to pick it up. As he did, he let the piece of lead pipe that had been concealed up his left sleeve slide down into his gloved hand.

Neither youth noticed the club or the subtle change in demeanour – cockiness at the perceived 'easy' target that had been presented to them blinded them to telltale clues. The shorter one swung a Timberland boot up into Han's face.

Han stepped back, dodging the blow with ease. As he straightened up, he swung the club down hard on short-arse's knee. There was an audible crunch and his lower leg flipped, swinging way beyond its normal arc of one hundred and eighty degrees.

Short-arse fell back against the wall, choking on a stunned sob. Han was on him in a second, ramming the pipe into his face, crunching bone and tearing the top lip. The lip, complete with unkempt whiskers, hung from the youth's torn cheek like a long dangling bogie. Han turned to his equally surprised friend who was now struggling to tug a knife out of the waistband of his trousers.

Han paused for a moment, saying, "Hurry up, lad. I don't have all day."

"Fuck you! Gonna fucking gut yer!" With that, the youth thrust the lock knife towards Han's face.

Han tossed the pipe at the youth, which confused him, causing him to drop the knife as he made a clumsy snatch for the pipe. In that blur of motion, Han stepped forward, jabbed him in the throat with his fingertips and then grabbed the youth's arm by wrist and shoulder, twisted it and then snapped it at the elbow by bringing his own elbow down hard onto it.

As the youth tried to choke and scream at the same time, Han retrieved the knife in his gloved hand and unceremoniously slashed open the youth's jugular. He staggered back, clutching at his neck with his one working hand as blood gushed down the front of his white shirt. His mouth opened and closed, but he only managed a choking gurgle.

Han retrieved his lead pipe and quickly and quietly beat both youths to a gory pulp. Their dead broken bodies were still twitching as Han discarded the pipe and walked hurriedly from the scene.

Han's blood was still up as he emerged onto well-lit streets. He knew what he had just done was impetuous and down-right dangerous. Other than the untraceable pipe, there had been no planning whatsoever.

It was a stupid risk to take, especially now that he had Charlie. His impatience had gotten the better of him. How stupid! He had acted like a complete fucking amateur. It was inexcusable. He cursed under his breath and stomped angrily back to his car, avoiding CCTV and keeping one wary eye on his back.

He had to learn to control himself, otherwise he'd never make the magic number. There was still so far to go. He had hardly left the city limits of this epic journey and he was already throwing caution to the wind. Stupid! Stupid! *Stupid!*

After burning every stitch of clothing and then showering, Han scrubbed down kitchen and hallway, washing the floors, walls and skirting boards.

After the flurry of activity, he stood in the kitchen in a clean pair of boxer shorts, waiting for the kettle to boil. His mood had not improved with the dissipation of the adrenaline. What if that bouncer gave his description to the police? Sure, he had been well disguised, but it would give them a rough canvas to start working on. He had been very careful to stay clear of 'most' of the city centre's CCTV, but would that be enough if they had a description to go on to allow them to track some, if not all, of his movements?

He would have to scrub every inch of the car next to destroy any possible forensic evidence there. And then scrub the thing a dozen more times. He would probably end up cleaning the whole house a couple more times too, just to be sure. He could not allow a single shred of evidence to lead back to him. There was too much still to do.

It's not your time, son.

Those fucking words again! The *Planet Terror* mug smashed against the kitchen tiles before Han realised he had thrown it. He stared at the teabag amidst the shattered remnants of the mug for a while.

There had been something else this time. An image. Fleeting, like a single out of place frame in a film reel. Like that scene in *Fight Club*. A single frame of a pair of tits or whatever in a family film. That had been what it had seemed like. A face, yes, he was positive that it had been a face of a man of about his age now, looking down on him ... as a child?

This was absurd. He couldn't remember his father saying anything like that to him. And even if he did, why would that be so significant now of all times? Someone else? But who? And why? And why the fuck couldn't he remember?

In seething silence, Han cleaned up the mess and made a fresh mug of tea in an old and faded *Reservoir Dogs* mug that he found gathering dust at the back of the cupboard.

"Note to self: if this shit is going to continue, get a job lot of mugs."

***

Will Wright had spent the best part of a week surveilling the address that Leigh had given him. Carol Belmont showed up on the first day and it had taken all of his willpower to hold back and show a little patience. She wore drab ill-fitting clothes, sunglasses and a woollen hat, but he recognised her from the dozens of photographs he had seen of her. Some of those photos had shown her with her ex-husband, Steve Belmont and then many more portrayed her hospitalisation and injuries, and then finally a couple had been taken while she had still been under police protection.

It amazed him that this person was not still under protection. According to the file, Carol had grown increasingly hostile towards her protectors and had finally given them their marching orders. So now, she was all alone, albeit in Portree on the Isle of Skye. He could certainly understand her choosing such a remote location. She had been issued with a new identity, so unless you knew precisely where she was, there was not a cat in Hell's chance of finding her. But, with her history, coping alone day to day – even in such a remote corner of Britain – must have been terrifying.

She still dutifully informed Northumbria Police every time she moved (which was regularly), but apart from that and an occasional phone call to check up on her, that was it.

Will had kept his distance for a while, checking for anyone who might be watching her, whether it be the authorities or someone more sinister. It was a fool's hope, but he had wished that Whitman might have tracked her down and was already watching. It was a guilty thought – clearly wishing someone in harms way who had already been through so much – but he couldn't help it. It would have made things a whole lot easier, but at the same time, it was a chilling thought.

He had fought the Taliban on their home turf, both in pitched battles and in insurgent hit and runs. He had lived with the fear of improvised explosive devices on every street corner, under every car, buried in every road, strapped to any civilian; man, woman or child. He had seen several friends and colleagues killed or mutilated. He had coped with the snap of an AK47 round zipping inches from his ear, and a mine flipping his Snatch Land Rover onto its roof like a Matchbox toy. He had been through a lot, least of all the brutal murder of his father, and yet, the thought of confronting Hannibal Whitman – if he was truly honest with himself – made his blood run cold.

Being honest with himself was going to be vital with what he had embarked upon. He bloody well had better be honest with himself every goddamn step of the way. He would kill Whitman and he would fucking well enjoy it, but it didn't change the fact that the man scared the shit out of him. Accept it and deal with it, he kept telling himself. It was the same in a firefight. You accept the fear – use it, if you can – but you don't let it impede your mission or your duty.

Han Whitman had murdered nearly four hundred people, including three police officers, one of which he knew personally to be a tough son of a bitch ex-marine and experienced detective. Could he – one man – surely take on such a monster?

He had to stop referring to him as a monster. Whitman wasn't some supernatural creature of the night. He was just a man. He had had the advantage of preparation, planning and surprise, nothing more. He did not have special powers. He was clever and ruthless, but he was human and, as such, subject to human flaws. He made mistakes – he failed to kill Carol Belmont, for one. That could still prove to be a fatal mistake.

It was late afternoon and Carol Belmont had arrived home more than an hour ago. No more stalling. The time had come to take the next step.

Will crossed the street from the small holiday cottage he had been renting. The snow had stopped falling, but the footpaths were heavily laden and the road was little better than a rutted slush track with ploughed snow heaped either side.

His stomach started doing back flips as he drew nearer the front door to Carol's rented cottage.

With his heart pounding, Will gathered himself at the door before lifting a hand to knock.

The door opened before his knuckles touched wood.

Carol Belmont stood in the doorway in a heavy terry towelling bathrobe and brandishing a bread knife. "Who are you?" she demanded, the tremble in her voice betraying her bristling fear.

MELANIE LAURENT IS A BASTERD

...CARA

Date with Death

CHAPTER 5

With trembling hands, Carol Belmont handed Will Wright a mug of coffee. She had discarded the knife, but her hostile demeanour remained, despite having reluctantly invited him into her cramped living room.

She sat down opposite him on a floral armchair that had seen better days and gestured for Will to do likewise. Will sat on the room's only other chair, another floral delight, but with mismatched pattern and colours.

Carol self-consciously touched the scar along her jaw line, formed by Han Whitman's final volley of gunshots at the end of that fateful weekend, before he escaped into the night. It no longer ached, unlike her hip, which was especially prone to colder weather. The physical scars were ugly and constant reminders, but were mere shadows in comparison to the mental ones.

He opened his mouth to speak, but Carol spoke first. "I'm sorry for your loss. I really am," she said, her voice still trembling, even though at least some of her fears had been allayed. "I didn't know your dad very well, but he tried to help us – him and Detective Mitchell. They died trying to stop him. I ... I can't help you."

Will sat forward, cradling the steaming mug in his hands. His frame squeezed into the armchair made him look formidable and, seeing Carol flinch and withdraw, he quickly sat back once more. "Look, Carol ... do you mind if I call you Carol?" She shrugged and it reminded him of a wounded animal. He continued, his tone calm and reassuring. "I'm going to find the murdering bastard and I'm going to make him pay. I thought you of all people would understand that. He killed all your friends and neighbours and damn near killed you."

Anger switched places with trepidation as Carol hissed, "You don't know what you're talking about. You have no idea what we went through! He killed Steve, Jimmy, Sam, John ... everyone. I watched them die. And I looked into Whitman's cold – no, not cold – fucking dead eyes as he prepared to finish me off too. He's not human."

The terror returned in undulating waves, the shakes so severe that she had to put her mug down for fear of it being jerked right out of her hands. She choked back a sob and turned away to wipe fresh tears from her eyes.

Will watched her with mixed emotions. Heartfelt sympathy was tarnished with an irritated impatience. This woman was ... broken. That was the only word to describe her. But he needed her help. The chances of finding Whitman with her help were bad enough, but without her, it would be hopeless.

Taking a deep breath, Will got down on his knees in front of her and clasped her frail hands in his strong calloused ones. "He is human, Carol. He's an evil, twisted, murdering son of a bitch, but he is human."

Carol looked down at him, tears streaming unchecked. Several tears splashed onto Will's hands. "The ... *horror* ..." she managed, scarcely above a whisper.

Will squeezed her hands gently. "I know it's not the same, Carol, but I've recently finished a tour in Helmand Province. I saw a lot of death, including a couple of lads from my unit. I shot and killed three insurgents ..." His words trailed off, suddenly unsure of how to continue. But looking back at Carol, he noticed that he held her undivided attention, as if she were praying for some sort of connection, some way they could empathise with one another. So he falteringly continued. "One was still in his teens. He charged our roadblock and refused to stop. I had no choice but to shoot him. He was strapped with enough explosives to blow my whole squad to Hell, so it was the right decision. But that boy's face haunts me to this day. He wasn't even old enough to start growing a beard. Fresh faced. Terrified, bulging eyes …"

For the first time there appeared to be a begrudging understanding in Carol's bloodshot eyes.

Maybe this man did understand at least *some* of the suffering she had experienced.

With an exasperated sigh, Carol said, "Even if I wanted to help you, I can't. I don't know anything about him. I told the police everything I knew and it led nowhere; just dead ends."

Will shifted from his knees onto his haunches as the twinge in his left knee intensified into a throbbing heat. The roadside IED device in Sangin that tore up his Snatch Land Rover had opened it up like a tin can. He had been one of the lucky ones; the driver, who had been right beside him, took most of the force of the explosion. He died in Will's arms from massive internal injuries, the man's blood mingling with his own, under an unforgiving Afghanistan sun, as they waited for the med-evac chopper that arrived several minutes too late.

Dispelling the memory, Will said, "I think together we might be able to figure out one or two things that the police missed."

"How?"

"Because we both care more about this than anyone else alive." Carol's sullen expression was confirmation enough. "If we put our heads together I reckon we can find him."

Carol stared at him for a time, the fear in her eyes expressing more than words. Finally, she said, "And then what?"

"Then I kill him."

Carol emitted a sceptical snort. "He murdered a whole community, for God's sake, plus three policemen and John Bryce. John was one of the hardest blokes I've ever known – he wasn't afraid of anyone or anything. How the hell are *you* going to kill him? I know you're a soldier and all that, and you're probably pretty tough yourself, but come on! Are you serious?"

Will's features remained solid and unyielding. "Dead serious. You help me find him and you let me deal with the bastard. I don't want to put you in any danger, so as soon as I'm on his trail, we'll get you the hell out of there. No questions, no arguments."

Now Carol managed a hollow laugh. "Oh, you'll have no arguments from me. I've met him remember. I have no intention of ever crossing paths with him again."

***

Han's night out in Leeds city centre with Perry had been pretty mediocre. It had been the first time back in the city centre since executing the two would-be muggers, so he had felt a little on edge – a little exposed – all night.

The crack had been alright – the usual movie banter covering regular topics like George A Romero (his rapid skydive from grace after *Land of the Dead*, with such monstrosities (excuse the pun!) as *Diary of the Dead* and *Survival of the Dead*) to the latest gossip on Ridley Scott's prequel to *Alien,* with smatterings of Hollywood babes thrown in for good measure. Halfway through arguing who was hotter between Megan Fox and Emily Booth, Perry – somewhat pissed by this point – had gotten a bit rowdy, so Han bundled him into a taxi.

Perry shoved his head out of the window as the cab pulled away, slurring, "How could you diss the Foxster like that? Booth had her time!"

Han shook his head and offered a tired smile. Instead of flagging a second taxi, he opted for a slow walk in the cold and clear night air. This time he had no murderous intentions.

Midnight had gone the way of the samurai, and Friday night revellers were vocal and animated. Further up ahead, a couple of police officers were attempting to calm down a group of a dozen or so young men and women who were mouthing off at two bouncers outside the Adelphi.

As he drew nearer, the disagreement turned violent. There was a sudden rush of movement and the shattering of glass and then everyone started battering each other.

The two bouncers were being set upon by four youths at the door, while the two police officers found themselves surrounded by a seething mob. Han could just make out the larger of the two officers go down and his hat go flying. The second was fighting his way to him, using a baton to clear a path. The officer nearly made it, but two youths jumped on his back as he fended off a third. He went down hard.

Han observed the chaos for a moment with mild amusement. The bouncers were holding their own from their superior position at the door, but the two officers were taking a beating, kicks and punches landing all over their squirming bodies.

At that point Han thought, *fucking little bastards. They've got no fucking respect for authority.* The irony of this thought was not lost on him, but this was about common decency. "Fuck it," he said and promptly rushed at the throng.

None of the youths seemed to notice his advance – they were all busy having too much fun. And since there were no approaching sirens yet, they figured they had a couple more minutes of entertainment before they'd have to leg it.

A teenage girl was the first to note Han's looming approach. With a sneer, she spat, "Yer better back the fuck off unless you want some, you cunt."

Han's fist connected with the charming lady's nose with a delightful popping sound and Han continued into the crowd without so much as a second glance.

He kicked at the back of a knee, felling one sweaty twat with a shriek of surprise and pain. Then he landed a blow between the cheekbone and jaw of a second who was laying the boot into the smaller of the two officers. The crack confirmed a precision dislocation of the youth's jaw. He sprawled away, trying to scream obscenities, but only succeeded in screaming out in pain.

Another youth moved in, but Han turned to greet him. His playful smile and the excited glint in his eye caused the youth to halt abruptly. The look was predatory. The youth spun on his heels and ran.

Han chuckled and looked down at the dazed officer. "You okay, mate?" The officer's hat had been knocked loose and revealed a mess of blonde hair. When the officer turned to face him, Han realised it was a woman. And a bloody attractive one, even with the angry graze on one cheek. "Oh, sorry, I mean, miss." Han offered a hand, but she got to her feet unaided and went straight to her fallen colleague, limping slightly.

The rest of the mob had seen the tide turn and decided that enough was enough. They scattered in all directions, apart from the girl who was spark out on the pavement and one lad who had been pinned to the ground by one of the bouncers. His colleague shouted over, "Hey, pal, you're a true craftsman! You want a job, no?"

Han offered the bouncer a cheery wave and followed the female officer. She was easing her unconscious colleague into the recovery position, whilst radioing for backup and an ambulance.

A police van arrived moments later, followed by an ambulance. It was only after her colleague had been transferred into the ambulance when she finally turned her attention to Han.

As she sized him up, Han asked, "Your leg okay?"

She nodded and Han could see that she was replaying the events over in her mind. After a moment, she said, "Thank you. Things turned a little hairy there."

Han shrugged. "No problem. How about you buy me a drink sometime to thank me?"

Her stare was unyielding, but it only held for a moment and then she revealed a warm smile. "You're a bit full of yourself, aren't you?"

Han managed a fairly respectable attempt at looking coy. "You're very beautiful. I'd kick myself later if I didn't at least try."

"I might be married, dating or gay for all you know."

"You're not wearing a ring, so you're not married or engaged. I don't care if you're dating or gay – they're just obstacles to be overcome."

"Bullshitter too, eh?" A colleague called over to her. "One sec, sarge." Turning back to Han, she said, "Give me your name and number. I'm going to need to interview you about this incident anyway, so we'll take it from there, eh?"

"Well, just so long as I don't end up getting sued by Vicky Pollard over there."

The officer glanced over at the teenager who was now sat up on the curb, being treated by a paramedic with a police officer standing close by. "Don't worry about that."

His heart skipped as he gave the police officer his real name. Sometimes he had to concentrate hard to make sure that he didn't call himself Han Whitman. The name was so synonymous with who he was – who he *really* was. After giving her his address and telephone numbers, he said, "So, can I ask your name? You know everything about me, except for maybe my inside leg measurement. And let me tell you, I'd happily surrender that too."

She smiled again and it had a playful slant to it. "Cara." She held out her hand.

Han took it in his. It was petite and warm, but her grip was firm. "Nice to meet you, Cara."

***

Han was fidgeting like an old woman while he waited for Cara to turn up, swilling his second Jack Daniels around in the glass until it resembled some sort of space anomaly from *Star Trek*.

He had chosen Henry's for its more laid-back atmosphere for their first date. First *proper* date, that is. You couldn't really count an interview at the local nick.

The fire was giving off a cosy front room vibe and the clientele were older and quieter. Wine and cocktails were the order of the day.

Why was he so nervous? Sure, he hadn't had a shag for six months. *Jesus, was it really six months?* What the fuck had he been doing? What a wanker. Thank God for the internet. How long had it been since he'd had more than the occasional short fling or one night stand? That would have to be over a year … Lisa.

Bloody hell. Moving on. Before that, Vanessa? Christ, they'd been together six years, but that had ended over three years ago. Two meaningful relationships in nine years. Married men have more relationships in that length of time!

So, maybe he had every reason to be nervous. Cara seemed … potentially more than a casual fling. There was something about her. There was a spark in her that … enticed him. Hopefully not in a siren sort of way. He wasn't keen on Greek girls anyway …

Just as his drink threatened to suck the whole planet into it, Cara appeared in the doorway. She was dressed in a figure-hugging short dress of flame red that immediately reminded him of Shosanna Dreyfus.

It took him a moment to recover before he stood up and motioned her over to his booth. "Hi," Han said and felt rather sheepish.

"Hi back," Cara said with an easy smile. She sat down opposite him and eased back in the leather chair. Relaxed. Confident. Usually how Han felt, but not tonight.

"What can I get you?"

"I'll have a JD and diet coke please."

Han cocked an eyebrow. "I like your style."

"Some people say that it's not a very girly drink, but then I'm not that much of a girly-girl."

Han couldn't help but cast an approving look over her. Toned, but with distinct feminine curves. "I'm sorry, but in that dress I beg to differ. You look stunning." The compliment came out before he realised it and he felt suddenly quite embarrassed by it. "Sorry."

Cara laughed. "I'm not one of those women who can't take compliments. Keep em coming, mate." As an afterthought, with a flicker of lashes, she added, "And thank you."

Han returned with two drinks. After knocking back the remnants of his second, he cradled the third.

Cara watched him for a while as she took a couple of sips, savouring the taste of Tennessee. Then, seemingly businesslike once more, she said, "You know, I had a look through the CCTV footage from the other night." She paused to gauge his reaction.

74

Han shrugged. "I hope I'm not in trouble, officer."

Cara smiled. "Not at all. I'm just at a bit of a loss. I did a little digging – sorry, force of habit – and you've got a clean record; not even any minor stuff as a kid. The casual – and I have to say extremely skilful – way you tackled those youths smacks of a bloody competent fighter. There's no record of military service and you don't have the face of a boxer. Are you Daniel Craig?" She laughed, but the question was serious enough.

"To be honest, I did hesitate at first, but then I just saw red. Bloody yobs like that think they can get away with anything. So, I didn't really think after that and, as I said in the interview, my actions are all a little blurred to be quite honest. But, to answer your question, I used to do quite of bit of boxing and mixed martial arts – lucky enough never to get the nose broken. I was also a close protection officer for a while."

"Really?" It was Cara's turn to cock an eyebrow.

"It's no big deal – it sounds more glamorous than it actually is. I was in my mid twenties and, as the cliché goes, somewhat disillusioned with my life. I saw an ad in the back of FHM of all places for a residential bodyguard and surveillance training course. I borrowed the money from my brother, who thought it was one of the most stupid things I could possibly go and do, next to drama college that lasted all of a couple of terms. I packed a bag and headed off into rural County Durham. It was an intensive course over twenty-one days and nights, run by a couple of ex-SAS guys. I only did a few UK-based contracts, so it didn't really blossom into a great and glorious career, but the course was a great laugh and I met some top blokes. The training was top notch too."

"And there was me thinking you were average Joe shop owner, when in actual fact the mild mannered janitor act is just a cover."

Han laughed and took another gulp of his drink. "I'm a number one super guy."

"My hero," she said, smiling. "You know, you could actually be in line for a Queen's Commendation for Bravery award for what you did."

Han coughed and nearly spat whiskey all over Cara, blocking it with his hand just in time. Still coughing, he managed, "As Eddie Murphy used to say before going all U rated, get the fuck outta here!"

"I'm serious," she replied, now laughing. As an afterthought, she added, "Films are a thing for you, aren't they?"

"I'm not a subtle man."

"No, I think I counted at least half a dozen film references in your interview."

Han sat back and smiled. "Ah, what have we here? A potential contender for the title?"

"I'm a dark horse," Cara said with a wink.

"Aren't we all, kiddo?"

Taking another sip, she said, "So, let me get this straight … you went from drama school to secret agent to video shop owner?"

Han laughed and said, "Well, there were a few other hurdles along the way – a call centre, which, no matter what anyone else tells you, it really is the worst job in the world, followed by a few years as an IT sales rep, which wasn't the worst job in the world, but probably the dullest. Then a stint in retail and then the rest is history."

"Well, it's certainly varied," Cara said. "Apart from some bar work, I went straight from Uni into the Force. Boring in comparison to you!"

"I've only known you a few days and I've already seen enough to know that being a copper is far from boring."

Cara knocked back her drink and, with a playful expression, said, "Fancy lining up a few shots?"

"Now, you're *my* bloody hero. What you doing for the rest of your life?"

"Dying of thirst."

"Touché."

After shots of tequila, Jagermeister and Sambuca, they settled back with *Old No. 7*. A mutual interest in films had both quoting lines from some favourites, like *Pulp Fiction* and *Snatch*. Before Han knew it, he was drunk and laughing hysterically at Cara's impression of Christopher Walken as Captain Koons.

Laughing, Cara said, "No, no, I've got it this time." With a squeaky whining tone, she continued, "I hid this watch up my ass for two years …" She couldn't manage any more, laughing and coughing at the same time.

"Pathetic! You didn't even quote it right!" Clearing his throat, Han said in his best creaky voice, "I hid this uncomfortable piece of metal up my ass for two years."

"We're not all total movie geeks," Cara said, still laughing as she knocked back another drink.

It was nearly 1am when they shared a taxi, detouring to drop Cara off first. As the taxi pulled up outside a neat row of terraced houses converted into flats, she leant in and kissed him on the lips. It took Han by complete surprise, but the soft touch of her warm lips made him instantly reciprocate.

Cara waved briefly from the door as the taxi pulled away.

Han fell back against the seat with a look that was a mix of surprise and exhilaration. The night's developments cascaded over him as the kiss played on a loop in the background. My God, that kiss …

The driver, a young Asian man, interrupted his thoughts, saying, "Unlucky, mate. Thought you were in there."

Han smiled. He certainly didn't feel unlucky. The night couldn't have gone any better. "First date – no need to rush things."

Dear Diary, Han mused to no one, but himself. Ginger serial killer starts dating copper and then awarded bravery award by Her Majesty … Now that was some pretty funny shit, right there!

He had quite a few JDs and several shots swilling round inside him, but that wasn't the only reason he was buzzing. Cara loved the same films and had the same wicked sense of humour. She was sexy, confident and intelligent. Yep, Cara was pretty fucking cool. He couldn't help but add in conclusion … pretty fucking dangerous, given his 'alternative' lifestyle.

What exactly was he doing? Psychologists would babble some shit about him wanting to be stopped on a subconscious level. No, he was damn sure that wasn't the case. And it wasn't about sex, although he had to admit he did fancy the hell out of her, and would be a politician-level liar if he didn't admit that he would love to get her into bed. Christ, he'd have to be a flaming queer not to want that. In fact, she could very well be capable of converting them too! No, it was more likely that he just loved pushing it just that little bit extra, the fucking knobhead that he was! But, he had to admit, the excitement he felt about Cara seemed to equal that of the excitement about Phase Two.

***

As Han embarked on a new relationship, whilst continuing his increasingly candid online conversations with Charlie, Will and Carol began their search in earnest. This involved first wading through the mountains of paperwork related to the case, acquired with significant personal risk by Leigh Simpson.

For Carol, it was as if she was reliving those fateful events in Haydon all over again. There were frequent tears or tantrums. Photographs and descriptions were the worst. She would lock herself in the bathroom or take extended breaks to chain-smoke at the kitchen door that led out into a secluded backyard.

Carol's fragile state continued to frustrate and sadden Will in equal measures. At times, he would try to console her, sometimes helping, more often than not actually exacerbating things. Other times, he would leave her be – give her some space. This was generally the path of least resistance, but it left Will feeling inadequate, or worse, resentful. He had to be patient. This was extremely hard for her. He had to tread carefully. But the crying and screaming put him on edge – he couldn't help it. It felt like nails scraping down a blackboard.

Three days of scrutinizing every word of every report and dozens of telephone calls under an investigative reporter guise had led them nowhere.

It was Carol who noticed something that had been staring them in the face. Will had set up a whiteboard that was now covered in marker pen scribbles, linking lines, sketches and photographs. Carol was tapping the whiteboard, her features

78

scrunched up. "What happened to the DNA evidence collected from Haydon?"

Will looked up from the stack of witness reports and frowned. "That's a good question."

"It was signed in to Central Submissions in Ponteland before it was to head to the FSS lab in Wetherby, but then no record of it."

Will hunted through files until he came upon the relevant one. "There's a note here that it is still under internal investigation. Evidence casket #145959 logged in at 14:42 15th January by a DCI P Clarke. No further record after extensive investigation. Possible indexing error."

Carol was shaking her head in disbelief. "They lost what was probably critical DNA evidence?"

"Aye – some sort of clerical error. They're still looking for it." Will could not believe it either. The most high profile case since Jack the Ripper and they go and lose all the DNA evidence gathered from the scene. Unbelievable.

A phone call to Leigh confirmed it. Heads had rolled and there was still an active investigation into the error and into finding the missing casket. The DCI – Peter Clarke – had been cleared of any wrong-doing. Unfortunately, Northumbria Police Headquarters in Ponteland had literally tens of thousands of evidence caskets, so the job of finding one incorrectly indexed casket amongst so many was the proverbial needle in a haystack scenario.

"Whitman told me that he had covered all his tracks, but there could've been a chance in that casket."

"He lived in Haydon for six months," Will said. "There was a very good chance of him leaving something behind, regardless of how meticulous he was. Fuck!" The files Will had been holding in his tightening grip scattered across the room.

Carol visibly flinched at the outburst and tears began to well in her eyes.

Will instantly dropped his head in shame. He knew how fragile she was and how difficult all this was for her. He still could not help himself. "I'm really sorry, Carol. Just a little frustration, that's all."

Carol turned away from him, wiping a tear with a shaking hand. "I'm going for a tab."

***

WHAT ARE WE GOING TO DO ABOUT THIS SCUM? The words seemed to pulsate on the monitor in the Live Messenger window. Han stared at the sentence. It was what he had been waiting for and yet something stayed his hands from an immediate reply.

HARRY?

Cara had leapt to mind. He had to shake his head briskly to dislodge the inconvenient thought. He was being stupid, of course. Cara was becoming one part of his life and this was another – they were separate and would remain so. SORRY, MATE – HAD A PHONECALL. He took a deep breath then typed, I'M READY. DO YOU HAVE SOMEONE IN MIND?

Charlie's reply flashed up almost immediately. THE PERFECT CANDIDATE. AN A GRADE SCUMBAG – CHILD RAPIST AND MURDERER, SENTENCED TO 10 YEARS AND SERVED LESS THAN 5. HE'S BEING RELEASED ON PAROLE THIS FRIDAY FROM WAKEFIELD.

Han looked at the screen for some time. There was no reason why Cara coming into his life should blur his work on Phase Two, but it did in some intangible way. It was ridiculous of course. Jesus, even Lisa never had an effect on Phase One, so why would Cara this time? He instantly regretted thinking about Lisa and shook his head to dislodge unwanted images.

Irritated with his sudden indecision, Han tapped out a reply. EMAIL EVERYTHING YOU'VE GOT. I'LL DO THE REST. He stabbed the ENTER key with such force that the keyboard bounced off the desk.

WILL DO ☺

The smiley face said it all.

What was the matter with him? Charlie was a bloody Godsend, remember! This was what he had been waiting for, remember! This is why he had been wasting hours chatting online

80

to this bozo, remember! Christ, before Phase Two Han had never used Live Messenger or chat rooms in his life. He had always considered them tools for the sad and lonely. He had endured all that bullshit for this exact outcome. So why the trepidation all of a sudden?

Was it because he was now putting his trust in another person – a stranger – who could quite easily betray him? They did not know any personal details about each other, apart from approximate locations – both in the West Midlands, which struck Han at the time as a bit of a coincidence. It had been Charlie who mentioned his location first though, so that was clearly just a little paranoia on his part. Other than that, they knew precisely diddlysquat about one another. His email and internet were secure, but there was always a small risk.

Did this target mean that Charlie was a guard at Wakefield or was he just privy to this particular cons release? Questions and suspicions remained, which was never a bad thing. He wasn't exactly Mr Trusting. That would be suicidal in his line of work.

So maybe his apprehension was understandable, but if he was going to be honest with himself, that wasn't the half of it. It was more than his concerns of working with a partner on this. His newfound relationship with Cara did play a major role too. They had only had a couple of dates and hadn't even had sex yet, but it felt right and he sensed that Cara felt that it was something too. It was something that he hadn't felt in a long time, maybe not since Vanessa.

He was being stupid. Women! They always make things more complicated! He swore to carry out Phase Two – partly for his own sanity, but also because it was right. The experiment was only half completed. Phase Two had to be completed, so that he could then move on with the rest of his life. It was as simple as that.

One thing for sure was that he had to get back on the horse.

***

Charlie had provided him with a recent photograph, as well as last known fixed address and known hangouts. He had also told him exactly when he was due to be released, which was 11am sharp.

Han stood across the street from the main entrance of HMP Wakefield, pretending to read a crumpled copy of *The Sun*. There was plenty of comings and goings of visitors and deliveries, so no one was taking notice of a solitary man in a thick overcoat and baseball cap under a sign saying *Clarke's Brewery*.

There was a warm yeasty smell emanating from the compound behind him that tantalised the taste buds. *Stay focussed*, he chastised himself. Follow the not-so-good Mr Barker, tie up, torture and murder said twat then back home for a bite to eat, gym then shit, shower and shave, before off out to meet Cara. Perfick, as Pa Larkin would say.

The target appeared five minutes later. He was lean and tattooed, with a rucksack thrown over one shoulder. There was an air of arrogance in his swagger as he walked quickly away from the prison, without so much as a glance back.

Han followed at a safe distance.

Barker continued at a steady pace, until reaching a bus stop. As he checked the timetable, Han hung back at the street corner just out of sight. The ex-con swore loudly, dumped his pack at his feet then slumped against the wall.

No bus for a while. That's irritating. The bus would pass him first before reaching the bus stop, so Han stayed back out of sight and waited, pretending periodically to play with his mobile phone.

Five long and tedious minutes passed before a bus appeared up ahead. Hoping it was the right one, Han ran round the corner and reached the bus stop just ahead of it, pretending to be out of breath.

As soon as Barker moved to flag it down, Han approached, saying in a wheezing gasp, "Just in time, eh?"

Barker ignored him as he waited to board.

Ooo, get you, Han thought to himself. *You'll acknowledge me soon enough.*

Han boarded the bus behind Barker and paid the same fair. He then sat at the front for a quick exit.

They both disembarked at Thornes Park and Barker took off at a fast walk down a path lined with mature horse chestnut trees. After passing the athletics stadium, Barker veered off into a forested area.

Han weaved through a mixture of walnut and lime trees, trying to maintain a safe distance, but the thick foliage made it impossible to keep his eyes fixed on the target. Barker frequently dipped in and out of view, so when Han rounded a particularly expansive walnut, whose heavily laden branches dipped right down to the forest floor, he was taken aback to be confronted by Barker.

"Who the fuck are you and why are you following me?" Barker spat with bristling menace.

The brisk walk had worked up a sweat on his brow, so Han palmed it away before speaking. "You ever thought of trying out for Olympic Race Walking?"

Barker threw his bag to the ground and took a step forward, fists balled up. "Answer the fucking question."

"I'm here to put you to death." That sounded a little melodramatic, but what the hell. It's all part of the fun. If you can't have some fun in your work, what's the point, eh?

The answer was so off the cuff that Barker didn't quite register it. "Eh?"

"I had intended to follow you back to your gaff, tie you up and torture the fuck out of you until I got bored or you died. So this is all rather inconvenient."

"This about that little cunt?"

"Partly, but that's not important right now."

"Fuck you!" Barker leapt forward.

Han was ready for him. He side-stepped and jabbed a punch into Barker's kidneys and then into his throat. As Barker doubled over, Han kicked him in the back of the knee, causing him to collapse onto the damp forest floor.

Han tracked round him as Barker lashed out in all directions. A quick kick to his side, followed by another side step brought

Barker's face in clear view. One solid kick crushed his nose and sprayed blood across the forest floor.

As Barker cried out in pain and frustration, Han took aim and planted the toe of his boot hard into Barker's temple.

"Mister Barker, you've been a wonderful contestant. Here's your bendy Bully and BFH. Th-th-th-th-that's all folks." As he squatted down beside the prone man, Han drew a small lock knife from his inside coat pocket.

After opening it with a sharp flick of the wrist, he slit Barker's throat then wiped the blade on Barker's grubby sleeve. As dark crimson mixed with soil and foliage, Han pulled on rubber gloves and went to work.

After checking the area, he emptied two tins of lighter fluid over the body and set it on fire. Despite the damp ground, the body took hold quickly, burning clothing away first and then bubbling and crisping skin. Han fed the flames with dry twigs and branches and then deposited the gloves into the fire and walked away at a brisk pace.

It hadn't exactly gone to plan. A quick execution was not exactly what he had had in mind, but needs must and all that. It was done, that was the main thing. Another one notched up against that elusive total.

As he walked onto Park Road Grove, his thoughts were plagued by Cara. Instead of elation or even a mild sense of achievement, Han found himself rather embarrassed by the event. Rather like sneaking out of a cheap hotel room after shagging a prostitute to go back home to the wife. *Jesus, what is this? I used to enjoy this shit!*

The need to engage in homicidal behaviour on a massive scale seemed to be losing its lustre. How irritating. *Is the mask of sanity slipping or reaffirming itself?*

***

Han showered twice when he got home and, as is customary for anyone in the habitual murdering business, disposed of his clothing in the usual way. Thank God for cheap clothing shops like Matalan! He'd be skint at this rate otherwise.

After the normal ablutions, Han set to work making a meal. Cara had called and suggested a night in, instead of a jaunt into town. Han had been out of the game a while, but he wasn't stupid enough to miss the potential hint linked to said change of plan.

Cara didn't seem to be particularly fussy with food and wasn't anything annoying like a veggie, but he decided to play safe anyway with a tomato and feta cheese starter, followed by a seafood tagliatelle with a little chilli kick to it. *A playful but mysterious little dish*, he thought with mild amusement. He opted for wine, but had a sneaky bottle of Jack in reserve. Be prepared!

Cara arrived on time. Another thing he liked about her – she was rarely late or early, but always about on time. The first thing he noticed was what could've been an overnight bag. It was one of those bags that was too big to be just a handbag, but was still innocuous enough to the casual observer. Han clocked it and Cara knew he had, but neither mentioned it. This was a see-how-it-goes situation and that was fair enough.

The second thing he noticed was tight jeans over a perfectly formed bum as she turned to throw her coat onto the hallway coat rack. She turned back and caught him admiring her. She folded her arms across her chest and smiled. "You were properly checking out my ass there."

Han laughed. "Busted. What can I say? It's a particularly fine specimen."

"Oh, I have a feeling I'm going to have to watch you tonight."

"You'll get no complaints from me, darling."

The evening got off to a perfect start and continued in that vein. They managed to put away two bottles of wine before Han brought out the cheese board.

Cara had left the dining table and was perusing Han's iPod that was set into a docking station on top of his Hi-Fi. "Your taste in music is almost as eclectic as your taste in films," she said, glancing over her shoulder as he returned with the cheeses, along with the bottle of Jack and two shot glasses. "I see you've come prepared!"

"Damn right," Han replied as he poured out a couple of shots.

"Jesus, you've got Neil Diamond mixing it with Disturbed and pretty much everything in between."

"A person's taste in music, films or art should reflect their personality," Han said.

"Twisted?" Cara suggested with a wink.

"I was shooting for diverse, but I'll take what I can get."

"Well, as there's a lovely full moon tonight, let's have a little Creedence Clearwater Revival."

As the song started, Han said, "You want the Moon? Just say the word and I'll throw a lasso around it and pull it down."

I see the bad Moon arising,
I see trouble on the way,
I see earthquakes and lightnin',
I see bad times today ...

Cara laughed and moved towards him, swaying her hips to the music. There was a playful glint in her eyes, but the dilated pupils revealed more.

Cara snatched a shot glass out of Han's hand and knocked it back. Han followed suit as Cara moved in closer to him. Discarding the glass, Han slipped his arms around her waist and felt her press against him.

They moved together with the music, their hands exploring each other. Han kissed her neck. Cara moaned and suddenly her hands were grasping hungrily at his belt.

Passion overcame both of them and they fell against the table as they ripped at each other's clothes. Cara's blouse fell open and Han pulled up her bra, releasing her breasts. As he took her nipple into his mouth, she managed to yank his jeans and pants down.

Han tried to free one of his legs, but only managed to unbalance himself. He fell flat on his back, pulling Cara on top of him.

They both burst out laughing, sprawled on the dining room floor.

As their laughter subsided, Han stared up into Cara's wide, beautiful eyes. Her cheeks were flushed and she was breathing hard. "Christ, you're beautiful," he whispered.

"Nice of you to say, but ... I'll let you into a little secret – you've got me already, mate." With that, she kissed him.

***

You wanna see something really scary?

What had started out as a game had suddenly become at first weird and then down right frightening. The young boy's eyes were wide and staring as he was led through the open doorway where the strange sounds were coming from. He tried to pull back, but the man's grip was unyielding ...

Han awoke with a start.

"You okay, honey?" Cara's soothing voice asked from the darkness.

Han felt her arm slip over his damp chest. "Yeah, sorry. Didn't mean to wake you."

"I know me staying at your house is a big step, but I didn't think it would give you nightmares."

"Ha ha," Han muttered. As his eyes adjusted to the darkness, he turned and sought out her lips and kissed them, softly at first, and then with a growing fervour. She moved into his embrace and the touch of her bare skin on his instantly dispelled the remnants of his ill ease.

***

As Han decapitated a couple of soft-boiled eggs, Cara walked in to the kitchen in uniform. Han looked her up and down and felt a stirring in his boxer shorts. Even in uniform, she looked bloody

87

good. The shirt seemed to accentuate the swells of her breasts and, what would ordinarily be quite masculine trousers, seemed to hug her in all the right places.

The toast popped up and Cara went over and started buttering without a word. As she sliced them into soldiers, she said, "You've got quite the Mark Kermode grotto going on here."

"I did warn you – I'm a bit of a film freak."

They took the plates and two cups of tea over to the breakfast table and tucked in.

"Do you remember what your nightmare was last night?" Cara asked after taking a sip of tea.

Han studied her for a moment out of the corner of his eye, while he dunked a soldier into his eggcup. It seemed like a genuine enough question. "Not really," he said after a time. "I think I was being chased or something." That sounded like a lie to him, but Cara just shrugged.

"Poor baby," she said after swallowing some toast.

"Don't worry – you made me feel *much* better," Han said and winked at her.

"It was probably just a ruse anyway." Cara laughed at Han's shocked expression.

"As if I'd adopt such nefarious tactics!"

"As if you'd need to."

Han raised an approving eyebrow.

"And who the hell uses the word nefarious in this day and age? I hate to be the one to break this to you but Queen Victoria's dead."

Now Han laughed too and any perceived awkwardness was forgotten.

***

DCI Karen Carter sat in thoughtful silence in the driving seat as she ate her way through a cheeseburger and fries.

Next to her, Richard glanced down at his salad box and back to Carter's burger. In disgust, he jabbed some lettuce with a plastic fork and crammed it into his mouth.

With a mouthful of burger, Carter said, "Rich, you tell me; is our guy changing his MO or is Barker either one, unrelated or two, a copycat? And the Dixons? Unconnected or not?"

Richard swallowed and wiped his mouth on a paper napkin, before saying, "Well, at first glance, Barker was quite different to the sex offender murders. The execution seemed less planned and more impulsive, like the two youths in Leeds city centre. Perhaps it was out of necessity. Barker was a newly released category C offender – served five years on child abuse and neglect charges that led to an infant's death. He wasn't on the sex offender register, but his crimes were related to child abuse. So there are similarities with Barker, but there doesn't seem to be any correlation or parallel with the Dixon murders, other than their collective run-ins with the law."

Carter finished her burger, and said, "So what conclusion would you draw from all that?"

"We have eleven murders in as many weeks. Three were on the sex offenders register, two were young offenders on the verge of blossoming careers in car theft and mugging, the whole Dixon clan – who between them, had triple figure convictions in … well, you name it – and then Barker just out of Wakefield, having served a woefully short sentence for causing the death of a child. I'd say that this isn't about one type of offender. I'd say that this is about criminals in general. We could have a vigilante or vigilantes on the loose."

Carter stared at him as he continued to munch on his salad. Richard was a bit of an enigma. He was pinched and intense and an obsessive fitness fanatic. He was also obsessively neat and clean and a bit of a god-squader. She was quite the opposite in a lot of ways. She certainly wasn't a bible-basher by any stretch of the imagination. Yes, she kept herself fit, but she ate shit, still had the occasional sly cigarette, drank far too much red wine, ate with her mouth open and was prone to wind … especially after red meat.

Two uniformed officers walked by. At the last moment, one – an attractive blonde constable – angled over to the front passenger window and gyrated provocatively, singing, "Sergeant! Oh, Sergeant! The things I'll show to you!"

Carter coughed to suppress a laugh then shouted, "Clear off, Willow!"

The two officers laughed and walked away.

Richard was staring out the window, his transfixed expression that of utter bewilderment. After a moment, he said, "What … was that?"

"Don't worry about it, Howie."

"And why does everyone insist on calling me Howie? It's rather confusing. Neither Richard nor Pembleton bear any relation to such a moniker."

She shifted in her seat and cleared her throat. Might have to stretch the legs in a bit. But first, she said, "*Woefully? Moniker?* Where were you brought up?"

"Kingston upon Thames. Why?"

Carter opened her mouth to speak, but then shook her head and opened the car door. "Never mind. Just going to get some air."

***

GOOD JOB, MATE, appeared in the Live Messenger window from Charlie.

The news had broken of the charred remains of a recently released ex-con having been discovered in Thornes Park. One theory that was being banded about in the press was a revenge attack for his crimes. That wasn't a million miles from the truth. A couple of tabloids were also suggesting a link to other recent murders. The word vigilante was quickly becoming a buzz word.

DIDN'T QUITE GO TO PLAN, Han typed.

IMPROVISATION IS AN ARTFORM, MA FRIEND.

Han smiled. You had to like this guy.

I'VE GOT THE NEXT ONE LINED UP FOR YOU.

The smile vanished – back to work. Han typed, SEND IT THROUGH.

CSI: Haydon

(HAPTER 6

His father's battered old Land Rover 90 had been as reliable as he remembered it to be. It was neither quick nor pretty, but it got you there and was built like a brick shithouse.

Will slowed down as he passed through Shillmoor. Dusk was setting in and a couple of lights had winked on to ward off the seeping darkness. He had only ever seen the tiny village on the news, but even he recognised that things had irreversibly changed since the massacre.

A barn that had been converted into a café and gift shop was the most noticeable change. Some enterprising soul was cashing in on the public's interest in the macabre. Several cars, including a Northumbria Police Land Rover were parked on verges and in the small number of parking spaces by the café.

Before reaching the turnoff for Haydon, Will pulled onto a short track that led to a gated field. He parked up and jumped out. Without the lights of Shillmoor, the Northumberland countryside was quickly taking on a dark and ominous tone. Although, perhaps he was just projecting his own ill ease.

Will suddenly felt quite lonely and, if he was honest, more than a little nervous. He actually wished that Carol had come with him, but that was ridiculous. When he had told Carol of his intention to visit Haydon she had lost it. The idea of Carol returning to this place was nonsensical. He could not imagine Carol setting foot in northern England, never mind anywhere near Haydon.

He knew that there was very little he could learn from visiting Haydon, but on some level, he felt that it was something he just had to do. It was more about laying a ghost to rest so that he could concentrate on the rest of his investigation.

He knew from Leigh that there was a twenty-four hour police presence in the village. Apart from that, the village had remained abandoned since the bloodbath. There was currently a legal battle with relatives over the release of property and land but, as it was technically still a crime scene and an ongoing investigation, no access had been given, apart from strictly supervised visits to recover personal effects.

The post office had been converted into an operations room, with sleeping quarters above for the four officers manning the post at any given time.

He had printed off a detailed map of the village and surrounding woodland from Google Maps and had marked it with all the main buildings, including the two pubs, the shops, the Herring residence, the Bryce farm and the Belmont residence.

Will walked with purpose through the woodland, heading towards Haydon. Full dark was upon him before he had covered half the distance. Rather than risk a flashlight, he popped night vision goggles on over his head – they were a spare set that he had picked up in Afghanistan and had neglected to hand in with the rest of his kit when he de-mobbed. He continued, using them to enhance his vision.

It started to drizzle and soon icy droplets were raining down from the canopy, soaking his beanie hat and combat jacket. As he edged closer to Haydon, his disquiet deepened.

Every tree, branch and shrub seemed to take on the appearance of a still figure, lying in wait. At one point, Will's heart skipped a beat as one scrawny pine looked exactly like a man standing in full view with his hands planted on his hips. The sort of casually arrogant pose that Will imagined Whitman capable of.

As he crept closer, he realised that he was holding his Fairbairn-Sykes Fighting Knife – another liberated piece of kit from his last tour – tucked behind his wrist, in readiness to strike. He had no recollection of even drawing it. His body had clearly just reacted at the thought of a confrontation with Whitman, without even consulting him. That was at once both comforting and bloody scary.

As the Whitman spectre dissolved before his eyes, Will cursed under his breath at his own jittery nerves. Close up, the tree was just a tree. He kicked it and moved on. The rain was coming down harder now, reducing visibility further.

On the outskirts of Haydon, he came upon a six-foot chain-link fence. Beyond it lay the place that had haunted his dreams for over a year. The place where his father and so many others had been brutally murdered by Hannibal Whitman.

It was almost inconceivable that he should be standing here now. He had dreamt so often of drifting aimlessly through these streets, calling out for his father. Those dreams had often ended abruptly with an indistinct face appearing at a window. The face was unrecognisable, but something about the luminosity in the eyes and the sneer on the lips convinced Will that it was Whitman, waiting and watching. Sometimes the figure would whisper, "Have you come to meet your father?" Then Will would snap awake, shivering in the early morning gloom.

He forced his train of thoughts back to the job at hand. Kneeling, he retrieved wire cutters from his pack and made short work of the fence. He peeled back a small section and crawled through then carefully replaced it, so that at first glance it would appear untouched.

After crossing a patch of unkempt shrub land, he made it to the backyards of a row of terraced houses that were in complete darkness, rain glistening off brickwork. He paused there, crouching by a rusted gate with only the sound of his breathing and the relentless patter of the rain for company. He cocked his head, straining to listen beyond the ambient noises.

He moved silently from street to street, pausing every few yards to listen out for new sounds. Nothing. The village of

Haydon was truly dead. It actually felt dead on some base level. It was just his imagination, but it felt as if nothing existed here anymore. Not even the wildlife.

Main Street was as deserted as the rest of the village, with the exception of ground floor and first floor lights on in the post office. Given the weather, he guessed that all four stationed officers would be holed up in there. Who in their right mind would be out in this weather in the middle of the night in such a Godforsaken place? Who indeed? He grunted a humourless laugh.

The feeling of nothingness was overwhelming. He felt disparate from the rest of humanity ... from real life even. He fixed his attention on those beacons of light. It wasn't much, but it was a reminder, an anchor. There were at least four living souls in this ethereal place. Unless someone had beaten him to it ...

"Get a grip, man," he hissed under his breath. He took a moment to gather himself then, with a resolute exhale, began a methodical search of all of the key locations.

***

"Here he is," Han said and waved at Perry, who had just walked into the bar, shaggy hair dripping from the unrelenting rain outside.

Perry walked over, grinning. "So I finally get to meet Han's new leading lady?"

Cara leant over to offer her hand, saying, "Hey, I'm the star of this show, buddy. He's my leading man."

Perry shook her hand and laughed. "Good for you." He took a moment to take in the woman in front of him. She was dressed in skinny jeans, a low cut *Van Halen* t-shirt and a leather jacket. She had brilliant blue eyes and a playful expression. "Jesus, you're gorgeous," he uttered.

Cara laughed and her cheeks flushed. "Why thank you, Perry. You're not so bad yourself."

"You're too good for this chump," Perry said, nodding at Han.

"Cheeky bugger," Han said, laughing.

Perry returned with a round of drinks and joined them at the table.

The bar was busy with early evening punters, but the mood was relaxed and conversational with low music and low lighting.

"So is your boss okay to work for?" Cara asked and nudged Han light-heartedly.

"He's a bloody slave driver."

"I bet!"

Han rolled his eyes and sipped his Jack.

"Nah, not really," Perry continued. "He's the best boss I could ask for and it's one of the best jobs in the world. I get to watch films all day."

"Yeah, but he's got a dream," Han said.

"Like Martin Luther King?" Cara injected with a smile.

Perry shrugged and knocked back half of his pint.

"Well, tell me then," Cara cajoled then, in exaggerated fashion, batted her eyelids and added, "Please."

"Okay." Perry leant forward on his elbows and, in a conspiratorial tone, said, "Well, my passion is films, like. I love em. My favourites are horrors and gangster flicks, but I love all films, even some of ya chick-flick types."

Perry took off his Parka and slung it over an empty chair. He was wearing his favourite *Pulp Fiction* t-shirt, with Uma Thurman languishing on a bed, smoking a cigarette. He had several tattoos on his arms, one of which was a facial portrait of Quentin Tarantino.

"I would've never guessed," Cara said and laughed.

"Yeah, I tend to keep it under wraps," he added. "The maestro himself started out working in a video store – that's what I want to do. I'm studying film and moving image production at Leeds. It's part-time, as I've got to work too, of course, but I've only got another year to go." The more he explained, the faster the words tumbled out and the more animated he became. "I'm working on a film project as part of the course – it's a tale of a woman's revenge against the sadistic gangster who murdered her parents. It's going to be shot in one room with only two characters and the story being told in flashback. It's only going to be a short,

95

but it's a start, eh?" He took another big swig of his pint and sat back with a deep sigh.

"He's quite passionate about it," Han said wryly. "But you should see his work – it's really good and I'm not just saying that as a friend. He's got an eye for it."

"Oh, you," Perry said in a mock show of exaggerated coyness. "I'm not the only one with artistic tendencies. Has he told you that he took some time out last year to write a novel?"

Han's expression froze. As Cara glanced at him, he managed a noncommittal shrug.

"You never told me that," Cara said, nudging him. "What's it about?"

Han sipped his drink. "Well … it's a thriller … a serial killer on the loose in the Nor … British countryside."

"Sounds right up my street," she said, clearly impressed. "I love stuff like Martina Cole, Patricia Cornwell, Ricki Thomas and Val McDermid. Can I have a read sometime?"

Han took another sip of whiskey. "Maybe. I'm not happy with it yet – it's a long way from being finished."

"I thought it was finished?" Perry injected.

Shut the fuck up, Han thought then said, "Yeah, the first draft. But it's a long way off from being properly finished. It needs a lot of fine-tuning yet."

Cara shrugged. "I can see it's your baby and you're not ready to share. I would love to read it sometime though … when you're ready."

"He's being modest," Perry said. "I bet it's a bloody masterpiece and he's just hiding it away."

"Oh, you," Han mimicked as he eagerly sought ways of changing the conversation.

Cara threw him a lifeline. "Do you two wanna get a room?"

"Nah, he's a crap shag," they both said in unison, which provoked fits of laughter. Han joined in, relieved.

Maybe writing a real novel wasn't such a bad idea. He certainly had the imagination for it and more than enough material to work with. It would have to be fiction if it was ever going to see the light of day though.

As Perry asked Cara whether she had read the *Dark Tower* series by Stephen King, Han pondered that idea.

Weekend at Seahouses

CHAPTER 7

Han notched up three more kills while his romance with Cara continued to blossom. It troubled him to admit it, but he was enjoying spending time with Cara more and the jolly old axe murdering less with every kill. The nightmares were returning with a vengeance too.

And those words ... those *fucking* words, *Not your time, son.* They just refused to die. It was easy to kill flesh – a knife could cut through it like warm butter, a baseball bat could crush a skull like a watermelon and a gun, well a gun – point and click, as they say! Pop the DVD in and press play. But those words ... they just kept coming. They replayed over and over every sleeping hour and now they were even encroaching on waking hours as well. There was no respite from them and there was no stopping them. They were relentless. What did they mean? Who said them?

The second phase of the experiment was supposed to sort all this shit out, so that he could move on with his life. When Cara came onto the scene, he had genuinely thought that everything was moving in the right direction, but that demon still whispered to him.

What the fuck was wrong with him? Now, some of course would scoff at a serial killer asking himself that, but what did they know? There was nothing wrong with Han Whitman. He was an ordinary bloke in every way. He just had a rather unusual sideline in mass murder. There were worse hobbies he could have. Trainspotting, bird watching and stamp collecting, to name but three off the top of his head!

He didn't remember anything about being led into some scary room as a kid, so what the hell was that all about? But it did feel like more than a dream – it felt like a memory. He didn't understand how he knew that, but he did. And that was a lot more unsettling than any nightmare that John Carpenter could conjure.

Han stared at the monitor.

GOT THE NEXT ONE LINED UP FOR YOU. The words seemed to glow and throb on the screen.

Han's fingers hovered over the keyboard for a time and then he typed, I'M GOING TO TAKE A BREAK. NEED TO RECHARGE THE BATTERIES.

He waited for a response and suddenly felt nervous. Would Charlie be disappointed? Angry? This was ridiculous! "Snap out of it, you knob-jockey!" he shouted aloud and slapped himself hard across the cheek. "Who gives a fuck what Charlie thinks? He's a decent enough bloke, but if he's going to be a knob about it, fuck him." Charlie maybe helping with the sarnies and sausage rolls and blowing up balloons, but this was still his party.

He heard the clip-clopping of paws in the hall and Jumanji nudged the door open with his nose. The Labrador looked at his master with a mixture of curiosity and sadness in his glistening eyes. He tentatively approached and rested his head on Han's lap.

"Sorry, boy," Han said and scratched behind the dog's ear.

Han glanced back at the screen to see that NO PROBLEM, MATE had appeared on it. Then, after a moment, Charlie added, IT'S JUST WE'RE DOING SO WELL – WE'RE ON A ROLL, MAN! ☺

Han chewed his lip. There's that bloody smiley face again. But at least he was being cool about it. He typed, I KNOW I'VE JUST GOT FAMILY AND WORK THINGS TO SORT AND NEED SOME R&R.

HEY NO PROBS. IT'S A PLEASURE WORKING WITH YOU. KICK BACK AND CHILL AND WE'LL TALK MORE IN A WEEK OR SO.

A week or so? Cheeky fucker. Old Charlie was becoming more demanding than Evelyn Draper, but lacking the seventies sex and Roberta Flack soundtrack. He'd come across one or two bunny boilers in his time – not quite as psychotic as Evelyn, or Alex Forrest for that matter – and he didn't fancy repeating the experience, especially not with a bloke. *Call me old fashioned.*

The more he thought about it, the more he realised that a little break was exactly what he needed. He was just a little overworked. After all, his last holiday had been, well, a working holiday, shall we say.

There were plenty of other pleasurable activities to try, as an alternative to murdering thugs and perverts. He had to admit, despite it losing its allure somewhat of late, it was still a damn sight more enjoyable than most of the murdering up at Haydon. That had mostly been a bit of a chore, truth be known. Several had nearly finished him. Lisa, Haley, John … Although, the Haydon Cock, Steve Belmont had been pretty bloody satisfying, like dropping the kids off after a prolonged period of constipation.

***

Cara was up for a weekend away and left it up to Han to surprise her. A spot of holiday cottage Googling brought up some lovely properties in rural Northumberland, including a couple in Rothbury.

Han was surprised by a brief tremor between his shoulder blades. The mere close proximity to Haydon was enough to set him on edge. "Maybe not," Han muttered and quickly returned to the search results. He wanted to get away from everything, not stir up old ghosts. He had enough chain-rattling going on around him as it was. No, perhaps something on the coast would be more conducive.

After another fifteen minutes of surfing, he eventually stumbled upon a two-bedroom cottage on the outskirts of the fishing village of Seahouses. It was only about a three hour drive and had a golden beach to walk Ju along. It looked idyllic.

It was available as a last minute booking and he paid by credit card over the phone.

***

As Han and Cara headed north up to Seahouses, Will returned to Carol feeling utterly spent. During his nighttime reconnaissance, he experienced almost every emotion on the spectrum, but a bitter concoction of grief and rage were the prevailing players.

He had wept, pounded walls, screamed until he felt as if his lungs would burst, and curled up into a ball, hugging himself against the creeping cold and his own tattered nerves. Later, he had been amazed that his presence had not been detected. What had begun as a professional covert incursion ended with Will blundering around, lost and dejected. It had not been a Royal Marine Commando's finest hour.

As he waited for Carol to open the door, all he felt was entrenched exhaustion. He let his kitbag fall at his feet, rested a palm against the doorframe and let out a deep sigh.

"You look terrible," Carol said, her trembling voice filled with both relief and concern. "Come in and let's get you something warm to eat and drink."

"I'll skip part one and go straight for the hard liquor, if you don't mind," Will said as he allowed himself to be led through into the lounge.

Carol had long danced with that devil and, although going through a rare dry patch, she located a bottle of shop brand vodka. Without a word, she poured them both a healthy measure.

She let him drain his first glass and top himself up again, before she finally mustered the courage to ask the obvious. "So … how was it?"

Will looked up from his glass. With a cynical snort, he said, "Oh, it was a blast."

Carol took a large gulp of vodka and, rather tetchily said, "I'm sorry."

101

Will sank into the soft chair with a tired sigh, cradling his glass on his chest. He couldn't even be bothered to take his damp jacket and boots off. He looked back at Carol. She was nursing her drink and avoiding eye contact. "No," he said finally. "I'm sorry, Carol. It was rough ... really rough. I'd take Sangin over Haydon any day of the week."

"I ... I can't even imagine what it must've been like for you," Carol said, a tremor dancing across her shoulders at the thought.

"No, out of everyone on God's Earth, I think *you* could imagine," Will said.

Carol drained her glass and filled both once more. "Was there anything ... helpful?"

"Not really, but ... I guess I needed to do it."

Carol sat back down and leant forward towards him. "You're a brave man, Will Wright; like your father."

Shaking his head, he said, "Stupid, reckless and stubborn might cover it better."

"You can joke, but that took guts. My ex-husband, Steve, was a womanising bastard, but he had guts – he was a fighter. It's what I fell in love with – he was my knight in shining armour." Carol took another big drink before continuing. "We went to the same school, but we'd never spoken a word to each other. We moved in different social circles, I guess you'd say. Then one night after school, I'd been held back on detention for smoking in the toilets, which was a pretty regular event. I was walking through the school – it was already dark – and two lads approached me. They nicked my tab and then started trying to feel me up. I started crying and that just egged them on more. But then Steve turned up out of the blue. They'd all been at football practice together. Steve battered the living shit out of both of them. I fell in love with him right then and, despite everything he did to me, I still love him now." She hadn't realised that tears were rolling down her cheeks. She wiped them away with an irritated swipe of her arm.

They sat in silence for a while, sipping at their drinks.

Carol finished her third large vodka and rubbed at her temples. "So what next, Sherlock?" She attempted a good-humoured tone, but it just sounded hollow.

"Sunderland," Will said after a moment's thought. When Carol frowned, he added, "That's where he bought his car – the police found that much out at least. The dealer couldn't help with a description – couldn't even remember whether it had been a man or a woman. He might know more, but just didn't want to get involved. We could try to coax it out of him."

"We?"

Will knocked back his drink and, with a groan, pushed himself out of the chair. "Come on, Carol. Let's do this together. It's a major city – it's nowhere near Haydon and I'll be with you twenty-four-seven. What do you say?" Will used every ounce of willpower to battle against falling back down into the chair and looked to Carol, his eyes beseeching.

He offered his hand and, hesitantly, Carol took it and then squeezed it tight. Her tiny hand was lost in his and that alone gave her the courage to agree.

***

DCI Carter stepped into her office and slammed the door with considerable force, rattling the blinds. Her cheeks were flushed and she was breathing hard.

Choosing his words carefully, Richard said, "I … take it your update meeting with the super didn't go very well."

"You think?" Carter snapped as she rifled through a desk drawer to retrieve a bar of Galaxy chocolate. She caught Richard's disapproving look and added, "Don't say a *fucking* word."

She slumped into her chair and starting biting off big chunks of chocolate.

Richard waited in silence, examining his nails.

Between mouthfuls, Carter said, "What does he fucking expect? He doesn't give us the resources, but expects immediate results. He can't have his cake and eat it!"

"No, you'd beat him to it, Ma'am," Richard muttered under his breath.

Carter shot him a glare that would've made a grizzly bear shrink away. "Don't get smart, *Howie*. And for the last time, stop fucking calling me ma'am! You got that?"

Richard cringed. He hated swearing as much as he hated raised voices. "Sorry ... boss?"

"Better." She cast aside the remaining few chunks of chocolate. Taking a deep breath, she massaged her temples and said, "Okay, where are we at here?"

"Well ..."

"It was a rhetorical question, Richard."

"Would you like a rhetorical answer?"

Carter glared at him once more, but then managed a half-laugh. "Well, at least we have that website – *Paedophiles Living Near YOU* – as a lead. The sex offenders were all on there, which at least links three of the murders. We need to check the ISP hits to each of their profile pages and then start wearing out some shoe leather."

***

A gusty wind blew over the top of the sand dunes on the beach, north of Seahouses' harbour. The sky had darkened prematurely.

The sand was kicking up and swirling at their ankles as Han and Cara walked back from Bamburgh. They had taken a leisurely stroll in the cool morning sunshine, following the coastline to the historical seat of the ancient Northumbrian kings. After visiting the castle and stopping for some lunch at Blacketts, they had then made their way back as the weather took a turn for the worst. The rain had held off so far, but the banks of bruised clouds rolling in from the sea foretold an imminent wet future.

Jumanji was trotting along ahead of them, only stopping to glance back every now and then to check that they were still visible. Cara zipped her fleece up to her neck and wrapped and arm around Han's waist.

"It's been a lovely weekend," Cara said. Her cheeks and ears were rosy from the biting wind.

Han looked at her as they walked and couldn't help but smile. "I'm really glad we did this."

104

"Me too." She arched her head up and kissed him on the cheek.

"What was that for?"

"For being wonderful."

Han squeezed her and said, "Oh, you don't know the half, hon." As he said it, he had to stifle a cringe. Luckily, Cara was staring ahead of them, towards the rocks and the outskirts of Seahouses, with a wistful look in her eyes. "Sorry I couldn't change the weather," he added as the first spots of rain stained the sand.

"A weekend at the seaside wouldn't be the same without howling gales and icy rain," Cara said and laughed as she wiped wayward strands of hair out of her eyes. "Didn't you say that your mum lived in the north east still?" she asked as they continued, picking up the pace.

"Yes, a little mining village north of Newcastle."

Cara turned to him, her expression hopeful. "We could … I don't know … maybe pop in to visit her on the way back if you like."

He should've seen that one coming a mile off, but he had let his guard down. The weekend had been so relaxing, so stress free. He had barely thought about Phase Two or Charlie, and those annoying words and sweaty nightmares had even taken a back seat.

The shock must have been written all over his face. Cara quickly added, "Don't worry – just a thought, that's all." She looked away, her disappointment clear.

Oh, bollocks to it, he thought. What did he have to lose? "Sorry, you just caught me off guard there a little. I hadn't really thought about it, but sure; that's a great idea."

"Really?" Cara stopped and turned to him.

"Yes, really. Haven't seen Mum since her birthday last April, so it's perfect. I'm sure she'd love to meet you." Was this really a good idea? It felt both right and insane at the same time. He had never let anyone in to the family, not since Vanessa.

"Really?" He had never seen Cara so unsure of herself. Her usual confidence had deserted her. She nervously flicked hair out of her eyes. Her guard was clearly down too. This was getting serious.

Han offered her a reassuring smile. "Of course! What's not to love about you?" Oh shit, he'd just said the L word. Fuckfuckfuck*fuck*.

Cara's face quite literally lit up. She threw her arms around him.

He could feel the warmth of her body pressing against him and the rapid beating of her heart as her hair danced in the wind. He suddenly felt like they had been transported to *From Here to Eternity*. Did that make him Burt Lancaster or Philip Ober? Either way, he should've been running for cover, or at the very least, terrified to the core. But as it turned out, he kissed her head and said, "I love you." And, Goddamn, he actually meant it.

Cara kissed him repeatedly on the lips and, breathlessly, said, "I love you too."

Cara looked down to see Ju nuzzling her leg. Laughing, she said, "I love you too, Ju."

***

The Monday afternoon traffic on the A1 was light as Han and Cara headed south towards Newcastle. Cara was flicking through her iPod that was connected to the car stereo. She stopped on a Paolo Nutini track. *These Streets* began playing as Cara sat back in her seat and closed her eyes, a smile playing across her lips.

Han took his eyes off the road for a moment to glance at her. There was only one word to express her relaxed demeanour – content. There was also only one word to describe her – beautiful. Her loose golden curls, the angle of her jaw line, her slender nose with just a slight upward turn at the end, her crystal blue eyes and slim neck. He let out a deep sigh and turned back to the road. He couldn't help but smile. He knew what he was doing could have serious ramifications, but it felt right. So why the hell not?

"So you've never seen your dad for years?" Cara asked, dreamily.

Han's eyes widened and his heart tried to break through his ribcage. His mouth had dropped open, but he managed to catch the gasp before it escaped.   He suddenly felt hot and claustrophobic.

"Hon?"

Recovering quickly, he glanced at her, saying, "Hmm? Oh, sorry, miles away. He left when I was young. He wrote and visited for a while then the visits died off and the letters soon after." He had to take a deep breath to fight off a nauseating feeling of vertigo. What was the matter with him? So he hadn't thought of his father for a *long* time. What the fuck was this?

"I'm sorry," Cara said and placed a hand on Han's knee.

He offered her a smile. "It's okay, kiddo. It was a long time ago."

"You don't know where he is?"

"Nope and not bothered either. I don't even know if he's alive or dead."

Cara cringed. "God, that's terrible."

"It's just the way it is, as Bruce Hornsby once said."

"Haven't you thought about trying to get back in touch with him?"

"No." That sounded a little abrupt. "Sorry, no, I've just got on with my life. Mum was a mess for a long time, but she's fine too. We've all moved on."

"Sorry, I don't mean to pry," Cara said then fell silent.

"It's no big deal." Han smiled. "I don't mind." That was a total lie. His mind minded a fucking lot. The nausea had dissipated, leaving a throb in his temples and a mood that had taken a rapid nosedive. He felt angry – not at Cara, but at … his father, of all people. What the hell? He'd never given two shits about him before. To be honest, he hadn't thought about him for … Christ, he couldn't even remember when the man had last crossed his mind. And now he was suddenly angry at being deserted. Was that right? *Gosh, therapy here I come!*

No, that wasn't right. He wasn't angry at his father for leaving. He was angry about something else, but he couldn't quite put his finger on it. Was this to do with the whole *not your time, son* bollocks? He couldn't remember his father saying something like that to him. None of it made any sense.

***

Han pulled up in front of a small two bedroom semi-detached council house. A people carrier that had seen better days was parked on the drive. Lights were already on inside, against the mid afternoon gloom.

Han got out, but Cara remained seated. He ducked down and said, "You coming then?"

A nervous smile played across Cara's lips. Shaking her head, she said, "I'm bloody nervous. Can you believe that?"

Han rolled his eyes. "Why?"

"She might not like me."

Now Han laughed, which felt good after the father episode earlier. "Get your sexy ass out of the car."

Cara smiled and conceded. "You know how to sweet-talk a lady."

The front door opened before they reached it. A tall woman with greying ginger hair greeted them, dressed in jeans and a t-shirt. Her eyes were wide with surprise. "I don't believe it!" she exclaimed with barely contained delight. She threw her arms around both of them and hugged ferociously. There were tears in her eyes when she pulled back. "And who's this?"

"Mum, this is Cara."

"Lovely to meet you, Cara. You are so beautiful."

Cara's cheeks flushed. "It's lovely to meet you too—"

"Bev. Come inside and I'll make us a nice cup of tea. Have you eaten? I've got a roast joint in the oven."

Han laughed. "You always have a roast on the go."

As Beverley busied herself in the kitchen, preparing additional vegetables, Han and Cara sat in the adjoining dining area, separated from the kitchen by an archway. Walls and surfaces were cluttered with photo frames and assorted ornaments. They sat on a small well-used sofa that was set against the far wall.

The smell of slow cooked roast beef enticed the nostrils and the gentle tones of Buddy Holly languished in the background.
Sometimes we'll sigh

108

Sometimes we'll cry
And we'll know why
Just you and I
Know true love ways …

Cara glanced around the cluttered room. She noticed a photo of Han, standing side by side with a similarly ginger man, but slimmer and slightly taller. "Is that your brother?"

"Yeah – that was at his wedding. He's older and more successful, but I got the looks."

"Oh, I don't know," Cara laughed.

As Beverley waited for the kettle to boil, she hummed along to the music, closing her eyes momentarily.

Han watched her, suddenly oblivious of Cara. A smile touched his lips as he remembered those lazy Sundays as a kid, listening to Mum's record collection from the old Bush record player in the veneered cabinet. Buddy Holly had been a particular favourite.

Cara opened her mouth to speak, but she caught the wistful look in Han's eyes and remained silent. She watched him, smiling, until the song ending broke the spell.

"This is such a wonderful surprise, son!" Beverley said as she prepared mugs of tea. "You could've warned me – I look a right mess!"

"Don't be daft, Mum. We were passing through and I thought you'd like to meet Cara."

Beverley stood in the archway, wiping her hands on a chequered tea towel. "It's a lovely, lovely surprise. I haven't seen you in months and then this!" Turning to Cara, she added, "He hadn't even told me about you yet."

"Is that right?" Cara said, showing mock disapproval to Han. Then to Beverley, added, "I'll make sure he gets up here more often."

Beverley seemed to study Cara for a time then, with sincerity, said, "My son always had good taste, but you, Cara, you are very special indeed."

"Aye, special needs," Han said with a wink.

109

Beverley flicked the tea towel at him. "Don't be so bloody cheeky, you. You're not too old to be put over my knee."

Cara laughed as Han said, "My teachers were always scared shitless of Mum. She once pinned one up against a wall and half strangled him."

Cara's eyes widened. "Really?"

"I'm embarrassed to say, yes," Beverley said and turned back to the kitchen to check on the simmering vegetables.

"My brother was getting bullied and Mum tried several times to get the school to intervene, but they did nothing. So after another fight, Mum storms into school full of Hell and eventually corners Karl's form tutor ... Mister Roberts, if I remember correctly ... and pins the little prick up against the wall."

"That was wrong," Beverley's voice drifted in from the kitchen. "I lost my temper."

"No it wasn't, Mum. You stuck up for us – you always did. When Dad was around and even more so when he left."

There was silence, save for the gentle bubbling of vegetables on the hobs.

Cara looked at Han, but he was looking down at his cupped hands. "There's nothing more protective than a mother," Cara said finally, trying to lighten the sudden sullen mood. "It's only natural."

The kettle boiled and soon Beverley was handing out mugs of tea. She sat down briefly with them to drink hers, asking the usual questions to Cara – what do you do, where are you from, how did you meet. She was soon up on her feet again though, busying herself in the kitchen.

Cara asked if she could help a couple of times, but Beverley would have none of it. She was the embodiment of perpetual motion. Or, in other words, a proper mum.

More aromas drifted in from the kitchen to mix with the beef; roast potatoes, onion and mushroom gravy, turnip, broccoli and carrots, not to mention homemade Yorkshire puddings.

"It smells absolutely gorgeous, Bev," Cara said with absolute sincerity. To Han, she mouthed the words, *fuck, that smells good.*

Beverley brought out plates that were overflowing with the biggest portions that Cara had ever seen. Telling them to start,

Beverley continued fussing in the kitchen. They took their mugs over to the small pine dining table.

"Mum, sit down and join us, for God's sake!"

"I'll just nip outside for a quick fag."

"I thought you had quit?" Han shouted after her as she disappeared out the back door.

"Don't you start – I get enough earache from your brother."

Han looked at Cara and rolled his eyes. "I won't say another word!"

Eventually, Beverley sat down with them with a far smaller portion and then played with much of it, while asking more about how Han was doing and asking more about Cara.

"It's nice to see a girl with a healthy appetite," Beverley said, smiling.

Looking at her empty plate with just a smear of gravy, Cara cringed. "It was the best roast dinner I've had in years."

"Mum's roast dinners are legendary. Travellers come from near and far – she was the inspiration for those Uncle Ben's sauce adverts."

"Sarcastic bugger."

"If we'd been a bit earlier we might've gotten to sample the beef dripping with some bread. Heart attack city, but bloody lovely."

***

Beverley hugged the two of them repeatedly as they stood at the front door. "Come back soon – the two of you. It's been lovely – it really has."

"It's been lovely to meet you, Bev. And yes, we will be back as soon as we can," Cara said.

"We haven't had a big family party for ages. We have to arrange one so that you can meet the whole brood."

"I'll give bro a shout and we'll get something arranged," Han said and gave her another hug.

Beverley kissed Cara on the cheek, which both surprised and delighted her. Turning to Han, she said, "Look after this one, son. She's a keeper."

Beverley stood in the street, waving for every last second while the car was still in view.

***

As they continued their journey south on the A1, Cara turned to Han and said, "Your mum is lovely."

Han smiled and nodded.

"I wish you could've met my mum," she added.

Cara's mother had died of cancer nearly ten years ago. Her father was still on the scene, but she didn't see him very often. Han glanced at her and said, "I'm sorry, hon. Me too."

Changing the subject, Cara took a deep breath then asked, "So ... what happened with your dad?"

Han rolled his eyes. "Well that didn't take long. I knew it would come up as soon as we got back in the car, so at least you managed to wait until we got back onto the A1."

"Fuck you," Cara said, smiling.

"My dad worked away a lot – he was a sales rep. He stayed away more and more and then eventually he never came back. It's no biggie."

"No biggie? I think you're understating things there a little. But I also think there's more to it."

Not your time, son.

The memory was like a spasm and it was as incomprehensible as it was unexpected.

"Are you okay, honey?" The colour had bled out of Han's face as if his throat had been cut. His hands gripped the steering wheel like they were throttling someone.

Han blinked and glanced at Cara. "Sorry, yes, just thinking back to that fab dinner." Recovering his composure, he added, "If you must know my dad was ... well, a bit of a drinker for a time. He and Mum used to have some horrendous fights. Sometimes it would spill over to me and my brother. As I say, it's no big deal."

"Doesn't sound like no big deal."

"Not as bad as you'd imagine. It was just … well, a bit awkward at times. Dad was pretty intolerant and Mum was very protective. Dad also liked women a little too much. That's all it came down to. After a while he left and … well, to be honest it was better that he did."

"Have you not seen him since?"

"Apart from those early visits when he first left, no. I've thought about him from time to time." *That's a lie*, Han thought. He hadn't really thought about him for years. But now, suddenly, he couldn't think of anything else.

"So, your father just walked out on the three of you and you never saw him again and that's … okay?"

"It is what it is, Cara," Han said matter-of-factly. The conversation was starting to irritate him, but to keep things good-humoured, he added, "I'm not one of these bleeding heart twats who want to blame everything on their upbringing. My mum was … and still is the most loving and caring human being on the planet. She should be fucking well sainted and I'm not shitting you. Me and my brother had a bit of a crappy upbringing for a while, but Mum made up for it in spades. I can't complain."

Cara didn't say anything for a while. She just laid a hand on Han's thigh.

That open doorway shot into focus. Strange sounds … animal sounds. Han shook his head to dispel the blurred, intangible images.

Who's your daddy?

CHAPTER 8

Han settled back into some semblance of routine, dividing time between Cara, the shop and Perry. The Seahouses trip, however, played on his mind. Not the trip as such – the conversation with Cara. His father.

Could it really have been his father who said those words to him as a child? Is that possible? Or was his mind playing tricks? Loads of people use the phrase 'son' to people they aren't actually related to. It was a widely used figure of speech. But his own whispering subconscious suggested something different. What then?

If it had indeed been his father, what had happened to cause him to say it and for his mind to have buried it so deep for nearly thirty years?

He was going to have to get to the bottom of this bullshit once and for all, otherwise it would slowly drive him insane. Heaven forbid that anyone think that old Hanny was losing his marbles. For one thing, he had no idea how to get to Neverland to retrieve them.

"Ah, putrefaction!" Robert Downey Jnr's voice announced quite suddenly.

An IM box had popped up on screen to reveal a message from Charlie.

"For fuck's sake," Han muttered as he read the message.

HARRY, OLD BUDDY, HOW GOES IT? HAVE A NICE HOLIDAY AT THE SEASIDE?

What? Seaside? Is this fucker following me?

Typing, he replied, OH AYE? HOW DID YOU KNOW WHERE I BUGGERED OFF TO? FOLLOWING ME, EH? HAHA. He tried to make it sound good-humoured, but he found himself leaning close to the monitor, his features pinched and expectant.

DON'T GET MUCH HOLIDAYS MYSELF, SO I ALWAYS ASSUME PEOPLE RUN OFF TO SUNNIER CLIMES.

Sounded innocent enough, but he was getting increasingly wary of old Charlie. That was crazy though, wasn't it? Charlie had handed a string of scumbags on a plate to him, and allowed him to execute each one. So it could hardly be some elaborate sting operation, for Christ's sake. He wasn't a big lover of the boys in blue (girls in blue being a notable exception!), but even they still had to, for the most part, stick within the confines of the law. There was no logical explanation for Charlie's continued involvement, other than to kill off the scumbags and make the country a better place to live in. That was his stance from the start. They were in it together; partners in crime. If Charlie double-crossed him, he'd be signing his own death warrant as well.

A little caution was healthy enough, he guessed, especially for serial killers. He was used to working alone, that was all. This was still a new and unusual working relationship. He had to keep things in perspective. He couldn't allow prudence to descend into paranoia.

HOW'S WORK? EVERYTHING OK YOUR END? Han finally typed.

AYE DON'T WORRY ABOUT ME – EVERYTHING PEACHY. GOT ANOTHER ONE FOR YA.

"Fine," Han muttered aloud in resignation. "Jesus, this is turning into a bit of a chore."

115

A knock at the door startled him and roused Ju from his slumber in the bedroom.

Cursing at the interruption, he quickly typed, BRB and then stomped downstairs. Yanking the door open, he said, "Yes?" It came out a little more terse than he would've liked.

A slightly dishevelled woman, perhaps in her early forties, was standing in front of him. His skin prickled as his instincts screamed 'cop'.

"Hi," Karen Carter said.

Recovering his composure, Han said, "Sorry for my curtness. Problems at work. How can I help?"

Carter offered a warm smile and said, "No problem."

After a brief introduction, Han led the detective through to the kitchen. "Cuppa?" he asked as he started to fill the kettle.

"Love one, thanks. Nice house. You live here alone?"

It was delivered as a throwaway remark, but Han knew damn fine that there were no throwaway remarks when it came to coppers. "I've got my Labrador for company," was his simple reply as he prepared two mugs. "So, how can I help, officer?"

"You may have heard on the news about the recent murders – several of whom were on the sex offenders register."

Ah-ha, Han thought. *Here it comes.* "Of course – the papers are saying that it might be a vigilante or something."

"It's one possibility," Carter said. "Have you heard of a website called *Paedophiles Living Near YOU?*"

Han stopped and turned to her. Her expression gave nothing away – just open curiosity. "I have and clearly the reason you are here is because you already know I have."

Carter nodded. "Yes, we know you viewed the profile of the first victim – an Albert Livingstone. I'm here to ascertain why."

Han continued making the tea and said, "Well, I appreciate the no bullshit approach, officer." He handed Carter a mug of tea and sipped his own then added, "I'm happy to tell you."

"Thank you," Carter said and sipped her tea.

"A friend told me about the site and I went on just out of curiosity really."

"Fair enough. So why did you search under a Wakefield postcode and why did you view Livingstone in particular?"

Outwardly, Han offered a noncommittal shrug while inwardly his mind raced. "I dunno really. I felt kind of weird even looking at the site – felt like I was some sort of intruder. I started to type my own postcode, but then … shame or embarrassment, I guess … I changed it to a postcode of an old girlfriend. Dunno, it just popped in there. If I remember rightly I think I just clicked on the first name that came up."

Carter studied him over the rim of her mug. He was a cool, casual customer alright. He gave off the right mix of mild embarrassment and genuine concern. His explanation made sense and, according to the records, he had only viewed the first victim – at least from his home PC. "That all sounds feasible," she said finally. "But you can understand our concerns. We have to follow every lead thoroughly."

"Of course – I totally understand," Han said. "I feel pretty stupid now."

"That sort of website plays on public fears. I can understand why people would have a look, but that sort of thing doesn't help – it can only be destructive."

Han pulled off a rather believable look of sheepishness. "I know. I'm sorry for wasting police time – especially in such a big enquiry where your resources are probably already stretched."

This guy was good alright. Changing tact, she asked, "How did you react to seeing Albert Livingstone?"

Oh, good question. "He just struck me as a normal-looking bloke. He could've been anyone's neighbour or work colleague. Quite disconcerting really. You just don't know who to trust these days."

"You got that right," Carter said. She drained the rest of her tea and suppressed a belch. Setting her mug down, she added, "The enquiry is ongoing, so I may need to speak to you again, but that's all for now. Thanks for the cuppa."

Han showed the detective out and then leant back against the front door. He let out a sigh and thought, *close call.* Thank God he switched to the internet café with number two. They would be

117

following that one up as well, of course, but he had covered his tracks well enough there. Still … close call.

He returned to the bedroom office and sat down with a sigh.

A response from Charlie was waiting for him. NO PROB, BUD.

Han chewed his bottom lip for a time, hands hovering over the keyboard. After a moment, he made a decision and typed, SEND IT THROUGH, BUT IT'S BEST IF I LAY LOW FOR A LITTLE WHILE LONGER. WILL GET BACK ON TASK AS SOON AS POSS.

UNDERSTOOD, was Charlie's reply.

Did he understand? Han wasn't arrogant enough to brush off a visit from the law. He had learned from experience that the police were not to be underestimated. Just because he had bested them a few times in the past, it did not mean that he was going to throw caution to the wind. On the contrary. No, extend the sabbatical by another week or so and then get back to it when he was positive there was no further interest in him.

**

Will and Carol pulled up into the grubby car lot of Chris's Chariots on the fringe of Sunderland's city centre. Neglect was evident everywhere, from the faded signage and grime, to the sorry-looking collection of ageing vehicles on display.

As they jumped out, they noticed a salesman striding over towards them from a portacabin.

He was wearing what had once been an expensive suit, but threadbare cuffs and shiny elbows betrayed its age.

"I see you're a bit of a four-be-four connoisseur," he said, with a nod towards the Land Rover that was still making its usual metallic settling noises. "Looking to replace the old warhorse?"

"Actually, no. We've come to talk to you about Hannibal Whitman." Will figured that there was no point in beating around the bush.

Chris rolled his eyes and retrieved a packet of cigarettes from a coat pocket. As he lit one with a disposable lighter, he said,

118

"Police, journos or nut jobs?" Before either could answer, he said, "I'm guessing nut jobs."

Carol spoke. "We're running an independent investigation – civil courts." Her face flushed, suddenly feeling foolish and embarrassed.

Will glanced at her, eyebrow cocked in surprise, along with a hint of admiration at her improvisation.

Chris seemed oblivious. He drew on his cigarette a couple more times as he digested this fresh development. Then he flicked the half-smoked butt away and said, "Well that's a new one on me. Nowt's spoiling, so step into my orifice."

Will and Carol followed him into the dingy and draughty portacabin, where Chris slumped down into a chair behind a shabby and coffee ring-stained desk. The room smelled of cheap coffee and body odour.

There was only one unoccupied chair, but neither opted to sit in it. Will started. "We're hoping that you might remember more about Whitman and your encounter with him than you did when interviewed last year."

Chris finished pouring himself a cup of coffee from a thermos flask, before turning his attention back to Will and Carol. "If anything, I'm going to remember less than I did back then. I'm not getting any younger, son." He took a loud slurp of coffee and sat back into his protesting chair. With a satisfied sneer, he added, "And why would I tell you even if I did?"

"For the families of the victims," Carol said weakly. She pretended to glance out of the window to allow herself a moment to compose herself, gulping back the lump in her throat.

Will caught the gesture out of the corner of his eye. Keeping the salesman's attention, he added, "Please, even the smallest detail could prove useful. If you could just take us through the encounter in your own words – it could prove extremely useful in our investigation." He was surprising himself with how official he was sounding.

Chris shook his head. His tone condescending, he said, "You come in here with some bullshit about a civil action against Britain's biggest mass murderer and all you've got to offer is a quick

119

tug on my heart strings?" He laughed and leaned back in his chair, placing his hands behind his head. "You're gonna have to do better than that, pal."

Carol opened her mouth to speak, but Will interrupted.

"Fuck this," he spat and slapped the plastic cup off the desk. Steaming coffee splattered Chris across the face, causing him to cry out in shock and pain.

Before he could react any further, Will sprung over the desk and pinned him by the throat against the chair.

"Will!" Carol was shouting, her voice shrill with panic.

"I'm not playing his fucking games." Glaring into Chris' gasping red face, Will said, "You're going to describe in great detail your encounter with Whitman or I'm going to torture you to death right here and now."

Will loosened the chokehold slightly and Chris managed, "Fucking prick! Not telling you jack shit!"

With his free hand, Will grabbed one of Chris' hands that were struggling at his throat. In one quick movement, he gripped the index finger and yanked it back and to one side, popping it loose from the knuckle.

Despite his throat constriction, Chris managed an impressive scream.

"Do you appreciate the situation now?" Will asked, maintaining an even tone. He relaxed his grip on the man's throat and released his injured hand. Chris immediately clutched it to his chest, gasping and blowing on it, as if burned by a boiling kettle.

"Mother fucker," he spat through clenched teeth.

Will leaned in close, ignoring Carol's protests. "Do I have your attention now?"

"Yes! Fucking yes, you bastard!"

"Good." He pulled up the vacant chair and sat across the desk with his arms folded. "Describe in minute detail everything from when you first set eyes on Whitman."

***

120

The sounds of gentle breathing were dispelled by Han's mobile phone bursting into Nino Rota, *The Godfather* theme. Han fumbled for it and, with eyes still closed, accepted the call, muttering, "What time is it?"

"Everything okay?" Cara asked, rubbing her eyes.

"It's me ..." It was Karl, but he didn't sound right.

Han opened his eyes and sat bolt upright. "What's wrong?"

Cara sat up and gripped Han's arm, hearing the alarm in his voice.

"It's ... it's Mum ..."

***

The late morning was bright and fresh as the mourners gathered at the graveside. The church service had been standing room only. Friends and family had travelled from far and wide to pay their respects to a much loved and respected woman.

Han stood with Cara clinging on to his arm, tears streaming down her face at one side and Karl and his wife at the other. They were all crying. Han had cried too when Karl had first broken the news that their mother had died in a house fire. It had actually been Cara who had set him off. She burst into tears, so Han had followed suit.

But now, surrounded by an outpouring of grief, he found himself unable to react in any way. He felt detached from it. He stood, staring fixedly at the hole in the ground that his mother was being lowered into. There would be plenty of time for anger and grief later, but all he felt as the casket disappeared was complete and utter disbelief. He could not get his head around it. Mum ... dead? She had burned to death in her bed, having fallen asleep with a lit cigarette. It felt more acute than denial – it felt ... false.

Slowly, the mourners filtered away. Han hugged his brother's wife and then Karl. Wiping tears from his eyes, Karl said, "I'll see you back at the house."

Han nodded and watched them walk back towards the car park, arm in arm.

121

Cara touched his cheek, drawing his attention. "I'm so so sorry, honey. I ... I just ..."

Han managed a thin smile of gratitude. He cleared his throat then said, "Can I have a minute?"

"Of course, hon. I'll wait by the car." She embraced him once more then headed off after the others. She glanced back a couple of times, her expression pained indecision, but she kept going.

Han stood motionless at the side of the grave, looking down at the casket. Mum *really* was dead. She was gone ... forever. A sob escaped his lips and he glanced around to make sure that he was alone. He clasped a hand over his mouth to stifle a second, but then his legs buckled and he fell to his knees, weeping uncontrollably with his head in his hands.

***

The last of the guests had long departed. It was gone 2am and Han and Karl were most of the way through a bottle of Singleton of Dufftown single malt whisky.

Cara placed a hand on Han's shoulder and said, "I'll take Louise up."

Karl's wife was lying on the sofa with her head in Karl's lap, fast asleep.

"Thanks," Karl said. As Cara helped her to her feet, he added, "I'm sorry we had to meet under these circumstances, Cara."

She managed a nod and led Louise out into the hall. She looked back at Han who was staring out of the window into the darkness beyond. With a sigh, she turned away and led Louise upstairs.

Han stood up and walked over to the micro CD player. He turned it on and pressed play. He had no idea what CD might be in there.

Just you know why
Why you and I
Will by and by
Know true love ways ...

Han stared at the small device as Buddy Holly's voice filled the room. His hand crept up to his mouth to stifle a sob.

Karl watched him and swiped away a rogue tear. "You okay, bro?" he managed.

"Not really." Han's reply was distant, dreamlike.

"Stupid bloody question, I guess," Karl added and sipped his whisky.

Han had to clear his throat before saying, "Mum was playing this song the last time I saw her."

Karl nodded slowly, eyes fixed on his glass. "It was one of her favourites."

Han finally tore his gaze away from the CD player. Wiping his face, he said, "Sorry ... I'll be alright." He knocked back the rest of his whisky then fished a crumpled packet of cigarettes out of his pocket. "Found these by the back door. Strange how even something so mundane and inanimate like these could evoke such ... feelings."

Karl stared at the packet then took another swig of whisky. "I bloody well told her for years ..." His voice trailed off and he turned away.

"It just ..."

Rubbing his eyes, Karl asked, "What?"

Han stared at his brother for a time, but then said, "Never mind. I don't know what I'm saying or thinking at the moment."

***

Han and Perry stood in the doorway, Han holding a glass of Jack Daniels loosely in one hand.

Perry shuffled from one foot to the other, with his hands buried into his jacket pockets. He felt useless. He had no idea what to say or how to help his best friend. How do you console the inconsolable?

Finally, he said, "I'm here for you, man. Whatever you need. Don't worry about the shop – I'll keep things ticking over. Take as long as you need."

Han nodded and swilled the whiskey around in his glass.

Perry rather sheepishly hugged him, patting his back a couple of times for good measure. "Take care of yourself, mate."

"Cheers, Perry." Han managed a tired smile.

After seeing Perry out, Han snatched up the bottle of Jack Daniels from the kitchen worktop and took it and the glass into the dining room.

The CD he had taken from his mother's house was resting by the iPod dock on top of the Hi-Fi. He took it out of its case and placed it into the CD player.

As Buddy Holly filled the air, Han knocked back another shot of Jack Daniels. He closed his eyes and, hugging the bottle and glass to his chest, he slowly swayed in time with the music.

He refilled his glass, but as he brought it up to his lips, his hand began to tremble uncontrollably. He slammed the glass and bottle down on the table then fell to his knees, holding his head in his hands and sobbing.

He composed himself as the next track began to play. He stabbed the power button, snatched up the bottle and glass and headed upstairs.

He slumped into the office chair and switched on the monitor. The PC was already on, so the *Inglourious Basterds* screensaver appeared almost immediately. The image was that of a battered Nazi helmet dangling from a baseball bat.

After drinking a shot and refilling his glass, Han banished the screensaver and logged in to Live Messenger. Charlie was online, but did not message him right away.

Han knocked back another shot of JD and typed, SORRY I HAVEN'T BEEN AROUND FOR A WHILE. I'VE HAD A DEATH IN THE FAMILY. IT HIT ME REALLY HARD. He felt weird telling Charlie personal details, but fuck it. What did it matter?

SORRY TO HEAR THAT, HARRY. IF THERE'S ANYTHING I CAN DO, JUST SAY. I'M HERE FOR YOU.

THANKS, I APPRECIATE THAT. He topped up his glass from the already half empty bottle and drained another shot. He rubbed his face vigorously then typed, IS THAT TARGET STILL VALID?

YES, BUT YOU DON'T NEED TO THINK ABOUT THAT RIGHT NOW. YOU JUST TAKE YOUR TIME, MATE.

"No, fuck it," Han said aloud. Han filled and drank again. NO, I NEED TO JUST GET ON WITH IT. IT'LL TAKE MY MIND OFF EVERYTHING ELSE.

WELL, ONLY IF YOU'RE SURE.

I'M ON IT, he typed then logged off. "Onwards and upwards," he muttered. He laughed, but he had no idea what he was laughing about. Then he choked back a sob and poured himself another shot.

***

Han was in a dark mood, not only because of his recent bereavement. His stotting headache did not help either. The drinking had gotten a little out of hand in the week since his mother's death.

What had seemed so clear in a Jack Daniels-fuelled haze last night, now, in the cold light of day, seemed stupid and impulsive. He was letting his heightened emotions cloud his judgement.

Yes, he had made a commitment to Phase Two, and he fully intended to see it through, but he felt that control of the experiment had been taken out of his hands. He felt that he was no longer working to his own agenda. It seemed more and more that it was actually Charlie's agenda.

He would sort out this latest target and then have a serious chat with old Charlie.

The new target troubled him somewhat as well. A nineteen year old lad, recently released and living in sheltered accommodation. His conviction seemed tenuous, with a history of mental illness and learning difficulties. Having said that, he was a convicted paedophile. He had had sex with a thirteen year old – consenting, according to the girl – but the law was the law. And rules is rules. The experiment guidelines were clear – anyone who, in the eyes of the law, had committed an evil act would be punished. And, for the statistic to count towards the Haydon tally, that meant execution. Still, little dumbshit Ryan played on his mind.

Han stood at a bus stop across the street from the indistinct terraced house that was Ryan's current abode. It was raining. Again. The rhythmic patter on the shelter roof helped abate Han's rising anxiety and focus his thoughts on the job at hand. He rubbed at his temples, willing the paracetamol to start taking effect.

A Ford Crap shot by, close to the curb, and kicked up sheets of muddy gutter water that splashed over Han's legs. He looked down at his drenched jeans and then back to the disappearing rear end of the car. Clenching his jaw, he turned back to the terraced house without a word.

The day just gets better and better. If he had managed to catch the registration plate, that fucker would've been a freebie. A joy compared to divvie Ryan.

Several young men and women entered and left the building, but none were the skinny, pale teenager that Han was waiting for. That got Han thinking; how many evil little fuckers were currently living in there? It would be nice to kill a few twats with one big fucking rock. But it would be difficult to trace who was guilty and who wasn't. It would probably mean dealing with half a dozen different agencies and he doubted Charlie had that sort of clout. Still, nice thought though!

It was mid-afternoon and Han was considering buggering off to find a little café for a bite to eat when Ryan finally made an appearance. He looked even frailer than he did in the photo and the look was emphasised by the grubby over-sized coat that swamped his slight frame. He barely looked sixteen, never mind nineteen. The *Harry Potter* baseball cap was the icing on the cake.

Han followed at a discreet distance. His plan was simple; follow until the opportunity arose to dispose of him quickly and quietly. He wasn't going to mess around or enjoy himself with this one.

It continued to rain. Harder.

Han realised that he was muttering to himself like Tam, that miserable old bastard in Haydon, used to. *I'm eighty-four and still grow me own veggies …*

Get a grip, Han, old buddy. He quelled a sudden urge to launch into Wookie speak, but the absurdity of it managed to crack a brief smile. His hangover had ebbed away too, so although he wasn't exactly upbeat, he was at least a little less downbeat.

Ryan clearly had nothing better to do. Han followed him up and down streets, in and out of shops (only browsing, never buying), into the park (too crowded), back up and down a few streets. All in the pissing rain. Little twat. At least he was making it easier to kill the irritating fucker. With his hangover gone, his appetite returned with audible gusto and he found himself searching for a deli or even a newsagent that he could quickly nip into without losing his target.

Then an opportunity abruptly presented itself. Ryan did the unthinkable; he entered a public toilet. To actually have a piss and not to suck off a fat old queer. Well, there's a first for everything.

Han followed him in at a discreet distance; not for the normal counter-surveillance reasons, but just so that anyone watching didn't think he was cruising for a fat old queer! I mean, he had a reputation to maintain. A public toilet, for Christ's sake! *Oh, the humanity!*

Ryan was pissing at the urinal, humming away to himself and casting his stream from side to side like a drunken Ghostbuster. Rather than a bit of Ray Parker Jnr (legend turned arse-bandit after teaming up with the fucking moustachioed 118 knob-jockeys), he was in fact attempting the humming equivalent of a lightsaber. This would surely be construed as a mercy killing! It took considerable effort to stop himself from shouting out, *I am your father, Luke!*

After a quick check to make sure none of the cubicles were harbouring George Michael, Han walked up behind Ryan, who was shaking, clearly blissfully unaware of the two shake rule. Sometimes this serial killing malarkey was a grubby old game. As Han raised his gloved hands, Ryan turned around.

With his hands inches from Ryan's neck, Han said, "Hi, Ryan."

There was no fear on the young man's face. There was only mild surprise and curiosity. "Hi. How can I help you, sir?"

Han lowered his hands and managed a half-laugh. "Well, you're polite, I'll give you that."

Ryan's wide grin had an almost maniacal quality. "Thank you, sir. My Gran taught me."

Gran? Oh, bugger, this was getting harder by the second. *Mercy killing, Han, ya great big Jessie. Focus!*

"Can I wash my hands now?"

"Err ... sure, kid," was Han's bemused reply.

Alternating between smiling and noisily smacking his lips, Ryan scampered (yes, that is probably the best verb to describe it!) across to the washbasins and began washing his hands with the meticulousness of a brain surgeon.

Han somewhat reluctantly walked over and stood beside him. With a sigh, he said, "Sorry kid, but I'm going to have to kill you now. I'd rather not, but it has to be, I'm afraid."

Finally a flicker of confusion from Ryan, but then he broke into that same slightly disturbing grin. He laughed – it sounded like an Orang-utan being punched in the stomach – and said, "You kidder! Okay! Do you mind if I dry my hands first, sir?"

Han bit his lip and said, "It'll be best all round if I just get this over with, I think."

The sickly naïve humour vanished and Ryan's bottom lip quivered – that had a bit of a primate quality to it as well. "Why do you want to kill me, sir?" His voice was reedy, trembling.

Han planted his hands on his hips and said, "I don't, as it happens, but you went and had sex with a thirteen year old girl. That's illegal, so you have to die. Sorry." It felt somewhat absurd tagging on the apology.

"Libby is my girlfriend – she loves me and I love her very much. We like all the same sweets and games and everything. We're going to get married when she finishes school." The unnerving smile returned, as if this simple explanation made everything okay. Like his imminent murder was all some daft misunderstanding. Silly Han!

"Err ... not sure you're grasping the situation here, kid," Han said. "Look ..."

Ryan continued to smile as if it were a protective barrier. It seemed to say, *I've explained everything, sir. It was a pleasure to meet you. Love and kisses to your mam.* Mum. Han rubbed his eyes to displace

128

the stark image of his mother, waving goodbye to them after their spontaneous visit on the way back from Seahouses. It stung like a leather strap across his back.

"I'm *sorry*," Han managed to say through his suddenly constricted throat. He sprang forward, gloved hands sinking into the soft flesh of Ryan's throat.

Ryan was gasping and quickly turning purple, but there was no fear in his eyes, only confusion, as if they were saying, *terribly sorry, old bean, but I think there has been some misunderstanding. Would you mind awfully taking your hands from my throat?*

The ridiculous thought of Ryan now morphing into a clipped British officer's accent caused Han to momentarily lose concentration, loosening his grip.

Ryan managed to say, "Sir? Please, sir, that hurts! Please stop!" Tears were welling in his bulging eyes.

The vulnerability in the boy's voice was palpable and made Han flinch. He gritted his teeth and squeezed his eyes shut. The image of his mother sprang back into his mind. "No ... no ... no," he uttered again and again as his hands squeezed harder and harder into the young man's flesh.

Ryan twitched and wheezed for several long minutes before Han eased his lifeless body to the cold concrete floor. Rising and stepping back, Han stifled a sob and then had to clamp a hand over his mouth to prevent himself from throwing up.

***

Han drove home in silence, eyes fixed on the road ahead and both hands gripping the steering wheel. He normally either listened to a local radio station or hooked up his iPod, but not this time. Ryan's wide, dying eyes played on a loop in his mind. Over and over again. *Libby is my girlfriend ... My Gran taught me ... Please, sir ... that hurts ...*

He knew this one would be ... let's say, awkward ... but no, it wasn't just awkward. Something had been odd from the start, right from viewing the file. Ryan had felt ... wrong. But, true to form, he did it anyway. His head had been screwed up at the time by the memory of his mother, but that was just a lame excuse. Han was rational; he didn't let something as trivial as emotion cloud his judgement. He murdered Ryan, even though it didn't seem right, just to notch up another statistic for Phase Two. Forever the consummate professional.

Did Charlie know that about him? Could Charlie possibly know *anything* about him? If he *did* somehow know more about him than he was letting on, what the hell could that mean? Was Ryan some kind of test? Something suddenly felt very wrong. Not just about strangling a poor young retard, but about Charlie and the bigger picture. Was the player being played here?

He suddenly realised the traffic lights ahead of him were red and several pedestrians were crossing. Slamming on the brakes, tyres initially lost traction, skidding on the wet surface. The car jerked to a halt inches from a startled old woman.

"Psycho!" she shrieked at him then shuffled onto the curb.

Han sat there for a moment, his heart racing. *Psycho? Jesus, lady, you don't know the half of it!*

He rubbed at his eyes to try to dislodge the barrage of images. Images of Ryan, of a crying little pig-tailed girl, his mother waving, but with a forlorn look, of Charles Bronson grinning that maniacal smile. *Killin' generals could get to be a habit with me.* Despite vigorous massaging, instead of dispelling them, it seemed to attract more. Faces from Haydon. Mandy … John … *Lisa.*

"Fuck!" he yelled. He wasn't even aware that he had said it aloud.

Honking horns alerted him to the changed lights. With an apologetic wave, he drove on. Red faced and sweating, he muttered, "What the fuck is wrong with me?"

***

Han stood at the kitchen bench, waiting for the kettle to boil with Ju sat at his feet, wagging his tail. Cara had called, but he couldn't bring himself to pick up, so he let it ring off and watched the screen of his mobile bleep periodically to announce a missed call and a waiting voice mail.

130

Cara was the best thing that had ever happened to him. She had been so supportive since his mother had died. He felt to speak to her now would somehow tarnish her and he couldn't have that. Cara was the one decent thing in his life and he had to protect that at all costs.

What had seemed so clear not so long ago seemed to have been turned completely on its head. What he *knew* to be right before now seemed wrong. He felt more lost now than he did before embarking on Phase Two. Phase Two was supposed to sort all this out once and for all.

For the first time *ever* Han questioned the experiment. Not just Phase Two, but the experiment in its entirety. Just what the fuck was it all about? Why the fuck had he started all this in the first place?

Of course, he knew the answer to that. The dream. It had been all so clear – the ultimate experiment to see just what a normal well-adjusted person was capable of if he put his mind to it. And to then return to normal life afterwards. Only he couldn't return to normal life. It wasn't over.

His mobile beeped again. Cara had no idea what she had gotten herself involved in. He held his head in his hands and cursed between clenched teeth. *Cara and Mum had hit it off so well too …*

He would have to call her back at some point, but now wasn't the right time. He would have to get his head together first, otherwise she would guess that something else was wrong in thirty seconds flat. Bereavement was a funny thing, affecting people in different, sometimes strange ways, but Cara was also a copper – she could see through the bullshit.

His thoughts drifted back to Ryan. There was a lot of shit swirling around his head, but his main concerns boiled down to one thing: was killing Ryan wrong? Thinking pragmatically, which Han was a master of, the rules of Phase Two were black and white, so the hit was just. In the eyes of the law, Ryan was guilty of having unlawful sex with a minor, despite the fact that mentally they were probably about the same age. A better lawyer might have … *fuck that. I can't start considering 'what ifs'. The whole fucking thing would go tits to the wind.* Had it already? *No, it fucking well hadn't. This was a setback, a glitch, that's all. Not FUBAR, just … Fucked Up … But Still … Recoverable. FUBSR. Doesn't have the same ring to it, but …*

"Do I look fucking bothered?"

Ju looked at him with that usual mixture of adoration and sympathy.

"Don't you start," Han said and knelt down to scratch the Labrador behind the ear.

As he sipped his tea, his mind turned to Charlie. He was a greater concern altogether. Was it possible that there was some bigger game afoot? Was their chance meeting just that or had it been orchestrated? Or was paranoia digging its little talons deep into his flesh? *Paranoid, mate,* he thought to himself. *You're just going a little stir crazy. Where's my pillow?*

Han drained his mug and came to a decision. Phase Two was officially on hold.

Han made a fresh mug of tea, took it up to the spare room office and fired up the PC. Charlie wasn't online, which made things easier. Han quickly typed up an email.

C,
Everything on hold. Will be in touch.
Take it easy,
H

Succinct. There would be all kinds of questions, but old Charlie boy would just have to get over it. Han was back in charge.

With a decision made, Han instantly felt like a weight had been lifted off his shoulders. He felt drained, but reassured. He sat back and managed a weary smile.

His mood improved further after a catch up chat with Cara. He made arrangements for dinner and a movie on Friday night then called Perry at the shop. Business was slow … no change there. LOVEFiLM? … *I don't bloody think so; bunch of corporate twats.*

Not wanting to dwell on poor takings, Han arranged a lad's night out. A few beers and a live band down the local. Just what the doctor ordered.

***

The man whom Han knew as Charlie stared at the open email on his laptop. A mere dozen words, but they changed everything. Initial surprise was quickly replaced with anger. How dare he screw with the plan? He had no idea who he was messing with, but he would … soon.

He considered the tactical use of some gentle persuasion or perhaps allowing him another short sabbatical – a little breathing space to get over the retard and the lingering loss of his mother, but no, not this time.

Was Harry going soft? The retard was a kiddie-fiddler, just like the others. This was all very disappointing.

The young upstart would have to be taught a lesson. He would have to learn who the monkey was and who the organ grinder was in this relationship. And maybe once he'd grasped that hard fact, just maybe then he would tell him the whole truth.

Two little amateur detectives fumbling around in the dark would just have to get a giant clue dropped into their laps. It was time to turn up the heat a little.

Charlie's face cracked into a self-satisfied smile.

***

DCI Karen Carter's office was bathed in darkness, lit only by the glow of her monitor that showed more than a dozen new unopened emails.

She couldn't bring herself to read them just yet. The open files of the deceased victims were splayed out, covering every inch of her cluttered desk, with the most recent at the top of the stack. A prison mug shot of Ryan stared up at her with curious, friendly eyes.

It was bad enough that the system had criminalised the poor kid, but then to be murdered by someone with a warped sense of justice or retribution was just horrific.

Not for the first time, Carter shed a few tears that splashed onto the papers in front of her. She had failed to protect a highly vulnerable member of the public. If she was brutally honest with herself, she couldn't give a stuff about the rest of the victims – they had all been grade A pieces of shit, every man jack of them. But Ryan was different. Ryan had been a child walking around in a man's body and had slipped through the cracks in the social and justice systems. He was the first *true* victim in this sorry mess.

And what did she have? She had plenty of leads, but nothing better than circumstantial. Her team had interviewed over two hundred witnesses and suspects and were liaising with more than a dozen different organisations, including Interpol and the FBI. But still nothing.

This vigilante – she was coming to the conclusion that this person was working alone – was covering his or her tracks perfectly. Always picking the right time and place, no witnesses and cleaning up afterwards. No trail whatsoever. Even the ISP trail hadn't led anywhere – just given them far more suspects than they could handle and, again, none of them any more than circumstantial. None had viewed more than one of the victims and none with any tangible motives. The majority were concerned parents, teachers, law enforcement, some convicted sex offenders and other members of the general public. No standouts.

It was annoying and stressful when it was just scumbags getting their just desserts, but now Ryan changed everything. Now it was personal.

***

The hotel bar was deserted, apart from the bartender, who was sat watching Humphrey Bogart facing off to Edward G Robinson in the middle of a hurricane on the TV, and Will and Carol sat in a booth.

They were hunched over their respective drinks and bathed in shadow, lost in thought. Neither had spoken for some time.

The second hand car salesman had managed a fairly sketchy description of a man with short hair, somewhere between late twenties and early thirties and with a stocky build. That was less than useless – Carol's description was far more detailed, and understandably so. The bastard's face was burned into her retinas. He had also given them the name of the taxi firm that had dropped Han off, but they had been about as helpful as a cream cake in Kabul. It all amounted to another dead end. They were running out of ideas. They were flapping around like a drowning bird in the sea.

Will still felt terrible about the violent encounter with Chris. He knew Carol was still in a fragile state, but he lost his temper and did it anyway. It had terrified the poor woman and had taken several hours for her to calm down. He also increasingly felt that he had betrayed her. He had dragged her along on this mad crusade with promises of retribution, but all he had given her was more pain and disappointment.

Knocking back his whisky, he called over to the bartender, "Can we get two more of the same?"

Carol looked up from the vodka she had barely touched. She could see Will wrestling with his torment. He was probably quite an intense man at the best of times, but the added stresses of hunting down his father's killer were clearly taking their toll. His anger had scared her terribly though. He was a soldier, a man of violence. And she had witnessed more than her fair share of that already. Still, she did feel an affinity with him, and for that, she managed to say, "We'll think of something, Will." She offered him a sympathetic smile.

Sighing, Will said, "I'm sorry, Carol. You didn't want to get involved with all this, but I dragged you along."

Tentatively, Carol reached across the table and touched his hand with the tips of her outstretched hand. It was a compassionate, almost motherly gesture, but it stirred something inside her, something long abandoned. She withdrew quickly, but Will caught it and held on. They looked at one another, neither daring to say a word.

The bartender brought their drinks and broke the expectant silence. Their hands parted as Will fumbled for his wallet.

***

135

As Will walked into the restaurant to meet Carol for breakfast, his phone beeped to announce a text message. Carol was already seated and offered him an awkward smile as he walked over. Before sitting, he pulled his phone out and opened the message.

Consignment #3450933443 for W WRIGHT awaiting collection from Home Delivery Network Sunderland Depot. 0191 5640924.

Will frowned. He hadn't ordered anything. He also could not recall having told anyone that he would be in Sunderland. Could it be Leigh?

"You okay?" Carol asked. She averted her eyes and fidgeted in her seat when Will turned his attention on her.

Will noticed the coy reaction, but pretended not to notice. He sat down, saying, "Not sure. I've got a package awaiting collection here in Sunderland. I'm not expecting anything and, with the possible exception of Leigh Simpson, I don't think anyone knows I'm here."

"Maybe Leigh found something?" There was a flicker of hope in Carol's eyes.

Will appeared unconvinced. Leigh would not be quite so melodramatic about it. Surely, she would just phone him? But if it wasn't Leigh, who could it be?

***

The Home Delivery Network depot was located in a business park in Hendon near the coast. It was a grey, listless morning and a biting wind was blowing in off the North Sea.

Will jumped back into the Land Rover, clutching a large padded parcel. Carol stared at it anxiously.

Will glanced from it to Carol. Apart from the usual printed delivery label, the outer packaging was innocuous. Well, it wasn't an Amazon package, that was for sure. Besides that, it was anyone's guess.

"Just open it!" Carol said, her impatience bubbling over.

He felt suddenly nervous. Was this a glimmer of hope? Some sort of lifeline? Or was it an IED? Would it lead them to Han Whitman or would it blow his hands off?

136

Annoyed with his indecision, he ripped it open without another thought. It didn't blow up, so that was a good start. He pulled out a folder thick with papers, with a typed note stapled to the front.

The file was labelled #145959 HAYDON: HAN WHITMAN CASE FILE. Will's eyes widened.

"Is that …" Carol chewed on a knuckle, words failing her.

"The missing DNA file," Will finished for her. "Err … yeah, I think it might be." The words tumbled out of his mouth, without his full comprehension.

"Did Leigh find it?" Carol managed to say with her mouth still wrapped around one knuckle.

Will read the attached note and then had to read it again before he managed to understand it. "Err … no."

William & Carol,

I hope this note finds you both well. I thought this file might aid your quest. Use it and consider what you already know about your quarry. Start your search where you can find an armoury of Royal assent.

Yours,

A Friend in Loidis

Will read the short note to Carol, who sat back, mouth agape. She felt suddenly lightheaded. "Leigh?"

Will shook his head. "No chance – Leigh doesn't piss about. This is someone else. Someone playing games." He glanced at Carol then back to the note, his brow furrowed.

Carol hugged herself as a shiver ran through her body. She opened her mouth to speak, but at first faltered. In a hushed, brittle voice, she uttered, "H–Han?"

Will read the note one more time then flipped open the file and thumbed through the contents. "It's definitely the evidence gathered from Haydon. I know Whitman is one sick individual, but surely he wouldn't help us to find him. If he knew where we were surely he'd just come and get us." Will cringed even as the words fell out of his mouth.

As Will struggled for words, Carol turned ghostly pale and the single shiver turned into a continuous trembling. "He knows where we are …"

Oh crap, Will thought. Carol was going to go into meltdown if he didn't wrestle back some control of the situation at once. Will leant across and grabbed her hands, squeezing them tight. Staring intensely into her wide eyes, he said, "No, Carol. He doesn't know where we are and he doesn't even know we're looking for him. This is someone else. Someone who wants to help us." Even as the final sentence rolled out, something about it didn't ring true. He didn't believe that it was Han, that much was true, but something in the note made him believe that this person was not a friend. Maybe someone who also had a grudge against Whitman.

Carol clung to Will's hands, as if she were at the edge of a precipice. Tears were welling in her eyes as she whispered, "Maybe we should just give the file to Leigh … and let the police handle it now. I really … don't think I can cope … with any more of this." She was gulping in air in between words as if she was having an asthma attack.

Will resolutely shook his head. "No, I'm going to handle it. I'm going to kill that bastard." The intensity in his words caused Carol to release an involuntary sob. Will flinched at the sight of her anguish. Adopting a soothing tone, he added, "I would like you to help me, Carol, but I'll understand if you feel you can't. If you can't, I'll take you back home right now and you don't need to have anything more to do with it. I promise."

Carol burst into tears, attracting furtive glances from a couple of van drivers standing near the open entrance to the warehouse.

Will pulled her to him, hugging her tightly. He cupped her head in his hands and said, "It's okay, Carol. It's okay, don't worry." She wept against his chest for several minutes, shaking uncontrollably as Will whispered soothing words to her and stroked her hair.

After a time, she managed to gather herself and sat back, wiping her eyes and nose with a balled up tissue. "It's so … tempting to do that, Will, to run back into hiding and to never look

138

back." She managed a bitter laugh that was strangled by another sob, before adding, "But I ... I can't run from it ... I can't forget it. It's inside me ... eating away at me like ... like a cancer. I don't think I can live like this anymore. The constant fear – it wears you down so much, so much that even just breathing becomes a constant battle."

She fell silent again, holding her head in her hands. Then, meeting Will's gaze once more, she said, "I ... I have to see this through ... with you."

Carol constantly astonished Will. She was terrified to her very core, that much was crystal clear, but she wasn't going to give up or run away. Not this time. This time, she was going to stand up and fight. "We'll see this through together," he said finally. After a moment of indecision, he leant over and kissed her on the lips. It was brief, but laced with promise.

Shocked, Carol stared back at him and touched a finger to where their lips had met. The moment that passed between them the night before had seemed like a surreal delusion, it had been so fleeting. At first, she had wondered whether the connection had all been in her imagination, and then later questioned whether anything had happened at all. But this was very real. Feelings that she had thought long dead, dead since Steve's murder, were suddenly rushing back.

She had always had a strong sexual appetite before, but any form of future sexual urge abandoned her the instant she set eyes upon Steve's blood-drenched corpse. Her womanhood had died with him. He had taken so much from her – her dignity, her sanity even – it only seemed fitting that he would take that too with his last dying breath.

She had felt friendship ... briefly, with John, Sam and Jimmy ... before they too were taken away from her. But she had never felt anything remotely sexual since that night, not even to pleasure herself. Last night had seemed so surreal that she questioned it, like she always questioned herself. The interruption had dispersed it like an unfinished spell. There were no interruptions this time.

A smile touched her lips, uneasy at first, but as Will returned it, it grew in potency. She felt heat rising between her legs and had to catch her breath to stifle a moan, the feeling was so intoxicating. "Get me back to the hotel," she whispered.

Will did not need asking twice. He flung the package into the back and gunned the engine.

***

Images of Ryan's sad, almost apologetic eyes played across Han's vision. He had to rub his eyes to dislodge them. The frequent images of Ryan's last gasping breaths were slotting in nicely with all the others. Oh goody. At least they were a respite from thoughts of his mother. But poor dead Ryan wasn't the only thing irritating Han.

Perry wasn't taking a blind bit of notice of him. He was too busy watching Megan Fox burning her tongue with a lighter. Admittedly, she was smoking hot, even with a crispy black tongue, but that wasn't the point.

"Perry! Stop fucking perving for one bastard second," Han snapped.

Perry turned to him and jabbed a finger at the flat screen TV on the wall where Meg was smouldering – in more ways than one. "Don't you see that? Are you dead? I know you're all loved up at the mo, but Jesus! Really?" He kept alternating his beady eyes between the TV and Han, waiting for a reaction.

Han stared at him. Perry's way of dealing with any form of adversity was to ignore it or joke about it. He had been exactly what Han had needed after his mother's death. Just the knowledge that his friend was there if he needed him was enough. Perry was a damn good mate. He tried to hold the intense stare, but then burst out laughing. Perry needed no invitation to join in.

Thankful for the levity, Han said, "Yeah, I know, I know. This shop shit is boring – especially when up against the Fox, but we've got to do this. Call it a crisis meeting. The shop is in trouble, mate."

Perry stopped laughing. His mate and boss had whinged on a semi-regular basis for years about fluctuating profits, cashflow and other mind-numbingly dull subjects, but this was the first time he had actually said they were in trouble. That couldn't be good.

"Sorry, man," Perry said, looking rather sheepish. "What can I do to help?"

Han stared at his friend. His sincerity was plain to see. There were maybe three people in the world who would do anything for him. His brother, of course, Cara too and then his faithful sidekick, Perry. His mum would've made four …

Where was it he had heard, *if you need to know the measure of a man, you simply count his friends?* With technically only one or possibly two of those actual friends, where exactly did he stack up against the Muppets? Bah humbug.

There was of course the cynical view that Perry was just worried about his own ass. *Movie Maniac* was the perfect job for a … how shall we put it … person of generally low personal aspirations (current and future film projects excluded) and an all encompassing passion for movies and online gaming. But Han wasn't feeling particularly cynical today, so Perry was a good (and rare) friend.

"We're going to try some offers, some fresh advertising, maybe a leaflet drop or two," Han said.

"Let me guess; you want me to trudge around in the rain sticking leaflets through doors?"

Han rolled his eyes, which prompted Perry to raise his hands and say, "Don't get me wrong – I'll do it. Just checking what you'd like me to do. Here to help, buddy." He offered a meek smile.

Han patted him on the back. "What you can do is start thinking of some promotional ideas while I stick the kettle on."

***

The sex was great. Well, to be honest, when is sex ever really *that* bad? A whole ocean full of female arms might have shot up into the air at that question, but as Will was a man, he could sympathise, but never truly comprehend.

The sex wasn't the problem. The problem was the intense awkwardness that followed. Will watched as Carol fidgeted with the belt of her bathrobe, while sitting in a chair opposite. Every now and then she glanced up, only to avert her eyes again when they met Will's.

Finally, Will slipped out of bed and walked over to her. She eyed his naked muscular frame and an embarrassed smile played across her lips. He crouched down to her level and took her hands in his. "Hey, you okay?"

Carol finally met his gaze. "Yeah, just a little … funny, that's all. I mean, I must be at least ten years older than you." She looked away, shame getting the better of her.

Will gently held her chin and brought them face to face once more. "Don't be silly. I don't give a damn about age differences or any of that bollocks."

"You're also the first person I've … been intimate with since Steve."

"Well, it's high time you tried something new then," Will said and smiled.

"Yeah, but …"

"Yeah, but nothing. What's happened has happened and I'm glad it did."

Carol stared at him, probing for deceit or uncertainty. All she saw was sincerity. "What now?"

Will shrugged and said, "No idea. Let's see what happens, eh?"

"Okay." She leant forward and kissed him tenderly.

After showering and dressing, they began pouring through the evidence folder. The file contained hundreds of samples and photographs taken from Haydon – bagged and tagged hair, skin and fibre samples, fluid swabs, fingerprint samples and footprint photographs.

"Will Leigh be able to test any of these to see if we get a match?"

"I'd guess that would be a possibility." Will mulled this over then added, "I don't want to jeopardise her job and I also don't want the police to get to him first, but we can ask."

They decided that there was no time like the present and telephoned straight away. They caught her on a day off.

"Anonymous?" Leigh was saying with growing concern. "This is serious shit, Will. We thought that casket went missing due to an indexing error, but now it seems like it was stolen. That could mean that Whitman had an accomplice on the Force working with him. And now this person has given it to you. How did this person know that you were looking for him and where you were? And why the hell is this person helping or *pretending* to help you now?" Her voice had risen to a shout and it sounded like she was pacing up and down in a virtual stampede, adding breathlessness to her edgy tone.

"I know, Leigh. This is all screwed up, but it doesn't change the fact that we now have the missing evidence and it could lead us to him."

"We also know damn well that Whitman loved playing games – his whole façade was one long one. This could be another one of his fucking games. He could be leading you two into a trap. I really think we should hand it over to the investigating team and let them bring this bastard down."

"No!" It was Will's turn to shout and it caused Carol to recoil in fright. "They had their chance. *I'm* taking him down."

"Please, Will ..." Leigh implored.

"I'll be careful, Leigh, I promise, but I'm going to do this my way. Now, is there any way to check some of these samples without bringing them to the attention of the investigating team and without putting you in an awkward position?"

"There might be."

***

After arranging a same day courier service to deliver the package to Leigh, Will and Carol continued their deliberations, their sexual encounter not forgotten, but set aside for now.

Carol scrutinized the note for the umpteenth time. "So, what exactly do we know about our *quarry*? And what's this armoury?"

Will stopped pacing for a moment. "There are Royal Armouries all over the world, but I think the two main ones in the UK are in London and Leeds."

143

"That doesn't narrow it down much."

Will took another look at the note then handed it back to Carol. "And what does *in Loidis* mean? Is it Latin or something?"

"You see, I was wondering about that too. We've got Wi-Fi here, haven't we?"

"Good idea." Will rummaged in his rucksack and pulled out a weather-beaten netbook. They both sat on the edge of the bed as he fired it up. Carol glanced at him and suppressed a smile. For now, at least, her fears had been allayed by a kind of adolescent excitement.

They both hovered over the screen as Google threw up search results. Top of the results was *History of Leeds in Yorkshire*. They both smiled. "It's the ancient name for Leeds," Will muttered, reading the brief description.

"Bingo. We make a good team, eh?" Carol said and nudged Will playfully with her shoulder. It felt good to be investigating – not only was it keeping her mind occupied, which was a good thing for more reasons than one, but it gave her renewed purpose. After so much pain and fear, she felt a small part of her self-esteem returning.

Will put his arm around her and visions of her naked flesh pressed against his shot to the fore. Suppressing the urge to kiss the nape of her neck, he said, "So we've narrowed it down to Leeds at least. That's a good start."

She felt his hot breath on her neck and felt goose bumps rise. "So … what do we know about him?"

"He's a murderer and he was pretending to be a writer. The police pursued the writer angle and drew a blank."

"He didn't have much of a discernible accent," Carol said then added, "That doesn't help at all."

They both fell silent for a time, deep in thought, mentally thumbing through all the evidence they had gathered, or, in Carol's case, horrifying memories of that fateful weekend.

"He was into films, wasn't he?" Will offered and dismissed it as soon as he had mentioned it. "Nah–"

Carol interrupted before he could move on. "He wasn't just into them – he was a right fanatic. That's all him and John ever used to talk about."

They both considered this for a moment then Will asked, "Okay, but how would we find a movie nut? Trail through geeky online film forums? Clubs?"

"He wasn't a pasty teenager … and he must've had money to be able to take time away for all those months. A rich family or someone who owns his own business maybe? Maybe he owns a cinema or something?"

Will cocked an eyebrow. "That's a possibility. Let's Google all the cinemas in Leeds."

A quick search returned a meagre selection and they noted down the few cinemas in and around Leeds.

Carol stared at the small list and sighed. "Doesn't look like any of them are independently owned and I think we can rule out a manager position."

"Yeah, you're right," Will agreed solemnly. "A manager job would've been too tying."

"Oh, hang on, what about the Cottage Road Cinema?" Carol asked, pointing at the screen that still showed the search results. "Bring that one up."

Will clicked on the website link and proceeded to trawl through the cinema's website.

Carol shook her head and pointed at the screen. "Dammit, look, it looks like they're part of the Northern Morris group, whoever the hell they are."

Will read through the section and said, "Yeah, but it's still a possibility though. No sense ruling it out just yet – we could check it out first."

With the screen returned to the Google search page, Carol noticed a banner advert for LOVEFiLM. "What about video shops?" she suggested. "Obviously not a chain like Blockbuster – the same manager issue would apply – but an independent, if any still exist."

"Yeah, that's worth looking at too."

Searches for *independent video shop in Leeds* and *independent DVD shop in Leeds* revealed loads of music or game shops, along with the usual chains, but only one independent DVD and game shop – *Movie Maniac*.

They looked at each other. "That sounds a little too close for comfort," Carol said, a shiver running through her.

They're coming to get you, Han.

CHAPTER 9

Han didn't get unnerved easily, but over a week had gone by and there had still been no word from Charlie, so it was a little disconcerting. He was expecting to be harassed into doing the next job or, at the very least, 'allowed' another short break. No word at all couldn't be good.

This person could potentially link him to the murders. Sure, identities had been kept secret and Han had been extremely careful from the off, but it was still a loose end and Han hated loose ends.

Charlie played on his mind as he closed up the shop for the evening. He had printed off the end of day reports and shut down the till PC. After switching off all the lights, except for the nighttime one, he headed for the door.

He had been spending more time than usual in the shop since his 'crisis' meeting with Perry. It felt good to be doing something productive, and it also helped keep his mind off his mother and Ryan. All the new marketing and promotion seemed to be paying some dividends – takings had improved a little.

Torrential rain drenched him in seconds as he locked the door and set the alarm. The darkness was held back a shade by dim streetlights. Cars sped past in both directions, throwing up sheets of rainwater and drowning out every noise, except for the unremitting drumming of the rain.

Han ruffled his collar and hurried down the street towards the car park. Behind him, further down the street, Will jumped out of the Land Rover and followed. The Land Rover waited, lights off but engine idling.

The car park was deserted and Han's Peugeot was one of only a handful remaining. He fished out his keys as he approached it.

Will made his move. He rushed him from behind, wielding his fighting knife.

The hammering rain concealed Will's approach, so Han only heard the splashing footfalls at the last moment. He spun to face the threat.

Will was the bigger man and cast a fierce bear-like figure emerging out of the darkness. A glint of steel, glistening with rainwater, was what alerted Han to the knife. He managed to block with his left arm, but felt the blade slice through two layers of clothing and the soft flesh beneath.

Han fell back, sucking in a breath. Will kept coming, spitting, "You're a fucking dead man, Whitman."

Somewhere in the back of his mind, being called Whitman registered, but there were more pressing matters. Han stepped back and managed a right-handed cross that caught Will a glancing blow on the chin. It was enough to stall his advance momentarily, allowing Han to move in with an upper cut with his left. The blow hurt both men equally. As Will staggered back, Han gripped his bleeding arm, hissing a tirade of curses.

Will recovered quickly and stepped forward – more cautiously this time – brandishing the knife in front of him.

"I don't believe I've had the pleasure," Han said, keeping some distance between them as he nursed his arm.

"I'm the person who's going to cut your shrivelled fucking heart out." Will was breathing hard and rainwater was dripping down his face and into his eyes.

"So who's this Whitman guy?" Han probed.

"Don't fucking bother." Emotion got the better of him and Will lunged forward, the tip of his blade coming within an inch of Han's nose.

Han stepped back and to the side then took another swipe. Will blocked and rammed his shoulder into Han's chest, sending him reeling backwards.

The Land Rover appeared, engine screeching as Carol over-revved in her panic. Han saw the metal grill looming and threw himself to one side. The wing mirror clipped his shoulder and sent him sprawling through muddy puddles. He landed hard on his side, knocking the breath out of him.

Will had stepped back as the car roared in between the melee. "What are you doing?" he shouted and started to move round the car to renew his assault on Han.

Carol shoved the passenger door open and yelled, "Get in!"

That's when Will noticed the police car. It had past the commotion and was now reversing back to the entrance of the car park with lights flashing. "Shit!" After one last glance towards Han, who was scrambling into the shadows, Will reluctantly jumped in and Carol gunned the engine.

Han watched the Land Rover bump over a raised grass verge at the far end of the car park as the police car pulled into it. An officer jumped out and the car gave chase.

The officer had spotted him, so Han made no attempt to flee. Instead, he collapsed back down on the ground, clutching his blood-soaked arm and, in a breathless gasp, yelled, "Oh, thank God! Help!"

***

Han stumbled out into the snowstorm, clutching his bleeding arm. With the blackness of the night as a backdrop, it felt like stepping into a television that was broadcasting only static.

The sirens were clearly audible over the rage of the storm. He didn't have much time. Half-blind, he staggered across to the Daihatsu Sportrak. Sucking in freezing air and wincing at the searing pain in his arm, he fumbled at the door and fell inside.

The urge to just lie there and await his fate was overwhelming, but he shuffled into a sitting position and gunned the engine. The snow chains bit into the drifting snow and he spun round and headed out of Haydon at speed. The sirens were coming from the Shillmoor end, so he took the northern route, past the Bryce farm that would take him to the border.

The Bryce farm buildings were mere dark smears, but his eyes lingered on them a moment as he drove past.

If it hadn't been for the combination of four wheel drive and snow chains he would never have made it more than five hundred yards outside of Haydon, but he had been well prepared. His flawless planning had held him in good stead, and, apart from a couple of unforeseen surprises, it could hardly have gone better.

The sun had crawled above the glacial horizon by the time he reached Selkirk, and the radio was awash with the breaking news of a massacre in rural Northumberland.

He continued without stopping, heading west and eventually to Galloway Forest Park. He discovered a deserted picnic spot and pulled in. The temperature was minus five, but the sky was a clear blue. Despite the freezing cold, Han stripped off and washed in a partially frozen stream.

With numb fingers and shivering uncontrollably, using a first aid kit, he tended his wounds and then quickly dressed in a fresh set of clothing.

He then drove on deeper into the park, lost amongst a sea of green, punctuated by the occasional loch or stream. He had not seen a single sign of life since turning onto The Queen's Way at New Galloway.

He took a service road to Loch Trool, a small loch deep in the heart of the park. After burning everything that could link him back to Haydon in a dugout hollow and burying the charred remains of the fire, he then gathered his backpack and supplies and drove the Sportrak to the edge of the frozen shore. After meticulously wiping down every surface, he then proceeded to fill the boot, back seats and passenger seat with as many rocks as he could squeeze in. He then half-deflated the tires and wound down the windows.

He then wedged a rock against the accelerator and watched as the 4x4 first cracked the ice at the water's edge and then slowly disappeared into the freezing black water. It stopped with its roof still sticking out and Han spat out a curse, but then it started to slide in the silt and it quickly vanished completely.

The water settled once more and it was as if the 4x4 had been sucked into some parallel world. Han stood at the loch side with his hands in his pockets for a time, thoughts of the previous few days finally given the opportunity to take precedence.

Rather than elation at his achievement, he just felt alone and cold. He was aching all over and exhausted, but he could not afford to linger. He hoisted his backpack onto his shoulder, wincing at the fresh wave of pain through his arm and then headed off at a brisk walk.

At the westerly edge of the park, he came across a small village on the A714. After a hot cup of coffee and a bacon roll in the House o' Hill Hotel, he took the first bus that turned up that was heading north.

The bus took him as far as Girvan. There, he checked into a small bed and breakfast near the golf club and then slept for twelve hours.

***

The police bought the mugging story, but surprisingly Cara seemed a little reticent. She had been full of sympathy, of course, and even took time out of her shift to visit him in A&E, where a nurse was finishing off the last of the ten stitches in his arm. But there had been just the slightest hint of distrust behind her beautiful eyes. She refrained from questions for the time being, but he was sure they would come.

That big bastard had carved him up like a Sunday roast, and might have finished the job if the cops hadn't gate-crashed the party. It's not often that Han was glad to see the police (present love interests excepted), but he was acutely aware that his attacker had had the upper hand. His chances would not have looked good on a betting slip.

151

A junior doctor had asked, with mild curiosity, about the previous wound on the bicep of the same arm. He had dismissed it, in the same cursory manner, as a mountain bike accident abroad, and no one had mentioned it since.

The police had not managed to apprehend his attackers. At the present time, Han wasn't sure whether that was fortunate or not. It would not be ideal for someone who somehow knew his alter ego to be questioned by the police; that much he was sure on. He had purposefully given a vague description, which, given the late hour and the weather, was easy enough for them to believe.

And so, to the sixty-four thousand dollar question: who the FUCK was that big bastard? And how the FUCK did he know that he was Whitman?

First things first. Why hadn't he – they, he corrected himself, as someone had been driving the Land Rover – gone to the police if they knew for certain who he was? That could only mean one of two possibilities. One, it was someone with a personal grudge, or two, they were paid hit men. As this wasn't a Hollywood action fest, and he certainly wasn't Bruce Willis, until evidence suggested otherwise, he was going with option one. But who? And how? And why now?

Charlie sprung immediately to mind. It was too much of a coincidence. He severs ties and a week later two people show up trying to kill him. He didn't have to see the dog with a guilty look on its face, cowering next to a steaming pile of shit to suspect the culprit.

Next question: was this a warning shot across the bow, or was it war? And also, how the fuck could Charlie know that he was Whitman or how to find him for that matter? Who the hell was Charlie?

Way too many questions and not enough fucking answers.

Cara had stayed the night and doted on him like a poorly child. He could sense her discomfort, wanting to probe, but not feeling that the time was right. There were quite a few awkward silences. She left for her shift the next morning after leaving some tea and toast by the bed for him.

Ju knew that something was amiss, so had not left his side since returning from the hospital. He lay between Han's legs at the end of the bed as he sat, sipping tea and deep in thought.

He used to enjoy a game of chess with his brother in years gone by and that is exactly what this felt like now. But what was his next move? Attack? Defence? Bluff? Sacrifice? He was a little short on pawns and the only pawn Perry knew was the wanking kind, so sacrifice was out the window. Fuck defence – that wasn't his forte. He'd been attacked, so he'd damn well attack back, but he had to pick his fight wisely, so a little Tom-Bluffery would be the order of the day first. Then followed by the mother of all counter-attacks. The Nazis had a great word for it – Blitzkrieg. Not that he was a lover of Nazis, but they certainly did have the flashier uniforms and a certain flare that you couldn't help but admire. Their downfall was having a leader that was a drooling lunatic. Always was going to be a bit of a disadvantage.

Winston – "We'll fight them on the beaches."

Adolf – "We'll fight them in our breeches."

He was acutely aware that his mind was rambling in all kinds of stupid and pointless directions. It was just all too much to take in at the moment. He had to clear his head and work out a strategy.

He lay back and closed his eyes, allowing recent events and revelations to flow over his mind. It didn't take long for darker thoughts to shoehorn there way back in. Mum, Ryan, Lisa ... *It's not your time, son.*

His eyes snapped open and, with it, came a decision. Han ruffled behind Ju's ear and climbed out of bed, wincing at the pain in his arm. He dressed carefully in jeans and a *Quint's Shark Fishing* t-shirt then sat down at the PC.

He logged in to Live Messenger and noticed that Charlie was online. Waiting. "Express elevator to Hell ..." he muttered.

After some further deliberation, he typed, THAT WASN'T VERY FRIENDLY. It wasn't exactly tactful, but he just couldn't summon the patience to string it out.

A response pinged back almost instantly, unapologetic and frank. CONSIDER IT A DEMONSTRATION.

"Motherfucker," Han spat aloud. Well, that confirms it. He was making no attempt to deny it. He clenched his fists a couple of times before typing, WHO WERE THEY AND WHY DO THEY THINK I'M THIS WHITM@N BLOKE? He deliberately added the @ sign as an additional precautionary measure. Yes, paranoia was running rampant, but you could hardly blame him.

THEY WERE A REMINDER OF YOUR DUTY AND THERE'S NO NEED TO PLAY GAMES WITH ME. I'VE ALWAYS KNOWN. The last three words seemed to hover in front of the screen, like a cheap 3D movie.

Always known? *What the fuck is this?* He stemmed the oncoming flood of questions and, instead, changed tact. He ventured, HOW DID YOU CONVINCE CAROL OUT OF HIDING? It was the verbal equivalent of hand grenade fishing, but what the hell. If it was someone with a grudge, she'd be at the top of the list.

I DIDN'T NEED TO. DETECTIVE WRIGHT'S SON DID ALL THE CONVINCING.

Han sat back, both shocked and oddly thrilled. So, timid Carol had teamed up with the late Detective Wright's son to be his would-be assassins. Well, it's a great big grudge pie and let's all take a hearty bite. Wright's son was in the armed forces, if memory served correctly from the media coverage. Alcoholic Carol and the toy soldier, eh? Interesting tag team.

Charlie sets the dogs on him and then tells him all about it, without any fuss or pretence. Was he trying to be both the punisher and the Samaritan? This was taking mind games to an Olympic level.

Who the fuck are you? He refrained from asking that, for now and instead, typed, WHAT'S YOUR ANGLE IN ALL THIS?

Charlie's response was unambiguous. SAME AS IT HAS ALWAYS BEEN. TO ASSIST YOU IN RIDDING THE WORLD OF SCUM.

Bullshit, Han thought immediately. NO, THERE'S MORE TO THIS. SPILL OR I WALK AWAY, DEMONSTRATIONS BE DAMNED.

154

His heart was thumping as he watched the notice at the bottom of the window, informing him that, *Charlie is typing* ... He didn't have to wait long. IT WILL BE HAN BE DAMNED IF I RELEASE THE TEST RESULTS OF THE EVIDENCE GATHERED FROM HAYDON, TOGETHER WITH SAMPLES THAT I'VE ALREADY OBTAINED FROM YOU. THE REAL HAN WHITMAN WILL FINALLY BE REVEALED AND YOUR COSY LITTLE LIFE WITH CARA WILL BE IN A WORD ... FUCKED. The words, although in the usual inoffensive Arial font, and with a pleasant sky-blue background, were no less menacing.

Han's fingers froze. *He knows about Cara! He knows everything about me!* And he's got that missing evidence. Could that be true? He knew he had been extremely careful cleaning up after himself as he went along, but his last minute departure might have left something. He had felt that the evidence getting lost had been an amazing piece of luck at the time. Maybe luck had nothing to do with it. Or was this just some sort of elaborate bluff? Something told him that Charlie was not the bluffing type.

This man/person seemed to know everything about his real life and his life as Han Whitman. How could that be possible? And how in Hell had he managed to obtain DNA samples from him?

Another message appeared from Charlie. I'LL ASSUME FROM YOUR LACK OF RESPONSE THAT YOU UNDERSTAND THE SENSITIVITY OF THE SITUATION NOW?

The words seemed to silently mock him.

He could not contain himself any longer. WHO ARE YOU? he typed as he fought to remain calm. *Stay cool*, he repeated to himself over and over. Losing it would only make matters infinitely worse. Whoever this person was, he was an extremely calculating and dangerous individual.

THAT IS NOT IMPORTANT RIGHT NOW, BUT ALL WILL BE REVEALED IN THE FULLNESS OF TIME.

His mind reeling, Han responded, WHAT ABOUT JUNIOR AND CAROL? THEY COULD GO TO THE POLICE.

NO. THEY WON'T, was Charlie's immediate response.

THEY WON'T BECAUSE I'LL KILL THEM, Han stabbed the keys, making the keyboard rattle with each murdered letter. THEY KNOW WHERE I WORK. THEY MIGHT KNOW WHERE I LIVE TOO. IF YOU WANT ME TO FINISH WHAT WE STARTED I NEED TO DEAL WITH THIS SITUATION FIRST. Han was breathing hard and leaned in close, glaring at the screen as he waited for a reply.

AGREED, Charlie replied. THEY HAVE SERVED THEIR PURPOSE. I WILL FORWARD THE ADDRESS OF THE HOTEL THEY ARE STAYING IN. THEY ARE BOOKED IN UNDER MR AND MRS WRIGHT.

Mr and Mrs, eh? Had Carol hooked herself a toy boy? Good for her – she certainly couldn't do any worse than that strutting cock, Steve. This could prove … interesting.

As the address of the hotel appeared, including their room number, Han began to feel that he was regaining some semblance of control of the situation. He could concentrate on taking Carol and Junior out of the picture first. Then, with some breathing space, he could consider his options with the seemingly omnipotent Charlie.

Charlie was clearly an adversary like no other, but he had played his cards, so at least Han now knew the rules of the game, and indeed that a game was afoot. He had damn well suspected that things weren't all what they seemed. It had been a niggling doubt even before Ryan. He had always trusted his instincts, but this time he had dismissed them as paranoia. Bloody idiot. It was a screw up, but, as he had well and truly demonstrated in Haydon, knowledge was undeniably power.

Things had taken a turn for the surreal, but they were not beyond repair. First things first.

***

After collecting the Beretta and his other more clandestine tools from their hiding place in a buried lockbox in the nearby graveyard,

Han drove straight to the hotel. When it comes to people hell-bent on revenge, there was no time like the present.

Charlie had clearly influenced the pair, but he was by no means in complete control, so who knew what they would do, given that their surprise pre-emptive strike had failed. Any transitory bravado that Carol had siphoned from the soldier would've vanished in a heartbeat. She would be clamouring for her hidey-hole, deep in the wilds of wanny, or whatever grubby little rock she had been cowering under.

He parked the car in a back lane, ensuring that it was not in view of any CCTV then walked the final couple of streets. It was a mild morning, but he kept his collar up and his baseball cap down over his eyes.

It was the kind of cheap and cheerful hotel that Lenny Henry raved about. Several people with overnight bags were milling around the lobby. A haughty middle-aged gent in a pinstripe suit was arguing with the receptionist over noisy neighbours. The young Eastern European girl was flustered almost to the point of tears. The fat lawyer-type was clearly used to more exclusive establishments, and certainly appeared to have the money to pay for them, which meant that he was either a right royal tight arse or he had been forced to endure slumming it with the lower classes due to unforeseen circumstances. Either way, if Han had had more time he might've just taught the arrogant prick a lesson. But, such was his lot, more pressing matters needed to be attended to.

Han strode through the lobby without a sideways glance. He took the stairs two at a time up to the second floor and located the room. Standing to the side of the door, he knocked. He listened and waited, hand inside his jacket, ready to draw the pistol. No movement, no voices. Nothing.

He knocked again, a little louder. Nothing. *Bollocks.*

The receptionist confirmed what he already suspected. They had checked out. *Double bollocks.*

Question was, were they running away or just re-grouping? Despite Carol's likely desperation to scarper to Timbuktu and shove her head in the sand, he was guessing that a combination of Junior and her own conscience would prevent her from doing that. The safe money was on re-grouping. After all, they had come out of the encounter unscathed, which was more than could be said for him.

First blood

(HAPTER 10

Will had managed to convince Carol to stay in the game, but only after switching hotels, buckets of tears and the healing power of vodka. A repeat sexual encounter was the last thing on both of their minds.

It was a no smoking room (like the whole country these days), but that didn't stop Carol from chain-smoking in it, only pausing to gulp vodka and light the stub of one cigarette on its replacement.

"That was our one fucking chance, Will!" Carol said for the umpteenth time. Her voice was hoarse from swinging between screaming and sobbing. "We lost our advantage. He knows we're after him now. Do you know what that means?" She choked back a sob by finishing off another shot and quickly refilling her glass. Her shuddering hands slopped some of the contents onto the carpet.

Will cringed as she downed another glass, but bit his lip. "Carol, it's a setback, but it's still positive ..."

Carol spat a mouthful of vodka across the room. Coughing, she managed, "*Positive?* How the fuck could it be positive? The biggest mass murderer in history is after us! And that's *positive?*"

"But that's just it – we went toe to toe with him and came away unharmed! I injured him – he's not the invincible mythical monster everyone thinks he is. He's just a man! I would've finished the job if it wasn't for the law showing up when they did!"

Tears were streaming down her face once more as Carol said, "But we had the element of surprise that time. Now we have nothing ..." She slumped onto the bed, spilling vodka across the bed sheets and her cigarette burning a hole in the carpet, before Will could stamp it out. There she remained, hands over her down-turned head, sobbing.

Will stood over her, his outstretched hand ready to comfort her, but instead, he lowered it. Better to let her get it all out. He thought about going downstairs to the bar, but dismissed it immediately. There was no way he could leave Carol alone, not in her current state, but also, in the back of his mind, he too was concerned that Whitman could be on their tail somehow.

Instead, he picked up the half-empty bottle of vodka and took a hearty mouthful. There was no sense in getting drunk, but he needed a couple of swigs just to calm his own nerves. He had managed to hide them pretty well from Carol, for obvious reasons, but that did not change the fact that he had very nearly shit himself.

Even though he had had the upper hand and had managed to wound the man, there had been something feral in Whitman ... he had seen something like it before in people who had taken lives and ... enjoyed it. Generation Kill, it was known as, coined by the book and TV miniseries. The desensitising of the men and women who fought the wars post-World War II. Video games and violent films had robbed modern soldiers of their sensitivities towards killing their fellow man.

He had seen it himself firsthand in Afghanistan. Soldiers laughing over the burnt corpses of children, taking pot shots at terrified unarmed civilians ... and worse. It was only evident in a minority of course, to suggest that it was anything more would be an undue stain on the vast majority of professional and courageous servicemen and women, whom he still felt a strong bond with, and would no doubt for the rest of his life. But, those who were affected could be more terrifying than the Taliban.

160

And yet, those trigger-happy, grinning like it's Christmas lunatics in Afghanistan only showed a glimmer of the sheer beast that Han Whitman had exuded in the few seconds of their encounter. That brief confrontation replayed over and over in his head, on a continuous loop, picking over the minute details. Was there anything more he could have done in the short time he had?

Christ, if only the police hadn't shown up when they had. This nightmare could have been over. He could have avenged his father's death, the deaths of all those others in Haydon. And, not forgetting Carol … Whitman had robbed her of everything. But, possibly cruellest of all, he had left her alive to endure the aftermath and relive the horrors for the rest of her life. He could have given her back some tiny shred of peace. So that the rest of her life could at least be tolerable.

And yet, with that said, he couldn't help but think in the back of his mind that Whitman would have gotten off lightly if he had managed to kill him there and then in that rain-soaked car park. That thought instantly made him both feel guilty and angry with himself.

Will took another swig and watched the frail trembling form on the bed. Her sobbing had diminished to soft whimpering. He preferred the shouting and screaming – that at least had some fight in it – the whimpering sounded so pitiful, so … hopeless. What had he been thinking, dragging her here? He should never have roped Carol into this. The poor woman had been through enough for several lifetimes with her ordeal in Haydon.

Of course, sleeping with her had only further complicated matters. And it wasn't just the sex – they had a bond that transcended their historical links. He could feel it – a kinship. Carol wasn't really his type, if he had a type. He had always gravitated towards the more outwardly confident woman who knew what she wanted and how to get it. Carol was a few years older, of course, but that didn't bother him. She was a sensual woman – she gave her all and wore her very raw emotions firmly on her sleeve. She tended to look somewhat dishevelled, but it was easy to see that she was still an attractive woman underneath that had just given up preening herself. That wasn't necessarily a bad thing either – he had dated some pretty appallingly narcissistic types over the years.

Carol had survived a cheating husband, followed by a very messy divorce, and then to top it off had been the sole survivor from the most horrific bloodbath in British history. She was either supremely blessed or horrendously cursed.

***

It took Charlie two phone calls to track down Will and Carol. Calloused hands paused over his laptop keyboard. The screen was bright in the dimly lit room and showed an open message box to an offline Harry.

Sacrifice his two pawns now or keep them in reserve? That was the question. Having them still at large would keep old 'Harry' at bay, but they did pose a small risk as a potentially unknown quantity.

Alive, they could still be manipulated. Dead, they were worthless. Alive, for now.

Charlie typed, H, DYNAMIC DUO LOCATED AND CONTAINED. ONCE THE TASK AT HAND IS COMPLETED WILL FORWARD DETAILS FOR EXTERMINATION. C.

Charlie sent the message then sat back with a creaking of old leather. Everything was progressing according to plan, with the slight irritation of Han's newfound respect for life. Still, Charlie had been manipulating him for some considerable length of time, so one little hiccup wasn't going to change anything. Besides, he had more than the Will and Grace card to play if needs must. It was time to ratchet Han's little Phase Two game up a notch. All the way up to eleven …

***

Han returned home in a rage. After slamming the front door with enough force to wake the dead, walking and otherwise, he

162

proceeded to tear through the whole house. He ripped posters, photos and postcards off walls, emptied drawers, dragged furniture into the middle of rooms, threw bedding and mattress onto the floor, examined light-fittings, telephone, everything he could think of. Throughout the rampage, Ju stayed at the back door, trembling and whining.

It didn't take long to find the first bug.

"You son of a bitch," Han snarled, staring at the tiny electronic device that he had just located in his bedroom behind his signed poster of Hannibal Lecter. "You sneaky piece of shit."

The bastard even had the gall to use more sophisticated kit than the cheaper devices Han had used to listen in to the residents of Haydon. These looked military or law enforcement grade.

Sweating and breathing heavily, he considered placing it back where he had found it and possibly using it to deceive Charlie. But even as he considered it, he begrudgingly had to dismiss it. Charlie would already assume that any bugs in the house would be compromised as soon as he dealt his hand. Not to mention, on playback, he'd probably hear him calling him a sneaky piece of shit.

"Fuck you," Han spat and stamped repeatedly on the small device until it resembled breadcrumbs.

He located another device in the kitchen by the kettle, and a third on his landline.

Movie Maniac hadn't been safe either from Charlie's surveillance. Han located bugs behind the counter and in the office.

God knows how long this devious prick had been eavesdropping on his life. Certainly over a year at the very least, but most probably longer than that.

***

As Han meticulously tidied up the disarray caused by his xenomorph hunt, Cara called to invite him round for a romantic meal at her flat. When asked why he sounded so flustered, he told the truth – having a bit of a tidy up, he had told her. It wasn't a lie.

As soon as she suggested the meal, Han knew the questions would come. And they did.

Before leaving the house, he noticed the short message from Charlie.

After unleashing a tirade of abuse, aimed at the undeserving monitor, he took several deep breaths and chose not to respond immediately. He would mull it over and reply tomorrow. He had enough on his plate. But what the fuck did 'contained' mean? Safely out of his reach, just in case they needed to be called upon again, was the answer of course. Fucker. The task at hand was going to take years at the rate he was going. There was no way he could have those two amateur sleuths poking around in the background all that time. The niggling concerns of a loose end would drive him batty. Not to mention the fact that the said niggling concern could turn into a total ass-rape at any time. Contained? My arse, as Jim Royle would say.

Cara had lovingly prepared a meal of asparagus soup, followed by a tender fillet steak. She was animated and chatty – more so than usual – and was fidgeting.

She managed to make it through the starter and serve the steaks, before reaching bursting point. "Just tell me; are you in some kind of trouble?" It was a simple question and it wasn't exactly unexpected, but Han's heart skipped a beat nonetheless.

Han put down his fork with a particularly inviting first bite of steak still skewered to it. "What makes you say that, hon?" He tried to sound amused, but it felt hollow, to him at least.

Cara studied him, like the good copper she was. She pushed her plate away, her food untouched. She ran a hand subconsciously through her hair and said, "I don't know – it's a few things really. You've been looking tired and stressed for a few weeks. You haven't been your usual upbeat self. And then there was the mugging. It just ..." She left the obvious unsaid.

It was Han's turn to scrutinise Cara. There was no malice or distrust in her flushed features, just genuine concern. He sighed and said, "The shop hasn't been doing all that well for the last six months or so, so that's what I've been a little stressed about. Mum's never far from my mind either. It's been getting me down a bit, but then that bloody mugging was the icing on the cake!" He laughed, brushing off the recent violence as if it were a parking ticket. "I mean, talk about kicking a bloke when he's down! At least the bastards didn't manage to nick anything." As an afterthought, he added, "Not that there was much to nick!"

"I thought you were Daniel Craig," Cara said as an attempt at humour.

Han was glad for the change in mood. "Bugger sneaked up on me from behind – didn't hear him because of the rain. Sneaky little ninja bastard. I'm not invincible, you know."

She seemed about to probe further, but then her guarded stance eased and she said, "You should talk to me if something's bothering you. Don't bottle things up – we're a partnership. Talk to me."

Han reached over and took her hand in his. "I'm sorry, hon. I didn't want to worry you with my crappy financial issues."

Squeezing his hand, Cara said, "Hey, I'm in this for the long haul, buddy. I want to help … if I can. I love you."

Han felt a lump in his throat and had to swallow, before saying, "I love you too."

***

DCI Carter stared at the daily update email and a name jumped out at her. She didn't make the connection at first, but then it hit her. Mr Cool and Casual had been mugged. A knife attack in a darkened car park to steal his shop takings.

Interesting, she thought. What were the odds of the same person appearing in two ongoing investigations? It was most definitely unusual. It could of course be a complete coincidence. The man was a shop owner and may well have been carrying cash takings at the end of the day. And she may well be just trying to clutch at any straw to find some kind of breakthrough in the vigilante case, but it was still intriguing.

Did he have a dirty secret in his past that the vigilante had found out about? That could be another motive for visiting that website. If he was indeed a potential target – that had managed to slip the net – it could mean that the killer could possibly target him again.

She had already carried out a background check on him, but it wouldn't hurt to do another more thorough check. Perhaps, if resources allowed, she could set up a low-level surveillance operation.

***

Will awoke with a start. His mobile phone was vibrating on the dressing table next to him.

As he reached over to grab it, he glanced over to Carol. She was sleeping soundly on the bed, the gentle sound of her breathing the only noise to compete with the vibrating phone.

He walked through to the bathroom and shut the door as he answered it. "Hi, Leigh."

"Hi, Will. How are you two doing?" She sounded tired.

Will grasped for the appropriate words and opted for, "Could be better. How's things at your end?"

"I've got the preliminary results back from the lab," Leigh said.

Will opened his mouth to speak, but closed it again.

"No matches from any of the databases, I'm afraid," she continued. "Drew a complete blank. There's a couple more still to come in, but I'm not overly confident. Whoever Whitman is, he isn't on the radar – he's never been fingerprinted or produced any DNA samples in the past, which means that the only way we could link him to Haydon would be by locating a suspect first and then taking a sample from him." The phone went silent for a moment and then she added, "I'm sorry, Will." Her fatigue was a feeble veil for the dejection she clearly felt.

Will wanted to tell her about their encounter and that they knew who and where Hannibal Whitman was, but he couldn't. For one, it would put her in an extremely awkward position. And, more importantly, she might decide to pull the plug and inform her superiors. She would be suspended and possibly face criminal charges, but she would do it in a heartbeat to rescue a stubborn friend from an extremely dangerous situation.

166

He wrestled with it for some time, even after he had thanked Leigh for her help and wished her farewell.

***

Leigh Simpson sat in her car, staring at her mobile phone. Her eyes were bloodshot from crying prior to telephoning Will. She had felt so useless and felt that she had not only let down Will and Carol, but also, more importantly, Tony Wright.

They had been lovers, but only one time. She had wanted more, and she felt that so had Tony, but they both didn't want to jeopardise their friendship. It was mostly true what she had told Will in that café. She couldn't bring herself to tell him the whole truth.

But now, Leigh stared at her phone with growing concern. Will had thanked her for her help and told her that it was okay, that they would still keep digging and not to worry. He had repeated the last part several times, like he was trying to convince himself, not her.

She didn't know Will all that well, but she had known his father, and it felt as though he was hiding something from her. Did he know more than he was letting on?

Leigh bit her bottom lip and glanced anxiously from her phone to the Northumbria Police Headquarters buildings spread out beyond the car park in front of her. Her concerns were building into a sense of impending doom.

Jailhouse blows

(HAPTER 11

Han sat at his computer and took a deep breath. He felt a lot more together after his night with Cara, so was now feeling more of his usual pragmatic self. He was still angry, but it was tempered with equanimity. Charlie was online and waiting.

He opened up a dialogue window and started typing, WHAT DO YOU HAVE IN MIND? He opted to avoid both the bugs and the Junior/Carol issue for now and get straight to the point.

THAT'S ANOTHER THING I LIKE ABOUT YOU, HARRY. NO BEATING AROUND KATE'S BUSH, came Charlie's reply.

BAD DREAMS IN THE NIGHT, EH? Han responded, stony-faced. Kate Bush? That would make it more likely that he was an older guy – no younger than late thirties maybe.

AND YOUR SENSE OF HUMOUR. I'M GLAD YOU'RE BEING THE BIGGER MAN ABOUT THE BUG ISSUE TOO – SHOWS GREAT MATURITY.

Han clenched his jaw, but refrained from responding. Instead, he closed his eyes and mentally thumbed through various Zen Buddhism teachings. One immediately sprung to mind ... *The greatest magic is transmuting the passions.* He repeated to himself over and over, until another message appeared.

168

BUT, YOU'RE RIGHT – ENOUGH SMALL TALK. I HAVE A PLAN THAT COULD POSSIBLY FINISH PHASE TWO IN ONE FOUL SWOOP.

Han frowned and slowly shook his head in disbelief. "Impossible," he muttered to himself.

THAT GOT YOUR ATTENTION, Charlie added. Of course, words on a screen could not show any emotion, but Han could almost sense an underlying gloating satisfaction.

"Okay, arsehole, let's hear it then," he said then typed, HOW? "Fuck it." Deciding that there was no need to hold back, not after everything Charlie had revealed, he added, THERE'S STILL AROUND 370 TO GO. He would have to check the tally though, as he wasn't sure of the exact number remaining. Sloppy serial killermanship.

HAVE YOU HEARD OF HMP THE WEARE?

NO.

WELL, LUCKY FOR YOU, UNCLE C HAS. IT IS THE UK'S ONLY PRISON SHIP IN SERVICE. IT WAS DUE TO CLOSE IN 2005 BUT RISING PRISON POPULATIONS FORCED ITS CONTINUED USE. THERE ARE USUALLY BETWEEN 380-400 PRISONERS BERTHED ON HER AT ANY GIVEN TIME.

Han gawped at the screen. *Jesus Christ.* He could see where this was going. AUDACIOUS, was all Han could think to type.

ONE 'AUDACIOUS' HIT COULD WRAP UP PHASE TWO IN ONE GO. THEN YOU CAN GET ON WITH YOUR 'NORMAL' LIFE WITH CARA. ☺

That fucking smiley face again. *Does he use that just to fucking piss me off?* Han sat, glaring at the screen. Despite calming mantras and pep talks, he could feel his blood boiling. *How dare this prick play me like this?*

He still had the same damn problem though. That problem was that Charlie was holding all the cards – he seemed to know everything about Han and Han knew absolutely nothing about him. In addition, he had his two amateur assassins as backup and God knows what else up his sleeve.

"Fuck!" Han spat aloud, causing a stir in the bedroom. On cue, Ju trotted in with his usual quizzical look on his cheery features. Han scratched the dog's neck, adding, "Sorry, Ju. You must be getting sick of me interrupting your dreams. Bet you nearly had Jinxy from next door cornered, eh?"

Ever the magical soothing influence, just with Ju's presence, Han managed to dispel the thickening red mist.

Charlie was a cheeky, devious son of a bitch, but he did have a point. One big hit would solve all his dilemmas over the continued experiment – getting it over and done with. Like pulling a tooth – one quick sharp stab of pain and then finished. Then adios muchachos – Han Whitman is officially retired. Cara, how about a nice long siesta in the sun somewhere baking hot with frozen margaritas on tap? On me. Call it a celebration. For what, you ask? For the Goddamn motherfucking Hell of it, that's what. Cue smiley face and roll credits.

Turning back to the screen where Charlie seemed to be waiting with saintly patience, he typed, SO WHAT'S THE PLAN?

GLAD TO HAVE YOU ABOARD – PUN INTENDED! HA-HA! I HAVE ACQUIRED DETAILED BLUEPRINTS, SECURITY AND STAFFING INFORMATION. WOULD YOU BELIEVE THAT THERE ARE ONLY 20 GUARDS STATIONED ON THE BOAT WITH AN ADDITIONAL 6 AT THE DOCK SECURITY POST?

I BELIEVE YOU, Han typed. BUT KILLING AN 'INNOCENT' IS FORBIDDEN IN PHASE TWO. HOW THE FUCK DO I WIPE OUT A SHITLOAD OF SCUMBAGS WITHOUT KILLING A SINGLE GUARD?

THAT HAD ME VEXED TOO FOR A WHILE. LET ME ASK YOU, HAVE YOU HEARD OF GAMMA HYDROXYL BUTYRATE (GHB)?

GHB? THAT'S A DATE RAPE DRUG, ISN'T IT? Ah, the plot thickens.

BING! CORRECT! IT IS UNDETECTABLE BY SIGHT, TASTE OR SMELL WHEN ADDED TO LIQUID AND IN THE CORRECT DOSAGE WILL RENDER THE AVERAGE PERSON UNCONSCIOUS WITHIN 5 MINUTES.

THE EFFECTS LAST UP TO 24 HOURS – GIVING YOU PLENTY OF TIME TO DO YOUR THING.

Han rubbed his chin, considering Charlie's formulating plan. He certainly had given it a great deal of thought. It could work. He found himself nodding, despite himself. He typed, OK, THAT SEEMS AT LEAST THEORETICALLY FEASIBLE. HOW WOULD WE ADMINISTER IT TO 26 GUARDS?

AFTER A LITTLE DIGGING AROUND, I FOUND A WAY TO TAP INTO THEIR WATER SUPPLY.

Han sat back, mouth agape. Could this actually work? Could he really complete Phase Two and, in turn, the whole experiment in one big hit? The more he thought about Charlie's plan, the more achievable it seemed. Actually, the more he thought about it, the more fitting and appropriate it became. After all, Phase One had been completed in one go, save for a couple of 'test runs'. Haydon had been Phase One, HMP *The Weare* would become Phase Two. The other few executions beforehand were just the warm up – like Mandy and Tess before the finale in Haydon. It made sense and it seemed right. He blinked several times and a smile touched his lips.

He could finish what he started and then put it all behind him and begin his new life with Cara. Everyone's a winner ... well, except for a few lowlife cons, but them's the breaks!

He didn't trust Charlie one bit, but he would have to cross that prick when the odds were more in his favour. He had no doubt that, for his own reasons, Charlie did want him to complete Phase Two, so he felt confident enough in Charlie's plan and his support in successfully executing it. What he didn't believe was that Charlie would allow him to lead a normal life after it. There would be more ... and something told him that it would only end with his death or imprisonment.

*** *

Charlie had indeed done his research. The files Han received in his inbox included detailed structural plans, security schematics, staff files and rosters, patrol routes and security protocols. It also

171

included web links for several GHB suppliers, along with details on dosages, and how and where to introduce it into the localised water supply that serviced the boat and the dock facility.

Pawing through the files gave Han renewed purpose and further restored a feeling of control, albeit a finite and temporary one.

There were of course still several nagging dangers. All the guards would need to ingest a sufficient amount to render them unconscious – the dosage would require at least half a glass of water to do the trick. With the summer months drawing in, a particularly hot evening would help enormously. So, he would have to plan the assault around the weather. Fitting once more – winter had helped him in Haydon, so summer would assist him this time. Providence, as Morpheus would say.

It was likely that not all the guards would be knocked out, so they would have to be dealt with in a non-lethal fashion. Tricky, but not impossible. Even those still conscious would likely have ingested some of the drug, which would make them easier to handle. He would have to time knocking out communications perfectly just in case though. He would need at least two hours to take out the livestock, so anyone left standing could not be allowed to call for help.

Sinking *The Weare* would have been easier, but that would mean moving all the unconscious guards onto the dock or into a lifeboat to ensure their survival. That sounded far too much like hard work, so bollocks to that. There was also the distinct possibility that the water depth wouldn't be sufficient. No, he would do it the traditional way. It would be more fun too. If this was going to be his last big adventure, as it were, he might as well enjoy it. After all, he was the good guy in this sequel … sort of.

Fail to plan and plan to fail, as his old dad used to say. His mouth suddenly felt dry.

It's not your time, son.

An image appeared before Han's eyes, as if he had been trapped in the dark for an age and someone had just turned the lights on.

"It's all part of the game," the man was telling him. He seemed impossibly tall to the young boy, a giant, a god. A god dressed in corduroys and a plaid shirt, with a Hamlet cigar hanging out of the corner of his mouth.

He glanced down at the boy and cocked his mouth into a crooked smile. It was a smile full of fun and mischief. What his auburn eyes lacked in good humour, they made up for with burning intensity in spades.

The man's big calloused hand enveloped the small boy's. It felt rough to the touch. He stepped forward. "Come on, son. You'll love it!"

Tentatively, the boy followed.

Han scrambled for the small waste paper basket under the desk and just managed to pull it out as he emptied the contents of his stomach into it.

Still alternating between retching and coughing, Han sat hunched over in the chair, with his face over the bin for several minutes, the acrid stench of bile filling his nostrils.

Ju had backed out of the room and was watching him from the landing, whining softly.

He finally composed himself and wiped his mouth on a tissue as he sat back, gulping in deep breaths and feeling utterly spent. His head was throbbing and there was a slight tremor in his fingertips.

Had his father ... He couldn't even bring himself to think it. Is that possible? It was just such a clichéd Hollywood drama type of bollocks, like *The Prince of Tides* or some such. No, it was absurd. If he had been abused by his dad, he would know ... Oh, okay, so all the fucking shrinks would argue that his fragile young mind blocked it out as a defence mechanism. And now, as an adult going through, what some might consider stressful times, his mind was finally processing those long suppressed memories and dishing them out piecemeal. Fine, that could be argued. But it wasn't Han. It was all so passé!

"Bullshit!" Han hissed and spat into the bin, causing Ju to back away into the bedroom. He picked up the *Reservoir Dogs* mug in his tight fist and raised it in the air, ready to ram it through the screen of his monitor. He held it there for a time then caught himself gazing at the iconic image of Harvey Keitel and Tim Roth

173

on the side of the mug. *Jesus, it's been ages since me and Perry have had a Tarantino night,* he suddenly thought.

He laughed at the disjointed thought and that brought Ju padding back into the room to nuzzle his nose in Han's lap. He placed the mug back down and petted the dog, mulling over the revelation.

My dad was a paedophile and he fucking fiddled with me? he thought, sampling the statement, like he would a first bite of an exotic dish. Could that be right? It just sounded like a load of shite. He could not get his head round it. It was more like a trite plot device, not real life … not *his* life.

Was this whole Phase Two shit about him getting back at Daddy? Hunt down known paedophiles and make them pay for what his father did to him? No, as soon as he considered it, he dismissed it. It wasn't even about paedophiles, it was about balance. Haydon was the yin and this was the yang. 396 for 396. End of story.

No, he didn't know what these supposed memories were, but they were nothing to do with Phase Two. Leave it at that, for now. He had enough on his plate, without thinking about hazy recollections. Bullshit traumatic childhood memories would just have to take a bastard ticket and wait in line. And it was a long fucking line.

***

Back on track, Charlie thought, with more than a little self-satisfaction. *And without the need to 'escalate' things unnecessarily.* He had thought that Harry would at least need a little nudge in the right direction, in the form of another lesson. It turned out that Harry was more fond of Cara than he had thought. Charlie was not surprised very often, but he was somewhat taken aback by that revelation. Little 'Harry' in love, eh? Who would've thought it? Especially after Lisa.

He had thought that he would have to get a little creative – maybe with that mutt of his. But no, he didn't even need to mention it. It was almost too easy. How many Achilles' heels could one serial killer have? It did go against the grain somewhat.

He was also, if he was brutally honest, a little disappointed in Harry. He had hoped that he would be more ... pragmatic and single-minded about this whole process. He had hoped that threats against perceived 'loved ones' would have been met with scorn. In short, he thought it might have become more interesting.

Still, there was time yet. There was still the big reveal – that would be fun. And he had yet to decide what to do with his dynamic duo.

***

Two weeks passed by with Han preparing for the big bash. He had scarcely shown his face in the shop and only managed to see Cara a couple of times. He was telling both Cara and Perry that he was working on new marketing strategies, along with various online promotions. They had both been understanding, but he had noticed Perry was getting a little tetchy of late.

He had all the plans committed to memory, so that he could find his way around in the dark. He knew the ins and outs of the security systems and the water supply, and knew when and where each guard would be at any given time.

It was all coming together. Unfortunately, the nagging thoughts of his father were never far away. A quiet moment would frequently give rise to those fragmented memories and their implications. *It's all part of the game ... you'll love it ...* It was just one more thing to add to Mum, Ryan, Lisa and every other unfortunate to cross his path over the years.

He became aware that his mobile was ringing. He had no idea for how long. It was Perry. Glad of the distraction, he answered it.

"Hey, mate. How's it going?" He managed a genial tone.

"Alright, aye. You up for a few down the local Friday night?"

"Would love to," Han said with sincerity, "but I'm up to my eyes at the mo."

175

There was silence on the other end of the phone.

"Definitely next week though," Han added.

"Fine," Perry replied, clearly crestfallen. After a pause, he said, "We haven't been out for a drink in three weeks or so. What is it? Is it Cara? She must be holding you prisoner."

Holding me prisoner? Han mused. Aloud, he said, "You have no idea, mate!"

"Just don't forget who your friends are. Guys don't dump their mates for lasses. Bros before hoes and all that!"

"Nah, it's nothing like that, mate," Han said, rolling his eyes. "Once the shop's back on track everything will get back to normal. We'll have a proper blow out next week."

There was silence for a moment then Perry said, "Well, alright then. Just remember, we're all just prisoners of our own device." Perry had resumed his normal cheery self, but the undertone was clear.

Smiling, Han said, "But you just can't kill the beast."

Perry managed a short laugh. "I can't sneak anything past you. One of these days I'll catch you out."

Long after Perry had hung up, his that last statement seemed to hang in the air. *One of these days I'll catch you out* … It was an innocent off the cuff remark, but Han could not quite dislodge it.

Jesus! Since all the crap with Charlie, paranoia was fast becoming a regular pastime. *Get a bloody grip, man!*

Assault on The Weare

(HAPTER 12

Han did not have to wait long into the summer. A heat wave hit the first week of June. Temperatures soared into their thirties and the media quickly started to band about the usual 'hottest temperatures since records began' bullshit.

Final preparations kicked into overdrive.

A gaming convention at the Olympia in London became his excuse to Cara for going AWOL for a few days. He planned to book into the hotel and even register at the convention before heading to Dorset where *The Weare* was berthed. That would offer a sufficient alibi if someone did make a cursory enquiry.

He had also checked that the convention clashed with Cara's shifts. She had been disappointed, of course. She said she would have loved to have accompanied him. A romantic evening out in London would've been a real treat, she had said. She even chatted animatedly about where they could have gone to dine and what shows they could've seen, feigning a disappointed pout.

Cara's ill ease seemed to have ebbed away over the last month and their relationship appeared to be right back on track. With the final whistle in sight, Han was feeling more optimistic than ever.

Perry was still being a bit of a mardy sod, especially at being told that he had to hold the fort at the shop, while he swanned off to have fun at a gaming convention. Han managed to placate him in the end by promising to pass on any freebies to him.

After booking in to the hotel and registering at the convention, Han left his car in the hotel car park and hired a cheap runabout with false ID. He then headed straight out of London and onto the M3.

Han reached Portland Harbour by mid afternoon, giving him plenty of time to scout out the lay of the land.

The south coast was basking in a balmy sunny afternoon, with only a gentle breeze coming in from the sea to ruffle the collar of his gaudy Hawaiian shirt. A pair of fake *Police* sunglasses and an *Outpost #31* baseball cap (a replacement for the one he had to burn after his impetuous Leeds city centre soirée) finished off the holiday persona.

Gulls squawked overhead, lazily drifting on the thermals. Han smiled and drew warm, salty air into his lungs. It was the first time that he had felt genuinely at peace for months. If he were truly honest with himself, the last time would have been pre-Mandy. He was starting to believe that he had turned a corner and things were now going to start working themselves out. It had been a tough old eighteen months or so, but the endgame was in sight. Sure, there would be one or two loose ends to tie up and kill later, but, in his current positive frame of mind, they were but minor glitches.

He massaged his arm – it still felt a little stiff from the stab wound, but it was otherwise fully healed. He was building up a nice little latticework there. He would have to try to be a little more ambidextrous in future knife-fights. Still, it would be a nice talking point on the beach.

His mobile burst into dramatic life. *Just when I thought I was out … they pull me back in …* "Hey, broheim," Han said. "Not a great time for me at the moment."

"Hey, bro," Karl said. "Sorry, I know you're down at that convention – hope it's going well. We're having a family get together next weekend. Are you and Cara up for it? It would be good to see you."

178

Han smiled. The thought of seeing everyone would do him the world of good. There would probably be a few tears later on, but hopefully some laughter first. "We'll definitely be there. The convention finishes tomorrow afternoon and then the schedule is all clear. It'll be great to see you. We'll come up early and we can have a session in that gym of yours first. I'll have to warn you though – I've gotten myself back into shape since I last saw ya."

"We'll see about that! That's fantastic – you can stay in the spare room. We'll make a full weekend of it, eh?"

"Definitely. See you soon, bro." Han disconnected the call and smiled. Karl had sounded delighted. In the back of his mind, he always felt that Karl was just a little disappointed in his younger brother. It wasn't the case at all. He was just disappointed that they didn't see more of each other, especially after Mum's death. Well, once all this bollocks was finished, he would rectify that.

***

A silver BMW 5 Series was parked some hundred yards away from Han as he chatted to his brother on his mobile phone. Inside, Carter and Richard observed with varying degrees of interest.

Richard was still unconvinced of any possible connection to the vigilante case, but Carter was the 'boss', so he had no choice but to pander to her.

Carter watched from behind sunglasses as Han laughed, turning at one point in their direction, but then turning away again without taking any notice.

She was not overly convinced that this man had anything to do with the vigilante killings either any more. The longer they had kept tabs on him, the more her original suspicions had diminished. Several weeks had passed without incident – no further vigilante murders and no suspicious activity around Cool and Casual. But it was the only vaguely credible lead she had, so it was better than nothing.

She had been amazed that she had been allowed the latitude to pursue the man half way across the country, but the brass were getting desperate for results, so had indulged her.

"Don't get me wrong," Richard began, "I'm happy for a pleasant jaunt to the seaside – particularly when I'm getting paid for it, but I can't help thinking that we could be putting our finite resources to better use."

Carter kept her eyes on the target. With a sigh, she said, "I'll be the judge of that, along with those above me who are ready to drop the axe at any given time right on my sorry ass." As an afterthought, she glanced at him and added, "*Finite?*" She shook her head and turned back to the target.

"I don't see the problem with adopting a more diverse vocabulary," Richard muttered under his breath.

"Get a grip, *Howie*," Carter said.

"You still haven't explained the *Howie* moniker," Richard said with an irritated *humph* at the end for added effect.

"You don't watch many films, do you?"

"No, most of them are trashy and amoral," Richard said and folded his arms, as if to emphasis the point.

"Well, that's why you don't understand your *moniker*."

"Just explain it to me. *Please.*"

Carter was about to tell him to grow up, but then caught the puppy dog eyes. "Jesus."

"Please don't blaspheme."

"You see!" she snapped. "That's what I'm talking about. Just when I started to feel sorry for you, you go and get right on my tits again."

Richard winced. "I'm sorry, but it's just who I am. I don't mean to offend or upset anyone."

Carter offered a resigned sigh and said, "When we get back, look up a film called *The Wicker Man* – the original, not the pointless remake. It'll explain everything." Before he could respond, she added, "Now, our guy here is supposed to be at a conference in London. Why, for one, is he now in Dorset of all places?"

Richard smiled at her, thankful for both the suggestion and for the change of subject. "Best guess would be an affair."

"He's in a relationship – with a beat copper, of all people – but he's not married. He wouldn't need to go to such lengths."

"I'm no expert on infidelity, but I'm guessing some people would go to extreme lengths."

I can't imagine you being an expert on women full stop, Carter thought. "Well, the least we can do is find out, eh? While we're here."

***

A sedate walk up a country lane brought Han to an old naval cemetery. Inland, behind him, was the sprawling complex of HMP Verne. In front, on the coast, was the docks and, in particular, the grey slab of floating excrement that was HMP *The Weare*. As a former naval troop ship that served in the Falklands War, she wasn't exactly a luxury cruise liner. She was squat, square and ugly.

For security purposes, not to mention aesthetic and tourism reasons, she was moored in a disused section of the harbour. That meant that she was all alone, and so served Han's purposes perfectly. Which, in turn, meant fewer chances for a prying ear to hear a gunshot or scream. The closest other vessels or buildings were more than five hundred yards away.

Han stood for a time, taking in the view. The sun warmed his face and the quiet was only broken by the distant sounds of gulls and the surf. Despite being surrounded on two sides by prisons, one floating and one the more traditional kind, the view was quite beautiful. The tranquillity of his surroundings seeped into his pores.

Maybe once the dust had settled, he could bring Cara here for a little break away.

He smiled. This might be rather fun. It had been a while since anything to do with the experiment had actually been enjoyable.

***

Darkness coated the harbour, the patchy street lighting woefully inadequate. A cloudy sky denied even the stars or Moon their glow.

Han Whitman walked past the grey/white battlements of Henry VIII's Portland Castle. It was a squat, functional castle, not like the grand castles of old, like Bamburgh or Alnwick, so looked almost like some sort of hybrid, crossed with a World War II bunker.

The streets were deserted, but Han stayed low and kept to back lanes and the interconnecting greenery that were brimming with plenty of shrubs and trees for additional cover. He took his time; no sense rushing things. With the endgame in sight, he was leaving no room for a rash error.

He past behind the last few buildings of Castletown and then made his way across moorland.

Even in the dark, without the aid of a flashlight, Han effortlessly made his way to the pumping station that serviced *The Weare's* water supply. It was little more than a locked shed.

***

Richard placed a hand on Karen Carter's shoulder, halting her progress. She glanced round, irritated. "What?" she whispered.

The darkness seemed to be pressing in on them. "I … I don't like this, Ma'am – I mean, boss. This isn't right. In fact, this is very bloody wrong."

Carter stared at him. Richard never swore, not even the likes of bloody or damn.

"We should call in local assistance."

"We've got nothing to *bloody* tell them yet. We observe from a *safe* distance and then evaluate the situation further. There are two of us, we're armed and we have a duty here. Got it?"

"I'm really not–"

"Grow a pair, How … Rich," she corrected herself.

Raising his voice a notch, Richard retorted, "I hardly think that's appropriate. But thank you for at least using my correct name, needlessly shortened though it may have been."

"For the love of–" Carter stopped midsentence as she caught movement out of the corner of her eye. Before she could react, a figure appeared behind Richard and grabbed him in a chokehold. In one swift movement, the figure yanked Richard's neck, which emitted an audible crack.

Frantically, Carter snatched for her sidearm. The figure was upon her in an instant.

***

A bolt cutter made easy work of the padlock on the shed and Han went to work on introducing the GHB into the water supply. He left the station as he had found it, even replacing the padlock with an identical replacement. An engineer would get a surprise when his documented combination didn't work.

From the small pumping station, Han dashed across the road to the harbour perimeter fence. Just beyond a couple of warehouses, silent and still in the languid water, lay HMP *The Weare*.

Using the bolt cutter, Han snipped a hole in the chain links then crawled through, dragging his rucksack behind him. He edged between the two warehouses and located the main telephone junction box at the rear of the guardhouse. After jimmying the lock, he snipped each line and then closed it once more.

He waited and listened. Above the gentle tones of the ocean, he could make out a television playing inside. Rippling applause was followed by some wannabe celebrity belting out a power ballad. Christ, sounded like some *X Factor* shit or some such. Maybe he'd kill the guard who put that crap on. That was justifiable, wasn't it?

He checked his watch. One guard would be in the middle of his rounds, that would take him along the dock and then around the perimeter fence. It was unlikely that he would have ingested much, if any, of the drug, so he would have to be dealt with first, before he discovered the hole in the fence.

Han kept low and skirted the building, pausing every few feet to listen. Flat against the side of the guardhouse, close to the front, Han stopped still and held his breath. About ten feet away, a guard was trudging along the railing at the water's edge. He passed the gangway that led onto the vessel and was heading away from it. He walked with a plodding resignation, reserved only for the most mundane of tasks.

Perfect. At that dawdling pace, he could intercept him at the corner of the first warehouse. He retraced his footsteps and then headed to the ambush site.

Han pressed himself against the prefabricated wall and drew a small aerosol out of a leg pocket from his black cargo pants.

Footsteps approached. As the guard drew nearer, Han could hear his breathing; deep puffing breaths, like a child in a strop. He clearly wasn't particularly happy with his current assignment. *Well, I'm sure we can liven things up for him.* Han smiled. His face was obscured by a balaclava, but his eyes and teeth appeared almost luminescent by contrast.

A boot fell into view and Han sprung into action. He stepped directly into the guard's path and aimed the aerosol right at the guard's nose and mouth, spraying immediately.

The guard coughed and stumbled backwards as the concentrated GHB took affect almost instantly, causing grogginess and disorientation. It would still take a minute or so to knock him out, so Han followed up with two solid punches to the face.

The guard dropped to the ground, unconscious. Before he could recover from the blows, the GHB would kick in, extending his time of rest to upwards of twenty-four hours.

Han snatched a key ring and walkie-talkie from his belt and left him where he fell. He was against the clock and he had a lot to do.

He quickly made his way back to the guardhouse and paused at the door. The television was still on, but no other sounds. With aerosol in hand, he opened the door and stepped in.

The guardhouse was one grade up from a portacabin. There was a large communal area, with cheap sofas and the television and a back kitchenette, with a small school-style dining set. A door at the rear of the room led to sleeping quarters, storage and toilets.

Two guards were asleep on the sofas. A third was sat at the dining table, staring into a mug of coffee with drooping, blinking eyes. He glanced up at Han with confusion set into his slack features. "Second cup ... don't know ..." was all he managed.

Han strode over to him and struck him over the back of the head with his police baton. No need to give him an extra dose of

GHB. This one was going to sleep for England. He had obviously felt tired and tried to combat it by drinking lots of coffee. Normally that would've helped, but not when using water laced with a very powerful date rape drug. Boiled water only marginally reduced the GHB's overall potency.

Han moved quickly through the door into a corridor. The locker room, toilets and shower rooms were all empty. Another guard was head down on the desk in the communications room and the final landward guard was asleep on his bunk in the sleeping quarters.

He could not have hoped for a better start. As a precaution, he sprayed each of the sleeping guards and paused only to collect up any visible walkie-talkies and mobile phones and to sabotage the radio. Then he was on his way, dashing across the gravel to the gangway.

After tossing the phones and radios into the sea, he used the keys from the first guard to open the locked gate that restricted access to the gangway. The gangway stretched most of the length of the vessel. Han headed for the main entrance at a fast jog.

The heavy external door was unlocked, as he had expected. Han pushed straight in. Sitting in a small cubicle behind a mesh window, a guard was reading a weathered copy of *American Psycho* by Bret Easton Ellis. *Apt*, Han thought absently.

The man looked up as Han approached at speed. "Who ..."

Han lifted the aerosol and sprayed a hefty cloud into the guard's face. The man leapt out of his seat, casting the paperback into the air. Coughing and already beginning to feel the effects, he shouted, "Help! Assistance!" as he scrambled, half-blind for the alarm.

"Assistance?" Han said with a grunt, shaking his head while he located the correct key to unlock the cubicle.

Disorientated, the guard was slapping a CCTV monitor and expecting the alarm to start sounding. Angrily, he snapped, "Sound, you fucker! Help! Help me!"

Han stepped inside the cramped cubicle and punched him several times. As the man keeled over, he gave him a swift kick in the side for good measure. "Prat," he muttered.

185

Han noticed a can of Coke on the desk. Well, he knew he wouldn't get everyone.

Scanning the bank of monitors, he saw no signs of alarm or distress. There did not appear to be any activity from the prisoners and he couldn't see a single guard walking around. Hardly daring to smile, he stamped on the man's mobile phone and yanked the microphone out of the radio set.

On the way out, he grabbed the guard's set of keys and shoved the first set into his pocket. The door led through into a secure waiting area, with office and administration rooms branching off to the left.

A plump guard was stood at a vending machine, weighing up the pros and cons between a Snicker or a Mars, no doubt. He paid no notice of the new arrival.

Han broke into a sprint and was on top of him before he fully turned around. He punched him once to pacify him then, with a hand tightly gripping the man's jaw, he sprayed the aerosol into his red gasping face. The larger man fell back against the vending machine, causing it to slam loudly into the steel wall. The sound seemed to reverberate around the room.

Irritated, Han punched him repeatedly in the face until the crunch of the man's nose shattering brought him back to task. He let the man slide down the vending machine to end up in a slumped sitting position.

He turned to see one of the office doors opening. A middle-aged woman was stepping out.

"Crap," he uttered and ran at her at full pelt.

She was groggy, so had clearly ingested some of the GHB, but was still compos mentis enough to realise acute danger when she saw it.

She tried to scream, but only a gurgle escaped her throat. She stumbled backwards, but Han was far too quick. He grabbed her roughly by the shoulder and sprayed her face. She started coughing and sank to her knees. He raised a fist to make sure, but then changed his mind and left her kneeling there, like a housewife at church on Sunday.

He swept through the offices, finding three more staff; two already unconscious and one just a snore away. He left them and checked the other rooms, finding sleeping quarters with several more guards asleep and one awake.

The young officer was sat at a small table, reading a Kindle by lamplight. He looked up. "Who are you?"

"A nightmare," Han replied, moving towards him quickly.

This one was alert. He jumped to his feet, kicking the table into the air at the same time. He cast the e-book reader onto a nearby bunk as Han batted the lightweight table aside.

The young man pulled out his baton and Han stopped. "Don't make this hard on yourself, kid."

The guard was wide-eyed, but he snapped back, "Fuck you! Wake up! Intruder!"

Han sighed and sprang at him. He blocked the guard's first blow with his arm, sending a burst of pain shooting up to his shoulder. Still holding the aerosol in his left hand, he punched him square on the jaw with it.

The young man reeled backwards, eyes watering and waving the baton wildly.

Grimacing at the pain in his arm, Han stomped over to him and sprayed a heavy dose into the guard's face. He then snatched the guard's baton out of his hand and battered him across the head a couple of times.

The young man crumpled.

"Stay the fuck down, hero," Han said through gritted teeth. He bent down to check his pulse. Still alive. Good. "Nice try though, mate. You've earned your rest."

"What's going on?" a voice said from one of the bunks.

Clicking his tongue, Han located the source and sprayed the man in the face, followed by a couple of punches for good measure. He then quickly sprayed the other sleeping men.

The rest of the guard and staff section proved uneventful. He moved on through a communal dining area and into a secure holding area. The guard at this post was already asleep. Han sprayed him anyway.

He then opened the door into a corridor with six heavy doors branching off each side, leading to the dorm-like cells. There was also one final door at the end of the corridor that led to showers, toilets and finally a solitary unit.

"Show time," he said aloud as he rubbed his sore arm. Still hadn't quite mastered ambidexterity. Well, at least it banished the lingering stiffness from the stab wound.

The cells were individually locked, so that would add a little extra time, but was better for control. So far, apart from the minor distraction caused by the wannabe hero, things were going swimmingly.

He dumped the rucksack and pulled out a sheathed machete. He drew the gleaming blade and tested its weight. Despite being eighteen inches long, it was remarkably light and manageable. After unlocking the first door, he stepped in and locked it behind him.

"Wakey wakey, eggs and bakey."

There were between thirty and forty cons per dorm room, sleeping in bunk beds three high in the dark and cramped room. The air reeked of sweat and farts.

His words were greeted with some random grunts and mutterings. He didn't wait for an invitation. He walked over to the first bunk and buried the machete into the sleeping man's skull. Blood splattered over his grey blanket. The body twitched a couple of times, but Han was already moving on to the next one.

He efficiently sliced the throat of the man above and despatched the one above him in the same way. He didn't really have the time to get too creative.

Most of the prisoners were not stirring – many would have been drugged in the same way as the guards – but some were finally starting to take notice.

"What the fuck?", "Fucker!" and "Shit!" was the general consensus of opinion.

Han hacked through several more as the mayhem grew around him.

Several prisoners were jumping out of bunks. Some were backing away, instinctively grouping together. Others were stepping

188

up to the plate, enraged at the disruption to their beauty sleep. Batter up …

A wiry tattooed boxer-type was first up. He had a flat nose and several visible scars on his arms and bare chest. He loosened his shoulders and raised his fists. "Let's have some then," he said and spat at Han's feet.

He didn't have time to piss about, so Han swung at the slugger's throat. He stepped back and to the side, alert and light-footed. "Too slow, bitch!"

Han swung again and gave the inmate an invitation to his left side. He was good enough to see it and moved in for a kidney punch. Han shifted at the last second and brought the machete down on the man's arm. It buried down to the bone in the prisoner's forearm.

As Slugger cried out in anger and pain, Han head-butted him, yanked the blade free and slashed open the man's stomach. Intestines spilled out onto the floor with an audible splatter, causing some shocked cries from several onlookers.

As Slugger crumpled, another prisoner tried to sprint past. Han slashed out, catching the man's ankle and all but severing his foot completely. The prisoner went sprawling, foot dangling loosely by a sliver of skin and tissue. Han buried the machete into the middle of the man's back and then turned to see a crowd gathering at the far end of the room.

"Fucking rip your throat out, you cunt," one bald-headed, barrel-chested ape snarled.

With Jean-Luc Fuctard leading, several others fell in behind him, their courage bolstered.

Han stopped and smiled. "Make it so."

Fucktard led the charge. His minions were confident in their leader, but not completely stupid.

Han's machete took the big man's head clean off at the Adam's apple and he stepped aside as the headless corpse blundered past, before collapsing in a heap on the floor, blood spilling from the stump to mingle with the pools that were already gathering from his earlier victims.

Several prisoners screeched in terror. Many of these plebs weren't hard nuts like Fucktard or Slugger – a lot were probably petty thieves, druggies or your usual spineless bullies. *Seeing any person get his head cut off right in front of you is a life changing event. I'm not talking about these sickos who look up beheadings on the internet, while sipping Horlicks from the safety of their armchair. I'm talking about standing right there and feeling the spray of hot blood on your face. And when the person in question happens to be a great big fucker, who everyone thought was invincible, then, well that's a whole new level of despair, I reckon.*

So, the mayhem instantly transformed into a hysterical rout. Han threw all finesse out the window – or, porthole in this case – and waded in.

In moments, he was awash with blood. Severed limbs littered the floor, along with dead and dying bodies. No one else tried to fight back – they scrambled away or just lay on the ground sobbing. A couple made it to the door and hammered on it, screaming for help.

Han let them scream. It made no difference one way or the other. He methodically picked through the remaining prisoners, despatching them without fuss and then put down any left that were still twitching from lesser wounds.

"Goddamn! I forgot how much fun this could be!" he yelled then turned to the two at the door and stole a moment to catch his breath. After knocking back a few gulps of bottled water, he was ready to continue.

Their screaming had stopped and they were both staring at him, backs against cold, unyielding steel. They were open-mouthed, with eyes that seemed like they would pop right out of their sockets. They reminded Han of cartoon characters and he half expected one to yell out, 'zoiks'.

"I'm afraid, lads, I don't have time to chat," he said, still breathing heavily. "So many to kill and so little time. Story of my life!" He laughed, but he was greeted with stunned silence.

Finally, one of the men spoke in a strained whisper. "P-please … please don't kill me."

Han sighed as he walked towards them. "I'm sorry, no can do. But, what I will promise you is that I'll make it quick."

One of the men fell to his knees with his hands covering his face, sobbing.

The one who had spoken shakily stepped forward to meet him. Clasping his hands together, he said, "Please, mister. I've got a little un that needs his da. I didn't know mine – he fucked off before I was born."

Han reached him and just shook his head slowly.

"Fuck you!" The prisoner lunged at his throat.

Han was ready for him. The machete sliced one of the man's hands off at the wrist and took three fingers from the other.

The prisoner's eyes grew wide as he stared in horror at his mutilated hands. Rather than scream in pain, he started retching. Before he could spray vomit onto Han's boots, he finished him off, hacking open his throat.

Han walked on as the prisoner toppled, gurgling to the floor. The last prisoner was huddled into a foetal position, shaking uncontrollably and whimpering like a wounded animal.

Han put him out of his misery. Before moving on to the next room, he checked his watch. It had taken him less than fifteen minutes to clear the whole room. On schedule and the pain in his arm diminishing, Han moved on to the next room.

Special guest appearance

CHAPTER 13

The figure sat amongst the long grass overlooking the naval cemetery and observed HMP *The Weare* through a Bushnell Night Vision Scope. Things appeared to be going like clockwork down there.

The figure had observed Han from the pumping station to disappearing into the vessel. No alarms had gone off. Prison service and police alike were still utterly oblivious to the slaughter happening at Her Majesty's pleasure. So far, everything was under control.

There were still plenty of risks, but as plans go this one was as foolproof as possible. Of course, there were additional resources, if required.

***

Han took a couple of deep breaths and opened the next cell door. Several prisoners were out of their bunks and talking animatedly. Others were sat up, listening to the debate.

As the door opened all eyes turned to Han.

"What the fuck's going on?" one prisoner asked, his tone demanding, but his eyes wide and fearful.

Then they noticed the blood-smeared machete.

"Oh my God," someone uttered.

"This ... this can't be happening!"

Han casually locked the door behind him and stepped further into the room. "Sorry, lads, it is happening. The time of your judgement is upon you. Now that everyone is coming up to speed, I was planning on launching into the Ezekiel 25:17 speech - you know, Jools from Pulp Fiction. Iconic speech. Anyway, now that I'm here I can't really be bothered, so let's just crack on, eh?"

"What do you want?" an older con asked. "I've got money ..."

"Sorry, mate. I don't want your money. All I want is to kill every mother fucking last one of you."

Those awake and still in their bunks immediately began scrambling out of them. Those already on their feet did one of two things; some ran to the extremities, hiding in darkened corners or under bunks, and the others grouped together, much like those in the first room.

"This is fucking mad!" someone cried, jostling to the back of the crowd.

"Madness?" Han asked. "This is Sparta!" With a roaring battle cry and machete above his head, he ran headlong into the crowd.

***

Will sat hunched over the wheel of the Land Rover as rain lashed at the windscreen.

Carol sat in the passenger seat, arms folded and eyes staring, unblinking, into the darkness.

Will glanced at her and offered a weak smile.

Finally, she muttered, "I can't believe you're making me do this."

A flicker of annoyance played across Will's face, but he quelled it and said, "I gave you the choice, Carol. I don't want to force you into anything." In fact, he would have preferred to do this alone.

Carol stared at him with an intensity that would have unnerved lesser men. "Sure, you didn't *force* me. But you made it very clear that you'd go ahead and do it on your own. What the hell was I supposed to do?"

Maintaining a soothing tone, Will said, "I can handle this. I really can. You don't have to do this."

Tears welled in Carol's eyes. "I have to. I can't lose you too. I … I love you."

Will tore his eyes away from the road. He opened his mouth to speak.

Carol turned away and said, "Don't say anything, Will. Don't say a word."

***

To say that Han was having a ball would be pretty accurate. He was knackered, but on schedule and uninjured, apart from the sore arm from earlier. It had been a hard slog, but there was only one dorm-cell remaining.

He stood outside the door, dripping wet with blood and dribbling gore. Tufts of matted hair and slivers of flesh clung to his clothes. He glanced down at himself and laughed. "Jesus, I must look like Leatherface!"

As he caught his breath, he fumbled inside his jacket for an energy bar. He washed it down with some more bottled water and took a deep breath. "Coming ready or not!"

There was a great deal of shouting and screaming coming from within. The slaughter in the first room had immediately alerted everyone else who had not succumbed to the GHB. As he had moved from room to room, the chaos had intensified, as the prisoners had to listen to the ever-escalating carnage.

He found some prisoners fighting each other or even offering some of their cellmates up as sacrifices to try to appease him, like some savage deity. The absurdity of it! Pathetic. Sub-human excrement. He should be getting paid for this shit!

194

He swung the door open and readied the machete. A small – almost Dwarf-like – man was hurled through the door at him. The squat little man's face was contorted in a scream.

The machete skewered him through the neck – more by accident than design – and gouting blood splashed across Han's masked face. As Han cast the dying man aside, he was rushed by several figures.

They were on him in seconds. A frenzy of fists and feet struck out as he slammed against the far wall of the corridor. Half-dazed, and with spikes of pain bursting all over his body, Han fought back, swinging the machete like a hoe, slicing flesh left and right. A hand flew off in one direction and the blade sliced open the chest of another person, before burying deep into the face of a third. The blade was wedged fast. As he tugged, the hilt sprung free from his slippery-gloved hand.

The man fell away with the machete still protruding from the side of his head. A prisoner immediately tried to wrench it free by stamping a foot onto the gurgling man's face and yanking hard.

More prisoners were jostling to put the boot in or throw punches at Han's thrashing form.

Time for plan B, she said! Han drew the Beretta 92 automatic and opened fire repeatedly until it clicked empty. Prisoners fell in all directions, some screaming, others immediately silenced. Han pressed the magazine release and slammed a fresh one home as the empty one clattered to the sodden floor.

The melee dispersed, prisoners wisely opting to run for it, instead of persevering with the lynching.

Han staggered to his feet and took aim at three prisoners who were dashing away from him down the corridor. He placed a round into the backs of two and the leg of the third, who fell forward onto his face. He scrambled frantically for the exit as Han took careful aim.

The bullet punched a hole in the back of the prisoner's head, spraying blood and brain matter onto the deck in front of him. His head flopped to cold steel with a soft *thunk*.

Han then turned back to the wounded around him. Several were moaning or crying and trying to claw away from him. After despatching those still bitching and twitching, along with the unconscious ones still in their bunks, he retrieved the machete and the empty Beretta magazine. He then took a moment to survey the scene. To say that it looked like a slaughterhouse would not really give it justice.

Mutilated bodies lay in heaps around him, interspersed with severed appendages and steaming viscera. There was so much blood that at first glance it appeared that the ship was slowly sinking into an inky goo.

He was breathing hard and felt as if he had been thrown down several flights of concrete steps. One jacket sleeve was hanging off and his balaclava had been torn across one eye. He could feel his face swelling and various joints beginning to stiffen. This was going to take some explaining to Cara.

One cell left; solitary confinement. The toilets and showers were empty, so Han limped through to the final door.

Final kill of the night, he mused then opened the door.

The cell was empty.

After checking under the bunk to make sure, Han stood and planted his hands on his hips. "Bit of an anti-climax," he said with a click of his tongue. But then realisation began to dawn on him and a wide grin spread across his face. He suppressed a chuckle and said, "Don't get ahead of yourself, old buddy."

After a brief final inspection, he headed back towards the exit.

***

The Land Rover pulled up next to a lockup garage in a dark corner of a deathly quiet industrial estate. Most of the units they passed on the way in appeared derelict. Only a few appeared to be still in use – a garage, a Chinese takeaway and a printer – but all were in darkness. No shift working here.

"I won't be a sec," Will said as he jumped out, leaving the engine idling.

"Why the hell do we need a lockup?" Carol shouted after him.

Will either ignored her or didn't hear her over the grumbling diesel engine. He dragged his kitbag out of the back of the Land Rover then opened a side door and disappeared.

Carol strained to see beyond the gloom of the doorway, but could not make out a thing and Will did not turn a light on, opting for a flashlight instead.

She bit her lip and waited, every so often tearing her eyes away from the doorway to glance around the deserted estate.

She didn't like this one bit. Will was acting ... distant and the anonymous message ...

High Noon

I've got to, that's the whole thing.

CHAPTER 14

Cara let the phone ring through to Han's voicemail once again. She sat on the edge of the bed, concern nipping at her features. "Hey, it's just me. I hadn't heard from you since going down to the convention. I'm just a little worried, that's all. Stupid, I know, but give me a call as soon as you pick this up. Love you."

She dropped the phone into its cradle and stared at it for a time. Something wasn't right.

Ju padded over from his basket in the corner of the room and placed his nose in Cara's lap. Absently, she stroked his neck, her thoughts elsewhere.

***

As he retraced his steps, Han checked every room and darkened corner one final time. This could very well be the end of Phase Two and the end of the experiment as a whole. He was going to leave zero room for error.

The thought of the experiment finally being over was building inside him, like the imminence of Christmas morning to a child.

He stopped dead in front of the exit, gazing out into a clear moonlit sky. The clouds that had aided his incursion clearly felt that they were no longer needed. A bright half-Moon, surrounded by a multitude of stars, greeted him.

A cool sea breeze caressed his face. The blood splattered across his balaclava was starting to dry now that he had stopped sweating. He felt an overwhelming compulsion to rid himself of the mask, but fought the desire. He wasn't out of the woods yet.

Could the experiment finally be over? It had been such a huge part of his life for the last three years or so. A quack might say a life-affirming part.

Looking back, it seemed like a right of passage that he had to go through. A hardship to endure to then reap the rewards of happiness and contentment with Cara afterwards.

The idea was both absurd and undeniable at once.

A right of passage that involved the systematic murder of nearly eight hundred people? That was quite a test! King Leonidas would've been impressed.

Could he now go on with a 'normal' life with Cara? Was that possible after everything he had been through? Everything he had *done*? Hell yes. He deserved it.

Haydon had been a complete success, but he had failed to understand the entire picture back then. It had left things … out of kilter. Phase Two had redressed that. The same number (well, actually one or two more in Phase Two, but who's counting?) of evildoers executed as the supposed innocents in Haydon. Balance restored.

Han walked out into the cool night. Wisps of steam rose from his saturated clothes. He made his way ashore and then headed back to the hire car, parked on secluded waste ground behind Castletown.

Of course, there was still the niggling issue of Charlie and his two intrepid enforcers. *If* Han could take his word, Charlie would handle them. But that was a big if. Charlie was a loose end. And worse, a loose end that he didn't trust one iota. He had no doubt that Charlie had sought him out from the start and used him like a little laboratory rat.

Han saw the little Skoda Fabia up ahead. He had parked it off the dirt track beside an unkempt hedgerow to break up its profile in case of any late night dog-walkers (or doggers, for that matter).

As he approached, a match-light illuminated a figure standing by the car. The man sucked on a cigarette until the flame took hold then discarded the match underfoot.

Han stopped and his hand edged slowly towards his pistol.

"Relax, mate," the man said and stepped forward.

Han recognised the voice instantly, but it was not until the figure stepped closer that he believed his own ears.

"Perry?" he asked, utterly incredulous, pulling the balaclava up to reveal his face. His shocked features were smeared with the blood of dozens of prisoners and badly bruised from the beating.

"Aye," Perry said and glanced over his shoulder, his hair flicking with the brief movement.

Han stepped closer, closing the distance. "You? You're ..." He couldn't find the words. His whole world seemed to spin.

"Yes, I'm ... Charlie." Again, a fleeting glance over his shoulder and then a quick draw on the cigarette.

Han's arms fell limp against his sides. "I ... trusted you. You were my friend ... my *only* fucking friend." *Perry hasn't smoked for over two years*, Han thought somewhere in the back of his mind.

Perry opened his mouth, but then hesitated. Indecision seemed to mar his features. Finally, he flicked the cigarette into the hedgerow and said, "Fuck this! Run, mate! It's a fucking trap—"

A gunshot rang out.

Perry fell forward into Han's arms. Han dropped to his knees, cradling his friend. "Perry! What the fuck?"

"Fucker shot me, man!" Perry managed then coughed violently, spattering blood into Han's face. "Some bastard ... calling himself Charlie ... dragged me down here. He ... I'm sorry, man. He made me ..."

"Don't talk, mate," Han said, feeling for the wound. The back of Perry's Parka was already drenched. "Hold on. I'll get help."

"Who ... *are* ... you?" Perry whispered. With the final word, his head lolled to one side and his eyes glazed over. A trickle of blood dribbled onto Han's sleeve.

"No ..." was all Han could manage in bewildered disbelief.

Another figure had stepped out of the car. He drew on a cigar then said, "Don't fret, Harry," the man said, his tone mildly amused. "Or should I say *Han?*"

Han looked up from his dead friend, his eyes moist. "Charlie ..."

"You named that tune in one." The man stepped further out of the shadows of the hedgerow. The glowing tip of his cigar cast a flickering orange light over the man's face. He was perhaps in his late fifties or early sixties. It was difficult to tell. The man was clearly in good shape and broad-shouldered, and held a revolver pointing down at the ground.

"Why?" Han uttered. "Why Perry? I did what you asked ..."

Charlie sighed. "That wasn't quite how that was supposed to go down. If Perry had played his part, it could've been so much more fun. But he had to go and spoil it."

Anger was quickly eroding away at his grief. Han gently laid Perry's body down onto the ground and slowly rose to his feet. In a low growl, he said, "I carried out your fucking plan to the letter."

"Yes, you did, old son. And very proud I am too."

Han stepped closer. Finally, after all the games, Charlie was in front of him. The *real* Charlie. And with each muffled footstep, a familiarity steadily turned to recognition. "*You* ..." was all he could manage before his voice deserted him.

Charlie's craggy face flourished a genuine smile. "Who else, son?"

A wave of nausea returned with a vengeance and threatened to forcibly expel the contents of Han's stomach. Swallowing hard, he muttered, "Dad ... what the ..."

201

Charlie laughed and sucked on his cigar. Blowing smoke as he spoke, he said, "You've come a long way, son. I really am proud of you."

"You ... you ..." Images crammed into his head like a migraine. The ferocity of it drove Han to his knees. Charlie watched, silently puffing on his Hamlet.

"Come on, son. You'll love it!" The man led the little boy through the open doorway to where the strange animal-like sounds were coming from.

He was very afraid, but Dad was with him, so he didn't have anything to worry about, did he? He was going to miss The Clangers and Chorlton and the Wheelies at this rate.

Dad was a big man and other men had always been scared of him. He had only seen his Dad raise his mighty fists once. A man had been chatting to Mam outside the post office. Dad had casually stepped out of the car — the Vauxhall Cavalier MKI — and strolled over to them with his hands in his pockets, whistling the theme tune to The Sweeney.

As he approached, he caught worried realisation on Mam's face and confusion on the man's.

"Get yourself in the car, Bev," he had said and then, without another word, he repeatedly punched the man in the face. As the man's legs gave way, Dad grabbed him by the scruff of the neck to stop him from collapsing. Holding him against the wall, he continued to pummel the man's face. Dad didn't say a word and, apart from ramming a fist into the man's blood-splattered face, appeared relaxed, ignoring Mam screaming in the background. There had been a sickening crack as the man's nose caved in.

That had been the one time he had seen Dad fight. He usually didn't need to. One look would send a bigger man in the opposite direction.

The room had been some sort of office. Like the warehouse around them, the office had been long-since abandoned and left to gradually rot. Graffiti adorned the walls, and a soup of trash and human excrement littered the bare concrete floor, amidst puddles of stagnant water.

The one broken window had been boarded up, so the room was gloomy and filled with long shadows, despite the bright sunny mid-afternoon outside.

Other than a dented old filing cabinet shoved in a corner, the only other piece of furniture was a large metal table in the centre of the room. Strapped to the table was a young man in his late teens. The strange scraping noises were

202

coming from his wriggling movements as he tried to escape from his bonds. An oily rag had been shoved deep into his mouth and held in place by duct tape.

"Dad?" the boy's voice trembled as he pulled back from the bizarre and scary sight. "I ... want to go home. The Clangers will be on soon."

"Don't worry, son. It's time you saw this. This is going to be our little secret. You can't tell anyone about this – not Mam or your brother. This is between you, me and him."

The boy struggled harder. "Please, no! I don't want to! I want to watch The Clangers!

"It's time you saw this," Dad repeated.

"Why me?" Tears were welling in his eyes.

Dad smiled and tapped some cigar ash onto the floor. His grip on the boy's wrist did not falter. "Because you're like me, son. I've seen it in your eyes. You're not like the ordinary trash, like this pathetic creature here. You're special. And I'm going to teach you."

"I don't want to ... I just want to go home."

"Grow a spine, lad." Dad dragged the whimpering boy over to the edge of the table. "Stand there and don't move a muscle. Watch and learn, lad."

The teenager's eyes focussed on Dad and grew wide. He frantically shook his head, his pleading words muffled beyond recognition by the gag.

"Sorry, kid. This isn't personal. You're going to have to just grin and bear it, I'm afraid."

Several implements had been laid out on the table beside the bound young man. Dad turned the boy. He was snivelling and trembling, but rooted to the spot. He offered the boy a mischievous wink then set to work.

Dad chose a Stanley knife first. With one hand, he held the struggling teenager's head steady. Carefully, with a surgeon's precision, he cut away the young man's eyelids. Despite being gagged, the young man's screams were unmistakable.

Seeing his father remove the bloody little flaps of skin and discard them onto the floor, with a noise that resembled a wet slap, was too much for the boy. He bent over double and threw up onto the concrete. Vomit splashed Dad's brown brogues.

Dad shot him a disapproving glance, but then continued about his business. With practiced ease, he cut around the man's nose and then, with a soft sucking sound, pulled the nose away from the face, leaving exposed blood-

smeared bone extruding from the centre of the man's face. Blood oozed down the teenager's cheeks like crimson tears.

At this, the young man fainted. And so did the boy.

Dad hauled the boy to his feet and gently slapped his cheeks until he began to stir. The boy immediately began retching once more, begging, "Please, Dad, don't! Stop, please!"

Dad's smile was filled with compassion. "Don't you worry, young un. It's not your time, son. Not yet. But it will be and I'll be there to guide you." With that, he turned back to the young man on the table.

Han was bent over on his knees, sobbing into his hands.

"Let it all out, son," Charlie said, shaking his head slowly.

It took Han several minutes to compose himself. Gradually, he rose unsteadily to his feet. "I'm not sure which is worse – thinking that you might've been a paedophile or that you ... you fucking exposed me to ... *everything.*"

Charlie recoiled in horror. "You thought I was a fucking nonce?"

Han gaped at him.

"I'm a lot of things, son, but I'm no kiddie-fiddler." With a deep breath, he said, "I saw something in you right from the start. You had potential, kid. You were special, like me. All you needed was a little guiding hand."

Han leant against the hedge for support.

Charlie examined the remaining stub of his cigar and said, "I've never been far away from you all these years. I've kept a very close eye on you. I've helped where I could and dropped a few hints here and there to guide you on your path. You may not realise it, even yet, but I planted the original seed for the experiment. I didn't choose the specifics, like Haydon, or even the parameters of it, but I gave the idea its legs."

Swallowing back bile, Han spat, "Bollocks. Everything I've done I've done of my own accord. The experiment was my idea and mine alone. You're not going to fuck with my head over this. Haydon was the initial test to see if it could be done and everything since has been to redress the balance. All you did was offer up some victims like sacrificial lambs."

204

Charlie sighed and stubbed the cigar out under foot. "Look, son, we're on the same side here." With that, he cast his revolver aside. It landed in a clump of weeds. He held his hands up as a show of submission. "This is me, son. And I'm being completely honest with you. At the end of the day, you can choose to believe what you want to believe, son. Haydon was your experiment. You were mine."

"Fuck you!" Han snarled and drew the Beretta. Aiming at Charlie's head, he said, "You fucked me over with Wright's son and Carol. You've tried to fuck with my head from the start. You killed *Perry!*"

A flicker of concern marred Charlie's relaxed demeanour for a moment. It vanished as quickly as it appeared. "You don't need people like Perry. You don't need anyone. People like us shouldn't have anyone close to us – they're just an unnecessary distraction. Believe me, I know. I don't want you to make the same mistakes I did."

"The same mistakes *you* did?" Han uttered in amazement. "You tortured and murdered someone right in front of my eyes when I was a fucking kid!"

"I saw potential in you, son. Instead of letting it die, I vowed to encourage it. I wanted to see if I could take a normal well-adjusted lad like yourself and turn you into a killer, above the feeble morals and laws of a totally inept society."

Han was shaking his head vehemently.

"That first time I tortured that kid in front of you was just the start. I took you on several outings as we called them. You were terrified at first – crying and puking the whole time – but you got used to it and you even started helping me in small ways. Not in the actual work, but by handing me a tool here and there when I asked."

"No …" Han whispered, rubbing the pistol against the side of his head.

"You remember some of it – you'll remember the rest in time. Everything changed when your mam started getting suspicious. We argued – she thought I was fiddling with you too at first, for fuck's sake. So much so, I had to make up a load of bullshit about other women and using you as an alibi. She bought it and we split up. That was the end of our outings, but not the end of your training. I kept close and would throw you a little suggestion every now and then. Over time, you obviously forgot the outings, which was a setback. But the teachings stuck."

"Bullshit! Fucking bullshit! You can't turn someone into a killer by the power of suggestion." He jabbed the Beretta at Charlie to emphasis the point.

"The outings started the process, but then it took nearly thirty years to take full effect, culminating in your decision to 'experiment' on the villagers of Haydon. It was little things – magazine cuttings I'd strategically leave for you, showing torture and murder, whispered suggestions in your room at night–"

"You snuck into my room?" Han said with a snarl.

"Countless times over the years – I've been in your current house more times than I can remember."

Han stared in stunned silence.

Continuing, Charlie said, "I made sure that you saw a mutilated dog or cat from time to time, articles on the innate savagery of man, the collapse of an amoral society and all that bollocks. With technological advancements, I started sending you emails with links to horrific murders, forcing pop-ups onto your computer with grotesque images. Like I say, it was a very slow burn. And, I have to say, I did lose faith on many occasions throughout the years. But you came true in the end, son."

"This is bullshit mind-games. Okay, so you're my dad and you're a fucking psycho killer, just like me. You might've even wanted to mould me into your image, but what I've done was my decision, not yours. So the fucking apple doesn't fall far from the tree – that doesn't prove a goddamn thing."

"As I said, believe what you want. The great thing is that both of our experiments were a success. You became all that you could be. Now we can move on together – father and son."

Han fell back against the hedge, tearing the sleeve of his jacket further. He glanced down at it, as if it were some sort of alien parasite. Returning his attention to Charlie, he said, "Are you insane?"

Charlie laughed. "Some might argue that's a moot point."

"I told you from the start. This shit ends with the experiment. Phase Two is over and so is all this. I'm going back to a normal life."

"You really think you can lead a normal life? You're a killer – a predator, just like me. You'll never be content with an inane existence."

"You're wrong – I switched this on and I can damn well switch it back off again. That was part of the point of the experiment in the fucking first place!"

"Who are you trying to convince, son? Me or you?"

Han opened his mouth to speak, the Beretta trembling in his grasp. Charlie spoke first, shaking his head. "You can no more switch this shit on and off than Oppenheimer can un-invent the atomic bomb. You looked down the rabbit hole, young un."

"Well, I'm going to fucking well climb back out of it and I'll ram 'Little Boy' up Oppenheimer's arse."

Charlie's calm façade wavered, his cheeks growing crimson. "It's not over until I say it's over, lad. All this ... this bullshit, as you call it ... was just the matinee before the main performance. Just think of what we can achieve together!"

"No!" Han stepped forward, thrusting the gun ahead of him. "I want my life back! I want to lead a normal life with Cara!"

"Impossible, son. This is our destiny."

"Our destiny?" Han scoffed. "Our fucking destiny? This ain't Star Wars, you wanker!"

Charlie's left cheek and eye twitched and his face reddened further.

"This is *your* destiny, not mine," Han continued. "If I'm to believe you, you're responsible for all this! You turned me into a killer."

With a snort, Charlie said, "You can thank me later, son."

"This isn't fucking funny, *Dad!*" The barrel of the gun was only a few inches from Charlie's face. "Maybe I wanted to be normal! Did you consider that, eh? You took that decision away from me and turned me into some ridiculous film cliché! The original experiment was supposed to be one rational person's decision. You've changed all that."

"You still made the final decision yourself," Charlie said, changing tact. "I just guided you, like your guardian angel."

"Angel of fucking death, you fucking lunatic!" Han ripped off the balaclava and cast it aside, wild eyes glaring.

"Now, given everything that's happened, that's a bit like the pot calling the kettle, don't you think?"

"You turned me into a lunatic! What's your excuse?"

Charlie shoved his hands into his pockets and shrugged. "You don't get it, son." There was only disappointment in his tone. "I don't need an excuse. I'm not a lunatic at all. And neither are you. We're the sane ones, you and me! It's them out there – they're the lunatics! Living their dull, petty lives in misery, eventually praying for the grave. They called all the great pioneers mad or heretics. It's not till civilisation moves on that they get re-branded 'enlightened'. This is all so new to you – you'll understand in time."

"I don't want to understand. I want my life back – the life you stole from me." His fingers tightened around the pistol grip.

Charlie's tone abruptly changed. "Get a hold of yourself, lad!" he snapped. Han could smell the tobacco on his breath and felt warm spittle splash his cheek. "You're not a child anymore. I've been looking out for you all your life. I even arranged for the Haydon evidence to go missing, you ungrateful little shit-stain! Do you have any idea what sort of risk I took for that?"

"And just how the fuck did you manage that?" Han scoffed.

"Haven't you worked it out yet?" Shaking his head, Charlie said, "I've been a copper since not long after leaving your mam. I wanted to keep an eye on you and the best way to do that was on the Force. I called in some favours and I managed to get assigned to the Haydon case. I wasn't lead; that sanctimonious prick, Hewitt, nabbed that gig, but I managed to get on the team."

"You're a fucking copper?" Han asked incredulously.

"Does that really surprise you? It's the perfect racket for guys like you and me, son. I switched evidence caskets before handing it in to Central Submissions. The indexing error was easy –

the desk clerk was up to his eyes, so never suspected a thing. So why don't you show a little gratitude and grow a fucking spine."

"I will fucking cut you down right here, you fucking piece of shit!" Han shoved the pistol into Charlie's face.

Charlie moved with startling speed for his age. He gripped the gun and brought the blade of his hand down on Han's wrist then followed up with a jab below Han's nose.

Han staggered backwards. Charlie cast the gun aside and came at him. He wasn't as big a man as he used to be, but he was still easily an inch taller than Han and thicker set.

Charlie slammed a punch into Han's face before he could recover then kicked him in the groin.

Han dropped to his knees, gasping for air. Fresh blood oozed from his nose and his eyes were watering.

"Look at you!" Charlie spat, openly disgusted. "I created you! I turned you into a god! And this is how you repay me? You're pathetic!" He kicked him in the side. Han keeled over into the dirt, moaning.

"I've had your back since you were knee-high to a grasshopper. And this? *This?*" Charlie kicked dirt at him and then strode back over to the car. He leant inside and dragged DCI Carter out by the scruff of her neck. She was bound and gagged, but her wide, frenzied eyes revealed her keen grasp of the situation. He manhandled her over to Han, who was still coughing and gasping, his already exhausted body struggling to recover from the fresh assault.

Charlie dumped Carter down beside Han. Jabbing a finger at her, he said, "These fuckers were already on to you, son. It was down to old Daddy to help out … once again. You *need* me!"

Han glanced at Carter and recognised her immediately. *Christ, they were on to me*, he thought absently. But that didn't matter anymore. Nothing mattered anymore. "Fuck … you," he managed between gasps.

Taking a deep breath, his tone regulated once more, Charlie said, "Look, son, why don't I put this bitch out of her misery and we can move on?"

"No!" Han spat. "She's an innocent! I will not let you harm her!"

"She's a copper who knows who you *really* are, old son, is what she is. Speaking as one myself, there really is no coming back from this. She was sent here to keep tabs on you and when she turns up dead, you are the number one suspect. You will be public enemy number one, old son. With your true identity, they would have you in custody inside of twenty four hours. They'll corner you quicker than that pathetic piece of shit, Moat. The rules go out the window, I'm afraid."

Han was shaking his head so fiercely that specks of blood were flying out of his nose. "It's over, Goddamn it! No more!"

"I can set you up with a new identity, so that you can continue your work. We can be a team, you and me! With me on the inside, we'd be unstoppable! And you want to go back to a *normal* life? You're worse than the pond scum out there! They don't know any better – you do! Perry was holding you back. And so is Cara – she's making you weak, can't you see that? Well, don't you worry about her, son. I'll sort her out." Charlie glared at his son and added, "And you know what, son? You'll thank me for it."

As he moved in to nudge Han with his boot, he added, "Now let's sort this one out." Han suddenly lunged forward and grabbed his leg. Pitching it upwards, Han jumped up and threw Charlie off balance, sending him reeling against the side of the car.

"Fuck you! You're not going to hurt another soul!" Han spat blood at him and raised his fists. "Come on then!"

"I don't want to fight you, son," Charlie said, struggling to his feet and nursing his bleeding head where it had struck metal. "We're on the same team here!"

"We're not even on the same planet, *Dad*."

"You fool!" Charlie came at him once more. He blocked Han's first jab and dodged his second. He moved in with a swift head butt that burst Han's already bloody nose.

Han fell backwards, but managed to parry two more blows. Charlie kept coming, breathing hard, but determination set into his weathered features. "So be it, son!" he roared and swung again and again.

Han drew his guard up to his face, blocking two more punches, but his exposed stomach took two more that caused him to cough blood over his attacker. Charlie kept punching.

Han was forced up against the hedge. He was blocking some punches, but most were hitting home. His head was swimming and his ears were ringing and still his father waded in.

Han collapsed and rolled into a ball. Charlie kicked him twice in the head and then stopped to catch his breath. Holding his side, he coughed several times and drew in some gulping breaths. "Christ," he managed. "I'm not as young as I used to be, man!"

Looking down at his balled up son, he said, "I'm not enjoying this, you know? I didn't want this. There's so much more to tell you – the Troy Consortium … our future together … you don't know the half of it." With a jab of his thumb towards the prone detective, he added, "I was going to dispose of that trash and then I wanted us to take out those two little prying pricks together. It would've been our first gig together. I was so looking forward to it! They're–"

Han was rising to his feet, spitting blood and a tooth onto the ground in front of Charlie. "Go to Hell," he uttered, blood spilling from the corner of his mouth.

"There'll be plenty of time for reunions later, son," Charlie said. "We haven't got much time …"

"You haven't." Han lurched towards him.

"Goddamn it!" Charlie shouted and raised his fists one more time. "I thought getting rid of your bloody mam would've knocked all this sissy shit out of you."

Han blinked and hesitated. "*What* did you say?"

"Your frigging mother. I took her out of the equation to aid your development. You were faltering – losing your way, so you needed a little nudge back onto the right track."

"You murdered *Mum*?" Blood sprayed Charlie's face as Han spat the final word.

For the first time, serious concern flashed across Charlie's eyes. "Look–"

Han came at him like a runaway train, an enraged scream on his lips. Han took a blow to the side of the head, but it didn't even slow him down. He anticipated another head butt and tucked his chin down in readiness. Charlie's forehead smashed off the top of Han's head, causing him to stumble backwards.

Han drove his fists into Charlie's stomach. Then switched to his face, punching until his knuckles bled.

Charlie was trying to raise his hands in defence, trying to speak through his broken mouth, but Han didn't listen. Talk was over. Charlie – Dad – had to die. He grabbed a handful of Charlie's hair and repeatedly slammed his face against the bonnet of the Skoda. Blood splattered over the bodywork and windscreen. He kept smashing it against metal until Charlie's body went limp.

He then dragged his ragdoll body over to the front driver's wheel and placed Charlie's bleeding head in front of it. He was groaning and his limbs were flapping incoherently.

Half dazed, Han fell into the driver's seat and started the engine. His whole body was shaking uncontrollably. Revving the engine, he yelled, "Why don't I drive you to Hell, Pops, eh? Get you there a little sooner?"

In a slurring gasp, Charlie managed, "Son …"

Han shoved his head out the open door and said, "Sorry, *Dad*, you've got to be heading off now. I *will* see you later though."

Revving the engine one more time, he leant into the steering wheel and then took his foot off the break. The car lurched forward and bumped over Charlie's head.

Charlie squealed like a wounded animal. The wheel tread tore off his ear and a clump of hair, but his head remained intact.

Glancing out of the open door, Han snapped, "For fuck's sake! Fucking cheap-ass cars!" He rolled the car forward, bumping over the head with the back wheel and then reversed at speed back over it.

Charlie tried to raise an arm to act as a pitiful shield, but his body was spent.

The wheel hit Charlie's head hard and this time it burst like a balloon. Blood and gore splattered in all directions. The wheel skidded briefly, churning up red-stained muck and then jumped forward into the hedge. Han's head struck the steering wheel, dazing him.

He sat there for a time, holding his head. Then, without a word, he fell out of the car and crawled on all fours towards the headless corpse of his father. "See? You see?" he muttered as he approached. Laughing maniacally, he added, "See that fucking head come apart, man!"

Hair and brain matter caked the ground all around him. The head had completely disintegrated, leaving only a mangled stump of neck with torn strands of skin and muscle trailing from it.

He glanced over at the detective. She was watching him with terrified, tearful eyes and trembling all over. The gag was being sucked in and out of her straining mouth with every hyperventilating gasp.

His hysterical laughter instantly distorted into gasping sobs. He slumped onto his side, holding his face with his bloodied and swollen hands.

"I was once like you are now, and I know that it's not easy,
To be calm when you've found something going on.
But take your time, think a lot,
Why, think of everything you've got.
For you will still be here tomorrow, but your dreams may not."
'Father & Son' by Cat Stevens

With snot and blood dribbling from his nose, Han crawled over to the trussed up detective. As he drew nearer, he could see her panic reaching new limits, muffled cries breaking the sudden quiet.

He held out a trembling hand to her and managed, "It's … it's okay. I'm not going to harm you … It's over."

"Hannibal Whitman," a voice said from somewhere in the distance of his mind, like a wisp of smoke.

Han stifled his sobs and looked up through blurred vision, his eyes blinking.

Two figures were standing nearby, one with a gun.

"Fucking die, you piece of shit," Carol Belmont said and spat at him. She raised the pistol with a trembling hand and took careful aim.

"Wait," Will said and placed a gentle hand on her wrist.

Confusion marred her features as she turned to face him. "What?"

"Not yet – he's not getting off this easy."

"What?" Carol repeated. The detachment she had felt in him on the journey down had solidified into something more – she could see it in his eyes. "Are you crazy? This is what we're here for. Both of us."

"Slight change of plan," Will said and snatched the gun from Carol's hand before she could object.

"What the hell are you doing?" Anger swelled over her initial confusion. She reached out to take it back, but Will stepped back from her, shaking his head.

"I'm going to make him pay for what he did," Will said. His tone was even, calculating, but his eyes were burning with an intensity that Carol had never seen before. "A quick execution isn't enough, not after everything he's done," he continued, his stance unyielding.

"Don't be crazy, Will. Please!" Carol gripped Will's arm. Imploring, she added, "He got away once before already. We have a chance to finish it right now, right here. To avenge your father and everyone else. *Please* don't do this, Will." Tears rolled down her cheeks. Everything that had seemed so clear a moment ago was unravelling before her eyes.

Han watched the exchange. It was a perfect opportunity to attempt an escape or to try to turn the tables. It would have been such a cliché, of course. But, unfortunately, Han's body was not up to either task. The slaughter and then subsequent family feud had taken every last ounce of energy out of him. He could do nothing other than observe and wonder what hand fate would deal him next. Would he be executed here or ... something worse elsewhere? The something worse would probably involve torture, so not good, but it would mean living and breathing longer, so could provide an opportunity later, if his body was able to recover a little. Unlikely, but you never know.

For a moment, when Carol had aimed the gun at him, he had accepted his imminent death without reservation. After Perry's

214

murder and the ensuing confrontation with Charlie, it had seemed … fitting. It's my time, he had thought. So be it. His only thoughts had been of Cara. She would find out about him. That upset him more than the thought of his impending demise.

"I'm sorry, Carol," Will said and the inevitability of his words struck Carol like a slap across the face.

"*No*," Carol uttered weakly. The single syllable was despair personified. She sank to her knees, holding her head in her hands.

Will hesitated for a moment, his hand outstretched. The shattered woman on her knees in front of him had started out as being a means to an end, but then had become a kindred spirit, and then a friend and finally a lover. He felt awful – disgusting, even – for deceiving her like this, but he knew she would not be a party to what he had in mind, and nor did he want her to be. What he was planning to carry out would taint him forever – far worse than Afghanistan did – and he wanted to protect her from that. Out of everyone involved in this nightmare, Carol deserved some peace at the end of it all. After he was finished, he would never feel peace again, nor deserve it. But his father would be truly avenged.

Han Whitman was going to suffer.

He withdrew his hand and strode over to Han, who was watching him with grim acceptance.

Will kicked him in the face, gouging a flap of skin from his cheek. He then kicked him several times in the chest and stomach. Han could barely muster the strength to attempt to soften the blows, never mind defend against them. He lay there and took it.

As Han moaned and bled, Will bound his arms and legs using cable ties.

Carol glanced over her shoulder at him, her bloodshot eyes with a desperate final hope in them. She opened her mouth to call to him, but then turned away and buried her head in her hands once more, weeping softly.

I ain't through with you by a damn sight. I'm-a get medieval on your ass.
~ Marsellus Wallace, Pulp Fiction

CHAPTER 15

Carol looked up through her damp fingers to see the Land Rover speeding away. In some small part of her mind, she thought that Will would change his mind at the last minute. She had been bereft of hope since Haydon, but the tiny shred had been rekindled through their budding relationship. As the rear lights disappeared into the darkness, so did that frail spark of hope.

She curled up into a ball and prayed for the Earth to open up and swallow her whole.

DCI Carter had observed the events with emotions that swung from terror to anger to anguish. With Richard's murderer dead and the other two men gone into the night, she finally gathered her composure and began struggling once more against her bonds.

It was futile. She craned her neck to see the woman who was moaning softly to herself. Carter recognised her – not hard, given that she had been skyrocketed into the public eye overnight during the aftermath of the Haydon massacre. She had been the envy of every reality TV aspirant. The vigilante puzzle had become a whole lot bigger and more complex, but the pieces were quickly falling into place.

Could it possibly be that Cool and Casual was not only the vigilante killer, but was also the infamous mass murderer, Hannibal Whitman? It just seemed too incredible to comprehend. But Carol Belmont and her former companion seemed to believe so, and so did 'Charlie'. They talked about the experiment ... Phase Two ... so much to take in, but now was not the time.

Carter tried to shout through her gag, but the sound was hopelessly muffled. Continuing to shout, she shuffled her body, edging closer to the Haydon survivor.

***

Will stopped the Land Rover outside the lockup garage. Dawn was fast approaching and greys were encroaching on the shadows. The cool air already had the beginnings of birdsong from warblers in the nearby marshland.

After unlocking and opening the door, he dragged Han Whitman out of the back of the Land Rover and threw him unceremoniously onto the damp concrete floor of the garage.

He flicked a light switch and, as a couple of overhead strip lights flickered, he bolted the door and turned back to Whitman who was groaning, but otherwise still.

One of the strip lights stabilized, but the second continued to flash, casting flickering shadows over half of the expansive garage. His kitbag was where he left it, on a long oily workbench that he had dragged out into the middle of the room on his previous flying visit. Apart from a couple more workbenches around the periphery, the garage was long abandoned. Trash littered the floor amongst stagnant pools of rainwater from the leaking roof.

The air smelled dank.

It was perfect for Hannibal Whitman's final resting place.

Will dragged Han over to the bench, saying, "I'm going to make you suffer to your last breath, Whitman."

"Oh, goody," Han muttered. Blood drooled out of his mouth as he spoke, splattering the concrete.

Will heaved him onto the bench, ensuring that every movement jarred Han's wounded body, finishing by slamming his head off the wood. "Before you die, you piece of shit, I will break you," Will snarled. "You will beg for the end when I'm finished with you."

Once in position, Will strapped each arm and leg to the corresponding leg on the bench, so that Han was splayed across it.

Han drew in a shaky breath then said, "So you're Detective Wright's son?"

Will flashed him an angry look.

"Surprised that I know?" Han asked. "Well, my piece of shit dad – the very same man who was helping you and Carol – told me. He was playing all of us – dropping you guys little clues here and there when I didn't tow the party line."

Will punched him in the face, further tearing the flap of skin hanging from his cheek. Fresh blood oozed from the open wound. "I don't give a shit what you've got to say, Whitman. You're a dead man. Save your fucking strength – you're going to need it."

Gritting his teeth, Han said, "That wasn't some passé attempt to bargain for my life, Will. Just thought you'd like to know the whole picture."

"I'm not interested in hearing anything from you other than agonized screams."

"Rather melodramatic, don't you think?" As Will rummaged through his kitbag, Han added, "I'm definitely getting a Theatre of Blood vibe here. Shame, I always wanted to be Vincent Price … looks like I might end up being Robert Morley. Let me just say that I'm not partial to poodle."

Will began retrieving a variety of implements out of the bag, including power tools, saws, hammers, a Stanley knife and a blowtorch.

Han drew in a deep breath and said, "Having said that, perhaps Saw or Hostel might be more fitting." He was aware that he was starting to babble, but it was the only defence mechanism he had left.

The last item Will pulled out was a small first aid kit. He opened it and took out a syringe. After squeezing a small amount

218

of liquid out and flicking the end to release any bubbles, he jabbed it into Han's arm.

"I'm not really into the drug scene, Will."

"You'll love this – it's adrenaline. It's to make sure you don't pass out on me, no matter what."

"Very thoughtful."

"While that's kicking in, I'll just get things ready, smartarse."

Will dragged a second bench over and laid out the extensive range of tools, along with improvised tourniquets.

"You certainly came prepared, Will. What happened to the neat execution plan – like in the car park?"

Will turned. "Glad you asked." Despite a neutral tone, his demeanour was bristling with malice. "Up to that point, all I wanted was to kill you. Details didn't matter. But when you got away I started thinking about how I would've felt if I *had* managed to kill you there and then. And you know what? I felt cheated. I felt that you would've gotten off lightly. I got so *fucking* angry." Will gripped the Stanley knife in a white-knuckled fist. "Carol thought I was angry that we had failed. No, I was angry that if we had succeeded *I'd* have failed me dad. He deserved better than a quick and painless execution. Felt like that would've been doing you a favour."

Han angled his neck to see Will's scrunched up expression. He had seen that look of absolute determination before many times. *I've created a monster*, he thought solemnly. "I suppose I can understand that. We all want to get the most out of our work, eh?"

"Keep talking, by all means, you fucking weasel," Will sneered. "You're making this all the easier for me."

Gripping the Stanley knife, Will strode over to Han and stood over him. He seemed to hesitate for a moment and Han caught a flash of uncertainty. But then, in a flash of movement, he buried the razor-sharp blade into Han's knee, cutting through cargo pants and flesh.

Han's body jerked and went rigid as he sucked in gasping breaths through clenched teeth.

As Will sliced around the kneecap, he said, "Not so talkative now, eh?"

Blood spilled over from the bench and splashed onto the floor as Will worked further under the knee, the blade scraping on bone here and there, but otherwise cutting through with little effort. It took ten seconds before the whole kneecap came away in Will's hand with a wet pop.

Waves of nausea assaulted Han as his rigid body fought to control the searing agony. He prayed for the sweet embrace of oblivion to take him, but the adrenaline denied him unconsciousness. With his jaw clamped shut, the only sounds were his nasal breaths and a low moaning from the back of his throat.

Will set the Stanley knife down on the bench and waved the bloody chunk of flesh and patella in front of Han's sweating and pale face. Han's pupils were fully dilated and staring feverishly.

He cast the kneecap aside and it landed with a plop in a dirty puddle. "You've got a pretty high pain threshold, Whitman," Will said. "That's good – it'll come in dead handy."

Han opened his eyes a fraction and glimpsed the Stanley knife. By shifting his arm slightly, he managed to conceal it.

***

Carter was gasping for breath and trembling from exertion, but she was in kicking distance of Carol, who had not moved from her balled up position. Her crying had dissipated and her stillness and silence was more disturbing than her hysterics.

Dawn was creeping over the horizon.

Carter kicked out at her with both trussed up legs. At the same time, she shouted through her gag.

At first, Carol grunted, but otherwise ignored her, but then she seemed to suddenly remember where she was. She sat bolt upright and stared at the bound detective. Wiping snot and tears from her face, her voice hoarse, she said, "Sorry ... I'm sorry, pet."

On her hands and knees, Carol crawled over to the detective and struggled with the cable ties. Fresh tears brimming, she said, "I ... I can't break them ..."

Carter tried again to speak through the gag. Cursing her own stupidity, Carol tugged it off, saying, "I'm sorry, I'm so sorry."

220

Carter drew in several deep breaths of unrestricted fresh sea air. "Thank you," she managed to say at last. "Carol, my name's Detective Chief Inspector Karen Carter. Can you find a knife or scissors to cut these ties?"

Carol glanced left and right, wringing her hands. "I ..."

"I *need* your help, Carol," Carter added, staring intently at her.

Carol met Carter's gaze and managed a hesitant nod. Her eyes fixed on the car and the gory remains of Charlie. Biting her bottom lip, she struggled to her feet and said, "Wait."

Carter watched her approach the headless remains of Richard's murderer. She thought about his cold body lying in a hedgerow, waiting for a jogger or dog-walker to discover it, his neck twisted at an unnatural angle. Why hadn't she just explained the Sergeant Howie nickname? She knew it bothered him. Instead of being a superior he could look up to, she ended up just being a bitch. Worse – a bitch with continuous PMT and wind. He had wanted to call for backup, but her pride got in the way. She had failed him. And a promising young detective had lost his life.

She bit back a sob. She would have to deal with that another time. Carol needed her and she needed Carol.

She heard Carol curse several times as she stepped over chunks of brain and skull to peer into the car. After taking what seemed like an age, she started to head back towards her with a penknife in her hands.

Before she reached the detective, Carol noticed a black object in a clump of weeds. She knelt down and scooped it up then crammed it into a coat pocket.

She reached the detective and carefully sliced through the cable ties.

"Thank you, Carol," Carter said as she massaged her bruised wrists. "I've got a million questions, but they can all wait. Do you know where your friend went?"

"I ..." Carol faltered, suddenly on unsteady ground. She felt a twinge of guilt.

Carter gripped Carol's hands in hers and winced at the pain in her wrists. "Look, I have a damn good idea what he's planning

221

to do, so we haven't got much time. You clearly care about him. If you truly do, you need to help me stop him before he crosses the line."

"I don't know …"

"I can bring this monster to justice and I can protect both of you. You'll never have to worry again. But let's do this right. If we don't stop him he'll be no better than that bastard. He'll have won, don't you see?" Carter's eyes were beseeching.

"I think … he's taken him to a lockup not far from here." Tears streamed down Carol's cheeks, but she made no attempt to wipe or hide them. She took a deep breath and nodded. "Let's go."

Carter resisted the urge to hug her. No time. "Right we'll have to take that." They both looked at the blood-splattered Skoda. It wasn't ideal, but beggars can't be choosers. As she strode over to it with Carol tagging behind, she added, "We need to find a phone – I've got to ring this mess in."

***

"How about these next, eh?" Will asked, brandishing a pair of garden shears. "There was a scene in a film … one of the Exorcist films, I think …"

Han was concentrating on his breathing, but a film question gave him something else to occupy his mind. "The Exorcist III … you're talking about the nurse?" he said in a rasping voice.

Will's smile was crooked, out of kilter. Han could see the extent that Detective Wright's son had wandered over to the dark side. He was in real trouble. "Yes! That's the one. That scene with the nurse and the shears scared the living shit out of me. Couldn't sleep for days."

"Yeah … was a good scene." Han managed a stiff nod.

Will opened the blades and slid Han's little finger between them. "Obviously I wouldn't cut your head off – well, not yet anyway – that would spoil all the fun."

"We wouldn't want that," Han muttered and closed his eyes.

222

"Glad we agree." The blades sliced through Han's little finger with minimum effort and the severed appendage rolled onto the floor.

Through gritted teeth, Han spat, "Fucker."

Will grinned again – it was a hybrid mix of rage and ecstasy. "Starting to get to you a little, eh? Hang in there, Han. I wouldn't want you going to pieces." Will laughed, but then brought a trembling hand up to his mouth and glanced around the room, uncertainty clouding his wrath.

Han forced his eyes open and glared at him. "Wouldn't want you to go to pieces?" he spat. "For fuck's sake, Will. Where's your originality?"

Will's head snapped round to glare at his prisoner. A moment later, a *snip* signalled the loss of the little finger's neighbour.

Hissing, Han repeatedly slammed his head back against the bench, until he could focus on his pounding head, instead of the fire in his knee and hand. "Now it's a party!" he screeched, half-laughing, half-retching.

"Was that original enough for you?" Will snarled as he cast the bloody shears aside and rummaged through the assembled tools. "Hmm, what next, Han? I think I've got a cordless drill around here somewhere. Or maybe an angle grinder."

"Go crazy, man …" Han choked back a sob. He shook his head and took several quick breaths through clenched teeth.

"Let's go for the drill," Will decided, as if he was choosing between a latte and a mocha. "We'll keep the angle grinder in reserve." He picked up the drill and pressed the trigger.

The sound sent a shiver through Han's body like an electric current. Gulping, he managed to say, "So … we're moving on to … The Driller Killer now then?"

As he gunned the drill a second time, Will said, "Bit before my time, that one. I did see that mad scientist drill a hole through a zombie's forehead in that Romero one though."

"Day of the Dead," Han offered, relieved for the fresh distraction. "The scientist was Logan … played by Richard Liberty."

Will shook his head. "Is there nothing you don't know about films?"

Han managed a grunt that turned into a wince and a sharp intake of breath. Speaking in short bursts, he said, "Isn't that ... a double negative?"

"I wouldn't know." With that, Will pressed the tip of the drill bit against the sole of Han's boot. "You think you've got soul, brother?"

"Just ... get on with it, fucknut."

Will pressed the trigger and Han immediately felt the drill bit bite into the rubber. The vibrations sent fresh sparks of pain through his knee and hand. He pressed his eyes closed and held his breath.

The drill bit took a second to work through the rubber and then burrowed into flesh. Han spat out the breath as the drill punched through bone and out through the top of the boot, spraying droplets of blood and fragments of bone over Han's legs and the bench.

Stars burst across Han's vision as searing pain pulsed through his entire body. His laboured breaths were frantic as his cheeks reddened and quivered.

Will bent over the shuddering form with a quizzical look on his face. As if speaking to a subordinate, he asked, "Are you getting a picture of the overall plan here, Han?"

Between wheezing pants, Han managed, "Oh ... I think ... so."

"I'm going to make sure every inch of your body is in agony before I finish you off. Maybe then you'll comprehend the suffering you caused to so many people."

"Get off your high horse!" Han blurted, his face contorted. "And drink your fucking milk."

Will threw his head back in a raucous laugh that was strained beyond recognition. Wiping tears from his eyes with his blood-soaked wrist, he said, "I'm no expert, but I don't think John Wayne ever said it quite like that."

"You ... really are ... a fine apprentice, Will. You're ... *hired!*" Han managed a laugh that was strangled by a gurgled sob.

"Why don't we ratchet this up a notch, eh, *mate*?" Will returned to his tools. Glancing over his shoulder, he asked, "What films can you think of that have used a blowtorch for torture?"

"None … spring … immediately to mind," Han muttered as his head lolled to one side and the room swam in and out of focus.

Will studied Han for a time and then set the blowtorch back down. "I think I better give you another adrenaline shot before you pass out first."

After injecting another dose, Will fired up the blowtorch and held it over Han's face.

Despite the intense pain, Han could feel the heat on his face immediately.

"And it burns, burns, burns …" Will muttered under his breath as he edged the flame closer. The flap of skin on Han's cheek began to bubble and crisp at the edges. The smell of cooking flesh stung his nostrils.

Will moved the blowtorch a fraction closer and the flap of skin and meat below it liquefied. A blackened hole appeared, revealing teeth and a flapping pink tongue. Han's mouth stretched wide in a silent scream as half of his cheek melted away.

"Two faces deserve two mouths, don't you think?" Will said then gagged at the smell. He took a couple of steps backwards, coughing. After extinguishing the blowtorch, he cast it aside. It skidded under a workbench and out of sight.

Han's body convulsed, straining and bucking on the bench, strangled animal cries the only speech he was capable of. The bench and surrounding area was awash with blood and a stinking haze hung in the air.

Will stared at the writhing man. The man whom, in the back of his mind, despite his reassurances to Carol, he had feared was indestructible. Han Whitman … the monster … the legend … but still only a man … flesh and blood. He now lay at Will's mercy, helpless, his flesh ruined and burnt.

The acrid stench brought tears to his eyes and he coughed a couple more times to clear his throat. The second cough transformed into a sob and he staggered back against the tool bench, rattling several implements. His stomach turned and he bent over double, emptying its contents onto the concrete to mingle with the blood and water.

With a throaty gurgle, Han said, "This … ritual torture … doesn't seem … to agree with you."

Resting his hands on his knees, watching yellow drool ooze from his open mouth, Will muttered, "Fuck you, Whitman." He wiped his mouth and straightened up once more, his face ashen. "You killed me dad. You're going to die, you evil cunt."

"Pot … calling … kettle."

Will lumbered over to his prisoner, his head swimming. "Fuck you! I will stick my fucking hands into that open hole in the side of what's *left* of your face and peel the whole fucker right off!"

"Do it, you … *pussy*." Han's head rolled to one side and his gaze fixed on Will. Red-black fluid trickled out of his slack lips and mingled with the seeping fluid oozing out of the charred hole.

"I fucking will!" He steadied himself against the bench for a moment and rubbed his face, which left bloodied smears on his forehead and cheeks. Then, taking several deep breaths, he reached down to Han's ruined cheek.

The garage door burst open, the timber frame disintegrating under the impact. Sunlight spilled in, followed closely by Carter and Carol, who both fell into the room.

Carter was first to recover, holding up a raised hand, she yelled, "Will, stop!" It was both a command and an appeal. "Don't do it!"

Carol had slipped in the wet and landed hard on one knee. Sucking in air, she gasped, "Please, Will! Please don't!"

Will's hands froze over Han's contorted face. His head dropped and he felt an overwhelming urge to cry. His voice a trembling whisper, he said, "I'm sorry, Carol. I have to do this."

Carter stepped closer, wiping dirt and sweat from her forehead. "No you don't, Will. You do *not!*"

Will glanced at her, his features awash with conflicting emotions. "It's too late."

"It's not, goddamn it!" Carter took another step closer and added, "Everyone will understand – we'll make them understand. He murdered your father."

Carol had risen and she limped closer, her hands clasped together. "Listen to Detective Carter, Will. She's on our side." There was no anger or bitterness in her tone, only fraught concern.

Will snorted and turned back to Han. "Nobody understands. This ... *monster* can't be tried. The system can't cope with someone like *him*. He has to die and he has to suffer to his very last breath ... which will be very soon."

"I understand, Will," Carol said and released an involuntary sob. "*I* understand!"

Tears rolled down Will's cheeks. With a strained sob, Will uttered, "Yes, I guess you do, Carol."

Carol stepped closer, wincing at the pain in her knee. She offered a hand to him. "Come to me, pet."

Carter glanced nervously over her shoulder and gave a brisk shake of her head.

Will was staring at Carol, their eyes locked. Her outstretched hand was so inviting, her eyes beseeching. He knew he had cared for her, but for the first time, he felt unquestionable love for her. It would be so easy to take her hand and walk away. But then he glanced back at Whitman and caught his cruel, intelligent eyes studying him. Despite the intense agony, the man was still lucid and observing. In that instant, the decision was made for him.

Will shook his head slowly and met Carol's gaze once more. "You *do* understand, Carol, but ... it doesn't change anything. If he lives he will become some kind of sick celebrity figure – probably have a fucking book deal by the end of the year. He *has* to die." With that, he turned back to Han and leant in towards him.

Han stared up at him. It felt as if his entire body was in flames. Through hazy vision, he could see Will's blood-encrusted hands close on his face. Then, he noticed something else on his furrowed forehead. "When did you become ... a Hindu?" Han murmured, scarcely above a whisper.

Will paused. "What?"

"Will!" Carol was lurching forward, but Carter had gripped one of her arms.

Will rolled his eyes heavenwards and realisation struck him. "Oh ... shit."

Carol watched, helpless, as the back of Will's head exploded where the high calibre sniper round exited.

"No ..." Carol uttered, falling to her knees.

"Stand down!" Carter yelled. "Stand down, goddamn it!"

Han blinked and drew in a shaky breath that caused the charred skin around the hole in his cheek to quiver.

Several uniformed officers – including a couple of armed response in full tactical dress – entered through the front and rear of the building. Paramedics with a trolley followed.

The medics instantly crowded over Han, under the watchful eye of one of the armed officers. After releasing his bonds and administering pain relief, they applied temporary dressings to his knee, foot, hand and face. As they prepared to transfer him onto the trolley, Han decided that it was now or never. The painkillers were taking the edge off the intense pain, allowing him to think a little clearer.

With his uninjured hand, Han grasped Will's forgotten Stanley knife and lashed out at the watching armed officer, slashing his forearm. The officer cried out and his pistol fell from his hands. The paramedics recoiled in shock.

Carter had been consoling Carol, who was still on her knees, crying. She glanced up at the outcry and her confusion turned to alarm. She started to shout out a warning.

Carol reacted without thinking. She drew the revolver that she had found near the Skoda and fired.

The gunshot echoed like a thunderclap.

It took a second to register, but then Han glanced down at his chest. He was sat up on the workbench and blood was spilling down and pooling around his crotch. He turned to Carol. The rest of the room seemed to have frozen. "I ... suppose that's ... poetic," he uttered, his tone mild amusement.

As time lurched forward, the injured officer was joined by a second and they both aimed pistols at Han's head as one barked orders into his radio. One of the paramedics rushed to the officer's aid as the other stood, dumbfounded. Carter gently eased the revolver out of Carol's loose grip. Carol continued to stare at Han, and he at her.

Then Han fell back against the workbench, arms dropping either side and the Stanley knife clattering harmlessly to the blood-drenched floor.

His vision was hopelessly blurred, but he could still make out several figures pressing in around him. Their faces were vague, indistinct, but he recognised them regardless. Mandy, John, Jimmy and Sam. Two more joined them, walling him in on all sides. Lisa was holding Ryan's hand. They all stared down at him with eyes like opaque glass. There was no emotion behind them, but the figures waited expectantly, silent and unmoving.

"What … do you want … me to say?" he said between shallow breaths. "*Sorry?*"

The paramedic dressing the officer's knife wound exchanged a glance with his immobile colleague.

Han managed a derisory snort that expelled droplets of blood from his nostrils. It wasn't exactly the finale he had in mind, but them's the breaks! Blood bubbled on his lips as they worked soundlessly for a moment, and then, his voice like a long drawn out sigh, he uttered, "Roll … credits."

Hello darkness, my old friend
I've come to talk with you again
Because a vision softly creeping
Left its seeds while I was sleeping
And the vision that was planted in my brain
Still remains
Within the sound of silence
'Sounds of Silence' by Simon & Garfunkel

It's all for you.

EPILOGUE

Late afternoon sunshine streamed into the bedroom. It was oppressively hot, despite only being dressed in light cotton pyjama shorts and shirt.

Cara sat on the end of the bed, cheeks flushed and eyes bloodshot from hours of endless weeping. She held the home pregnancy test in both trembling hands. Leaning in closer, she scrutinised it, as a scientist might a Petri dish swarming with bacteria.

A soft gasp escaped her lips and the small pen-like device fell out of her limp hands.

Jumanji had not stirred from his basket for several hours. The Labrador had not strayed from the front door for the first few days, only abandoning his post for brief periods for the call of nature. After a time though, he had padded, head down to his basket and remained there, his whine like a distant solitary ship's horn, adrift in a sea of fog.

Cara's whimper roused him and he trotted over to his new master, placing his cold nose into her lap. He emitted a soft whine.

The feel of his warm fur on her fingertips set fresh tears rolling down her cheeks.

Her hands then moved subconsciously to her stomach and remained there.

Music drifted in from the radio in the kitchen. It was softened by the distance, like a whisper in the dark …

Now you say you're lonely,
You cried the whole night through,
Well, you can cry me a river,
Cry me a river,
I cried a river over you.
'Cry Me a River' by Arthur Hamilton

THE END

BIOGRAPHY

Rod lives in the beautiful North East of England with wife,
Vanessa and he's not as mad as his writing suggests …

CHAPTER ARTWORK WAS ADAPTED FROM THESE POSTERS

Lightning Source UK Ltd.
Milton Keynes UK
UKOW051900060612

193954UK00001B/265/P